Waiting for Dusk

by

Nancy Pennick

Barb,

Follow your dreams!

Nancy Pennick

Nancy Pennick

F & I
by Melange Books

Published by
Fire and Ice
A Young Adult Imprint of Melange Books, LLC
White Bear Lake, MN 55110
www.fireandiceya.com

Waiting For Dusk ~ Copyright © 2012 by Nancy Pennick

ISBN: 978-1-61235-523-8 Print

Names, characters, and incidents depicted in this book are products of the author's imagination or are used fictitiously. Any resemblance to actual events, locales, organizations, or persons, living or dead, is entirely coincidental and beyond the intent of the author or the publisher. No part of this book may be reproduced or transmitted in any form or by any means, electronic or mechanical, including photocopying, recording, or by any information storage and retrieval system, without permission in writing from the publisher.
Published in the United States of America.

Cover Art by Lynsee Lauritsen

Waiting for Dusk
Nancy Pennick

Read a book.
Fall asleep.
Meet a boy.
Is it real or just a dream?
Katie's everyday life suddenly turns exciting when she travels back in time and meets the boy of her dreams. Thinking of nothing else, willing to leave the real world behind, she's determined to find out if it's all a dream or not. Returning again and again, Katie almost has her answers until one day her precious book goes missing.

Nancy Pennick

Dedication

To
Bonnie Urbancek McGarry,
the best friend a girl could ever have

Acknowledgments

To my wonderful husband, Ron, who only reads the sports page, but read my rough draft and encouraged me to finish.

To my son, Matt, my creative tech guy, who supported me along the way.
To my sister, Sue Gesing, and niece, Megan Gesing, who were the first to read my book and are my biggest cheerleaders.

To Ashley Dombrowski, who unknowingly was my inspiration to keep writing.
To Lynsee Lauritsen for designing the wonderful book cover that captured the essence of the book.

And finally to my publisher, Nancy Schumacher for giving my book a home and a huge thank you to her and everyone at Melange-Books who's helped me through this exciting journey, my first published book.

Waiting for Dusk

Chapter One

Boredom, boring, bored. Kathryn Roberts couldn't think of any more ways to say she was bored. Summer vacation was supposed to be fun. It was something everyone looked forward to and yet…she was bored. Katie sighed. She picked up her phone, looked for any new messages, and set it down. She strolled over to her desk and grabbed her laptop. As she flopped on the bed, Katie thought she heard a door slam downstairs.

"Katie! Katie! Are you home?" her mother called from the kitchen.

"Yeah, I'm home." Katie ran down the stairs and collapsed on the sofa in the family room. Her soft, light brown hair flowed over the pillow. It had streaks of gold from the summer sun, and was showing a slight wave from the humidity that hung thick in the air.

"What have you been doing since I left?"

"Nothing, I'm bored."

"Bored? Did I just hear you say that?" Her mother sounded irritated. "Well, all you do is stare at your laptop, stare at the TV and stare at your phone. When I was your age, I actually met my friends to do things. We went for ice cream, went to the beach, movies, you name it. We did things. I'll give you bored. You're bored of staring. That's what it is. Go do something."

"Easier said than done. Most of my friends are gone for the summer. Lindsey went to stay with her aunt at her ranch out west somewhere. Tyson's at basketball camp. Jordyn is in China on a cool vacation, studying her roots with her two moms. And me? I'm here."

Kate could tell her mother was gathering her thoughts and heard her calmly say, "We went on a vacation last year. If I remember correctly, someone said they would never go on a vacation with her nerdy parents again."

"Okay, sorry about that. What I really meant was that it was hard to be cooped up in a car with your parents for three weeks. The Grand Canyon was worth seeing, I guess."

Katie bounced off the sofa and gave her mother a hug. She knew she had to calm her down before she thought of some chore Katie could do.

"Apology accepted!" her mom stared into Katie's blue eyes. "Thanks, Blue Eyes. Now you can help me with dinner."

Katie rolled her eyes but didn't say anything. She didn't like it when her mother called her Blue Eyes, but kept quiet. Katie opened the refrigerator instead. "Just you and me?"

"Actually, no. I've invited Mrs. Johnson over for dinner tonight."

Maya Johnson was the Roberts' neighbor. They became close when Katie's mom was a college student and Maya worked at the university's library. Her mother spent a lot of time in the library and got to know Mrs. Johnson very well. They became like family.

After college graduation, Katie's mom married Jackson Roberts and moved away. A teaching opportunity opened up at the college so the family moved back home.

"So glad we moved next door to her. I know I was only three, but I remember how she baby-sat while you went to work." She was excited Mrs. Johnson was coming over to break up the monotony of the day

The doorbell suddenly rang and she knew who it would be.

"I'll get it!" Katie bounded out of the kitchen to the front door, opening it wide. "Mrs. Johnson!" Katie wrapped her arms around her and gave a quick hug.

She had always been like a grandmother to Katie. She called her 'MiMi' when she was little. As she got older, her mother insisted on proper respect and told Katie that she should call her "Mrs. Johnson". That didn't make sense because they were family.

"MiMi," Katie whispered in her ear.

"Child, I swear you grow taller every time I see you!" Mrs. Johnson's brown eyes glistened. "You should be a model!" She walked into the house and through to the kitchen.

"Maya," Joanna outstretched her arms, "So good to see you! How was your vacation?"

"Good to see you, too. My vacation was too short, just like all

Waiting for Dusk

vacations are. Now I'm back to the real world of paying bills, cleaning and grocery shopping."

She looked at Katie with a twinkle in her eyes, almost like she knew what Katie was thinking.

That is why Katie loved Mrs. Johnson so much. Even though Mrs. Johnson lived alone, she seemed to have a history that was fascinating, yet mysterious. She always told wonderful stories about how she and her husband traveled the country when they were young. They settled down in the house next door when Mrs. Johnson was expecting Carl Jr. He now lived on the California coast working as a marine biologist. Mrs. Johnson always took long vacations to visit him, and just got back from one of those trips.

"So how is Carl Jr.?" Katie's mother asked.

"Looking more and more like his father every passing year, God rest his soul."

Katie whispered the words with her under her breath. Mrs. Johnson looked at her and smiled. "So what have you two been up to while I was gone?"

"Mom is teaching a summer class, and I've been hanging out here at home with nothing to do. I guess I just got bored of staring."

"Bored of staring?"

"Inside joke," Kate's mother quickly responded. "Plus you know Jackson is gone for most of the summer on business. We really didn't plan a vacation."

Katie really missed her father. Jackson Roberts was a world traveler with business taking him far and wide. He wrote books, lectured and went on many promotional tours. Most of his books were nonfiction, from self-help to nature. Katie didn't have a clue how he got all of this knowledge and didn't really care. She just missed him because he would have made the summer enjoyable. There had been no word from him in quite a few days. Her mom said he was either somewhere with no service or he let his battery die again. Nothing new for her dad.

Mrs. Johnson, Katie and her mom sat outside to eat their dinner. They laughed and talked until the sun began to set. Katie excused herself at that time. "If it's alright with everyone, I'd like to go up to my room now. Glad you're home again, Mi…Mrs. Johnson." Katie stammered.

Mrs. Johnson chuckled. "Of course you are excused. Your mother and I need to make some plans to add some excitement in your life. First come over here and give me a kiss goodnight."

Katie skipped over to Maya and hugged her tightly. Maya kissed her cheek and whispered in her ear, "Sweet dreams."

Katie went upstairs, turned her TV on, grabbed the laptop and settled in for the night. Maybe Linds would call or Ty. That would be a bonus. Having Mrs. Johnson home for the summer was great because Katie didn't feel so alone. She could visit her during the day and maybe she could look for a summer job. Not that she wanted a summer job, but it would fill the days with something to do while waiting for her friends to get back in town.

It was close to midnight when Katie's mom came in to say good night. "Good night, sweet girl," she said and placed a book on Katie's nightstand. "Here's something to read. It may help put you to sleep."

"What is it?"

"Some romantic historical fiction. Just an old book I had. You loved to read when you were young, but I thought it was a little grown up for you back then. You're just the right age to read it now."

"Oh, thanks. Good night."

She glanced at the book on the nightstand and went back to what she was doing. *What am I doing?*

She looked at her webpage every ten minutes, updated her profile and watched some dumb short films people posted online. She sent texts to her father, Linds, Ty, Jordyn and a few school friends plus planned her outfits for tomorrow. Katie looked at the book again.

She didn't read books anymore. *What's my mother thinking?*

Katie wasn't really tired though. If the book could help put her to sleep, she'd give it a try. It was old but well taken care of. One could tell it was read many times as she flipped through the pages of the black leather book. Katie opened to chapter one and began reading.

Suddenly, there was a banging on her door. "Miss Kathryn, time to get up! You overslept. Get up!"

Katie turned over in the bed. Sun streamed into the room from the window.

Overslept? she thought. *Was Mrs. Johnson calling me?*

She got up, stumbled to the door and opened it. Although Katie was still groggy, she could tell something wasn't right. She looked to the left, and saw a long hallway with three more closed doors on her side, and then a large open doorway to what looked like a kitchen on the other side. She

Waiting for Dusk

looked to the right, and there stood Mrs. Johnson.

"Oh, MiMi...Mrs. Johnson! What's going on?"

"I'll tell you what's going on, missy. You're going to be late for work. And you youngsters have got to get my name right. It's Mrs. Johansson. YO-hon-sen!"

Katie blinked. She turned and looked at her room, then gasped. It was very sparse: bed on a metal frame, a dresser with a pitcher and bowl on it and a braided rug on the floor.

I must be dreaming. She pinched herself. "Ouch!" She looked forlornly at Mrs. Johnson...Mrs. Johansson. *She does look younger than Mrs. Johnson*, Katie admitted and said, "Where's the bathroom?"

Mrs. Johansson laughed. "You city girls." She pointed down the hall.

"Which door?"

"The one that takes you outside, Miss Kathryn. Just keep on walking and you'll see a little house. It's called an outhouse. Does that ring a bell?"

Oh, yes. It rang a bell alright. Katie was in Girl Scouts for awhile, and went away for an overnight summer camp. The camp had an outhouse. After that trip, Katie was a Girl Scout no more. "Yuck!" she screamed.

"Before you go out there, go fill this up in the kitchen and put it in your room."

Mrs. Johansson handed Katie the large ceramic pitcher. Katie decided to do as she was told. She went into the kitchen and saw a large pump over what appeared to be the kitchen sink. Mrs. Johansson stood in the doorway. "Start pumping," she laughed.

Nancy Pennick

Chapter Two

Katie filled the pitcher and when she turned around, Mrs. Johansson was gone. She carried her pitcher into the bedroom, poured the water in the bowl and then visited the outhouse.

What a dream! Whoever visited an outhouse in their dreams?

When she returned, she washed up in her bowl using the towel that was placed beside it, and then flopped on the bed. There was another knock at her door. She got up to answer it, and there was Mrs. Johansson again. "Here's your uniform. Put it on and be ready to go soon. You missed breakfast. I'll give you something to eat in the car. Mr. Johansson is pulling the Buick around to take you girls to work."

Work? Really? Katie could not believe she would have to go to work in her dream. She decided to play along and put the uniform on. It was a crisp black dress, almost floor length, black socks and shoes. She tied a stiff, white bib apron over the dress and was finished. There was no mirror to see how everything fit. Katie felt like she stepped back in time in the outfit. Perhaps it was an old-fashion or Amish restaurant.

Yes, that has to be it. All of this will make sense once I get there.

Katie stepped into the hallway and all the other doors were open too. Three girls about her age, dressed the same way, were in the hallway. Two of the girls were talking while the third leaned on the doorframe to her bedroom.

"Oh, hello. You must be the new girl, Kathryn. I'm Lucinda and this is Ruthie." She pointed to the girl next to her. "And that one," pointing to the leaning girl, "is Anna." She leaned in closer to Katie. "Not too friendly, that one."

By then, Katie decided to go along with anything that happened. She nodded her head but waved to Anna. Anna held up a hand and then quickly put it back down.

"Girls, girls! Oh good, you are ready. Mr. Carl is parked out front and ready to go. Have a good day and see you tonight." Mrs. Johansson scooped all four into her arms and gave them a group hug. "Do a good job." Her voice trailed after them as they headed out to the waiting car.

When Katie saw the car, she stopped short. "We're going to ride in that?" She stood with her mouth open. "Is that thing in working condition?"

Mr. Carl came around from the driver side. He laughed. "The car's not that old. I did buy it used this year but I needed more room to drive you girls from the boardinghouse to the hotel. This here is a 1925 Buick, holds seven passengers."

Katie just shook her head. *That's used, alright.*

The girls climbed in. "You know the car's not that old," Lucinda chimed in. She seemed to be the talker of the group. "It's only two-years-old. It's a very nice car, Mr. Johansson." She pronounced Johansson very exactly, in the proper, correct way.

Katie's head spun and she closed her eyes. *Please wake up. Please wake up.* She didn't wake up. All she did was bounce in her seat as they traveled along a dirt road. The air felt hot and dry. The landscape was filled with pine trees when she finally opened her eyes. She closed them again tightly. Thankfully it was a short drive.

Mr. Johansson pulled up to a door in the back of the hotel. The girls jumped from the car, waved good-bye and ran inside. All of them, except Katie.

Mr. Johansson turned around from the driver's seat. "I thought I only counted three going in." He smiled at Katie. "The first day is always hard. Don't worry. Everyone will help you. Most everyone's very kind. You'll have a good day. I'll be back to pick you up in no time."

Katie slowly got out of the car, tears filled her eyes. She wasn't in Kansas, make that Ohio, anymore. She said she would go along with whatever happened in her dream, and that was what she would do.

Chapter Three

Katie slowly opened the door to the back of the hotel, and stepped inside a very large kitchen. There was a lot going on with people running everywhere--servers, cooks, busboys.

A plump, sweet-faced woman ran up to her. "You must be Kathryn, the new girl. I'm going to have you work alongside Anna today so you can see how we do things. We run a tight ship. The vacationers come first. We must serve them and keep them happy. Now away you go."

Oh, great, I get to work with unfriendly, non-talkative Anna. What else can make my day?

Katie walked over to Anna. "You're stuck with me for the day."

Anna grabbed her hand. "Oh, no, Kathryn. You are stuck with me. Lucinda was trying greatly to get you to work with her. I'm a quick and quiet worker. I guess that's why Miss Betsy chose me. Harvey girl, in training, that's me. I'd don't know if I'll ever make it out to the dining room."

"A what? A Harvey girl? I never heard of that."

"Never you mind. Come on." And off they went to start the chores for the day.

The day went by quickly. Katie wasn't allowed to wait on the customers or vacationers, as they were told to call them, although Anna told her locals ate there too.

They filled the orders, scraped the dishes, took the dishes to the dishwashers and brought food to the cooks. By the end of the day, Katie felt very tired. During that time she discovered she liked Anna. She enjoyed her day and couldn't figure out why Lucinda didn't like Anna.

Miss Betsy interrupted Katie's thoughts. "Miss Kathryn!"

Waiting for Dusk

"Yes, Miss Betsy?"

"I would like you to get some more eggs for the cook."

Katie was a little surprised she was asked to do something on her own so early in training. She went to find Anna. "Anna, where's the refrigerator? I need to get some eggs."

Anna laughed." The..."

"Oh, you might call it the ice box or something like that!"

"I'm not laughing about the refrigerator or the ice box!" Anna smiled at her. "If we are out of eggs and you were asked to get them, you have to go out there." Anna pointed to the backdoor.

"Outside? Again?" Katie suppressed a scream.

"Yes, from the henhouse. I will go with you. Here take this basket."

At the last moment someone called Anna away, and Katie had to head outdoors on her own. She opened the door and looked around. Straight back from the hotel, across the road from where Mr. Johansson had dropped them off, was a henhouse and a barn. She hadn't noticed them earlier. The area was all fenced off and she couldn't find a gate. Kate clumsily climbed over the fence, thankful no one was watching.

Entering the henhouse she thought, *I can do this.* Hens sit on eggs and all I have to do is stick my hand under them and I should hit the jackpot.

Katie stared down her first subject. The hen did not seem too scary. She spoke softly to it. "Thank you, Mrs. Hen."

Reaching out her hand, she slid it under the hen and found two eggs. She continued on, having success and sometimes none, slowly filling the basket and trying to decide if there were enough eggs to satisfy Miss Betsy.

"Well, maybe just one more." She stared the last hen down, then reached in. That time the hen was not going to cooperate. It squawked and pecked away at her, then flew up and off the nest. That was more than Katie could take.

She ran out of the henhouse, climbed the fence and fell to the ground, always remembering to balance the egg basket carefully. She lay on her back by the side of the fence and laughed. Then she got very quiet. *Did I hear another laugh?*

Katie sat up and looked around. "Who's there?"

"Over here," the voice said.

Katie glanced over at the hotel, and leaning against the wall in the shadows was a boy about her age. She got up and walked toward him. She'd show him. Who was he to laugh at her? Look at all the eggs in this basket. *I didn't break one during my getaway.*

The closer she got to him, the more clearly she saw him. He wasn't a boy but almost a man. The cliché, 'tall, dark and handsome' fit him. His dark brown, wavy hair was long on the top, and shorter on the sides. A strand of hair fell into his eyes. His eyes sparkled and locked onto hers. Her legs felt like mush, and she stumbled. He reached out and caught her.

"Are you okay?" his voice was kind, concerned.

Katie tried to gain her composure. "Yes, yes. Are you one of the vacationers? Because if you are, I shouldn't be talking to you. It's against the rules." *Rules? What am I thinking? It's my dream after all.*

"No. No I'm not. I work here at the park doing an internship. My name is Andrew, by the way. Andrew Martin."

"I'm Kathryn, but everyone calls me Katie."

Andrew's brows crossed. "Katie doesn't seem to suit you. I think I shall call you Kate."

Katie thought Andrew was a little full of himself, deciding a new name for her.

"Then I shall call you Drew," she shot back.

"Drew, it is then!"

Kate found him charming. He had a strong laugh and a beautiful smile. It was hard not to stare at him—something she was good at, according to her mother. She felt she would never get tired of staring at him. She wanted to reach out and brush back the piece of hair that fell over his forehead.

Katie blinked and brought herself back to earth. "I need to get these eggs into the kitchen."

"By all means, don't let me hold you up. It was very nice to meet you, Kathryn, Kate."

"And you, too, Andrew…Drew." Katie started for the door.

"Kate. Are you staying at the boarding house by chance?"

"Yes. Yes, I am," She blushed and went inside. "Here are the eggs!" she called out to anyone who would listen.

Anna came running up and took them from her. "You were gone a long time but I covered for you."

The workday finally ended and Mr. Johansson was waiting in the

Waiting for Dusk

Buick when the girls came out after their shift. "Have a good day, girls? Meet anyone special?" he chuckled as he said it.

"Now, Mr. Johansson," said Lucinda. "You know our goal is to become servers in the dining room first and then meet someone special. And by the way, girls, I'm now an official Harvey girl! No more training for me." She squealed with delight.

Ruthie and Anna said all the right things to her, especially Ruthie.

"You are so lucky, Lucinda! You're the first to make it. You're so much prettier than me, I knew it would happen." She smiled brightly.

Anna looked at Katie and rolled her eyes. Katie was a little taken aback by what Ruthie just said, because Ruthie was very attractive. She had long auburn wavy hair, a little bit of a nose with a few freckles sprinkled across it and lovely green eyes.

Lucinda was just an average girl, not a raving beauty, but made up for that in personality. When Katie first met her, she thought she was lovely. Even though she had mousy brown hair, it was fixed in what might be the latest fashion for the day, a short bobbed haircut with waves. Her radiant smile made one feel it was only meant for them. She was nice looking, but not beautiful.

Funny, it reminded her of high school. Katie had met girls like her. The girl with the most mesmerizing personality could be very popular and have a group of friends hanging on every word. She began to see Lucinda in a different light. Why did she not like Anna? Why did Lucinda practically warn her away from Anna? She made a mental note to ask Anna later.

When they got home, Mrs. Johansson had dinner waiting for them. They talked and laughed with both Mr. and Mrs. Johansson while they ate. Katie felt so at home with Mrs. Johansson because she reminded her of MiMi. No, not reminded her of MiMi. She looked just like a younger MiMi.

Mrs. Johansson spoke, "Girls, remember that it's lights out at nine. You have a long day ahead of you tomorrow, especially you, Lucinda!" She gently patted the girl on her hand.

Each girl got up and thanked both Mr. and Mrs. Johansson for dinner. Ruthie hugged them both. Lucinda hugged Mrs. Johansson. Anna shook their hands. Katie was last. She wanted to throw her arms around Mrs. Johansson, call her MiMi and ask for her help in understanding everything. Instead, she just shook their hands.

"Good night and thank you," she said softly.

When Katie left the kitchen she found Anna waiting outside in the hall. "You did well your first day."

"Thanks." Katie blushed. "Anna, can you come to my room and talk?"

"Sure. If that's what you want."

"I want to ask you a few questions. First, what is a Harvey girl? And why does Lucinda hate you so much?"

Before Anna had time to answer, Lucinda was at Kathryn's door. "Party in my room before lights out! Come on, Kathryn. You too, Anna."

Anna's expression changed to a look of shock. "Oh. First, you have to put on your nightgown. That's how we do it," Lucinda called out as she left the room. Anna followed, giving Katie a slight wave as if to say see you soon.

You mean we're having a pajama party, like a sleepover? Katie rummaged through the dresser drawers in her room. She found a beautiful white cotton nightgown and put it on. She went down the hallway to Lucinda's room. Ruthie was already there. She too was wearing a white nightgown. Her creamy white skin glowed in the evening light. Katie sat down on the braided rug next to the bed. Lucinda and Ruthie were already situated on the bed. Anna came in and plopped down next to Katie.

"Kathryn, since you are new to our get-togethers, I will tell you what we do. We don't talk about work unless something special happened. If we do need to talk about work, we get that out of the way first. Then we tell stories and talk about our dreams."

Katie thought that was very strange. Why would you tell everyone what to talk about? Oh, right, it's Lucinda. We all have to do what she says. Aloud Katie said, "How long have you been here, Lucinda?"

"Since the spring. April second, to be exact. Anna and I came on the same train, didn't we, Anna?"

Anna just nodded.

"Anna always likes to do everything I do. She likes everything I like. Isn't that right, Anna?" Lucinda continued to badger her. "Not talking tonight?"

Without saying a word, Anna got up and left.

"Lucinda!" Ruthie said. "Sometimes we have to forgive those who

Waiting for Dusk

we feel trespass against us."

Lucinda, her eyes still fiery, turned to Ruthie. She grabbed a pillow and smacked Ruthie with it. "Pillow fight!" she screamed.

At that moment, there was a tap at the window. The girls grew quiet and all turned toward the window. It was nearing dusk and hard to see.

"Probably some creature," Ruthie said casually.

Then there was a tap, tap, tapping sound again.

"Unless it knows how to make a rhythmic tapping sound, I don't think it's an animal. I'm going out there to see," said Katie.

"Not a good idea!" Lucinda shouted after her.

By then Katie was down the hall and out the door. The warm night air hit her face. It felt good to get out of Lucinda's room. It was closing in on her, especially after the strange attack on Anna.

Katie was deep in thought, when she heard a sound. A footstep? She spun around to see Drew standing there. "Oh, I didn't mean to startle you, Miss Kathryn. You did say you were staying at the boardinghouse and I thought I'd come to see if you are comfortable. If you have everything you need."

That's a good line, Katie thought. He was so handsome in the moonlight she could have stayed in that spot forever. Drew walked over to her. "I have never seen anyone as beautiful as you."

"Lights out!" Mrs. Johansson called in the distance.

Katie couldn't help it. It was her dream after all. She fell into Drew's arms and kissed him. He kissed her back. They seemed to melt into each other as one. Right then and there Katie wished that it was not a dream and that it would never end.

Chapter Four

"Time to get up! Time to get up!" Mrs. Johansson knocked on Katie's door.

Katie groaned and rolled over. Then she sat up in bed. "Drew!" she said aloud to no one. She gasped.

She was staring at a pale sky blue wall. That was not the pine wall of the boardinghouse. It was definitely her bedroom. The large 3-D butterflies her father helped mount on the walls seem to flutter in the morning light. Her blue and yellow floral quilt was kicked off the bed, lying on the floor. Her cream color desk and dresser were in place. Even the black leather-bound book was on the nightstand. It was all a dream.

Katie put her head in her hands. It seemed too real but she knew in her heart of hearts that's all it was. She slid out of bed and opened her door. There in the familiar hallway stood Mrs. Johnson. "Oh, MiMi, it is you!"

"Who do you think it would be, child? The boogeyman?" Mrs. Johnson chuckled.

"Well, what are you doing here, since I don't need a babysitter anymore?" Katie teased.

"Your mother asked me to make sure you were up and dressed by the time she got home. She has a surprise for you."

"A surprise? What is it?"

"It's not a surprise if I tell you, is it? Now get yourself dressed and come down and have something to eat."

Katie went back into her room. *Should I tell MiMi about my dream? She's good at analyzing dreams and always makes me feel better.*

But it was different this time, it all felt so real, she decided against

Waiting for Dusk

telling her.

When Katie got downstairs, she found Mrs. Johnson in the kitchen. There was a bowl of cereal and a glass of juice waiting for her.

"Cereal? That's all?" Mrs. Johnson was known for her famous breakfasts and always made something special for her.

"You slept late and your mother wants you ready to leave when she gets home. You'll be eating again soon enough." Mrs. Johnson packed a picnic basket.

What was going on? A picnic? That's the surprise?

Katie's mom walked in the door. "Thanks so much, Maya. I don't know what I'd do without you."

"Oh, you won't ever have to find out." Mrs. Johnson picked up her purse, kissed Joanna on the cheek and went out the door.

"Wait! Isn't Mrs. Johnson going on a picnic with us?" Katie was a little disappointed. Maybe she would find the nerve to talk to MiMi during their outing.

Katie's mother put her arm around her. "No, it's just you and me, kid. I do have a surprise, though, besides the picnic. Since you turned sixteen, your father hasn't had much time to take you out for driving lessons. So today you and I are going driving...in the Mustang."

"Me? Drive the Mustang?" Katie was elated. That was a surprise.

"Yes, only when we get to the lake and you have plenty of room in the parking lot."

"We'll have the top down, right, Mom?"

"Yes, the whole way."

Katie grabbed the picnic basket and ran out to the garage, leaving her cereal untouched.

"Come on! Let's go!"

"Good thing I packed our towels and swimsuits already." Joanna called after her. "It's great to see you so happy."

Katie opened the special third car garage door. There sat the gleaming 1969 black convertible in all its glory. It had two large red racing stripes down the black hood that were about a foot wide. The black leather seats were soft and smooth.

"Mom, come on! You're taking too long!" Katie shouted from the car. She jumped into the bucket seat.

Katie heard the trunk pop open and turned to see her mother throw everything in. The trunk slammed shut, her mom hopped in the driver's side and started the car. It purred like a kitten, as her father always said. Katie leaned her head back on the headrest as her mother pulled out of the garage and headed for the open road.

When they got to the lake, Katie couldn't wait to drive the car.

"Let's eat lunch first, Katie. I'm starving!" Her mom parked and ran around to the back of the car.

Katie loved Mrs. Johnson's egg salad sandwiches and was sure that was what she packed for them, plus other surprises. They found a picnic table and sat down to eat.

"I'm sorry I'm neglecting you this summer, Katie. I didn't know I was going to have to teach a class at the University."

"I'm a big girl now. I'll survive."

"I guess I have to start thinking of you that way. You will always be my baby girl though." Joanna patted Katie's hand and dropped the keys into the palm of her hand.

Katie looked at her mom and felt a shiver of excitement go down her back. "Now? Really?"

"Now. Really."

Katie jumped up, cleaned off the picnic table and ran to the car. She slipped into the driver's seat. When Joanna sat down on the passenger side, Katie glanced at her and said, "What about Dad? Do you think he'll be alright with this?"

"Don't worry about Dad. I'll take care of him."

Katie started the car and slowly took it for a scenic drive in the parking lot. Afterward, they spent the rest of the day relaxing on the beach, going in and out of the lake, talking and laughing about past summers they had spent as a family.

"Wow, it's getting close to dinnertime. We should be going," Katie's mother said as she looked at her watch.

Katie reluctantly agreed. She enjoyed herself and hadn't thought about her dream. Now that she was going back home, she had an odd anticipation about reading the book again. She shivered.

"Are you cold, Kate?"

"What did you call me?" Katie said with a little more anger in her voice than she planned. It should be no big deal. But her mother had never called her Kate before. It took her by surprise.

"Well, my dear Kathryn, I think I called you Kate. Is there anything wrong with that?"

Waiting for Dusk

"No. Sorry, Mom. I guess I'm just tired." Katie did not want to go into a whole story about her dream and meeting a boy named Drew who called her Kate. They drove home most of the way without talking.

Katie unloaded the car, then helped her mother get dinner ready. They hadn't said a word for hours until her mom broke the quiet. "Are you okay, baby? You were having so much fun, and now it's like you are back to your brooding self. I'm ready to hear 'I'm bored' come out of your mouth again."

"No, just tired. I think I'll head up to my room for the rest of the night. Good night." Katie cleared her dishes, put them in the dishwasher and headed for the stairs.

"Good night, Katie. Love you."

"Love you, too."

When Katie was in the safety of her own room, she grabbed the book and lay down on her bed. Better put the television on. *It's a little early to think about sleeping,* she thought. *But why am I so tired? Maybe it was all that sun and water. I think I'll just close my eyes for a minute and then read another chapter.*

Chapter Five

Katie woke with a start. She looked around and saw the pine walls of the boardinghouse. Her heart skipped a beat. *I'm back! Why am I so happy about that?*

She wanted to see Mrs. Johansson, the girls, and even Mr. Johansson. Then there was Drew. Would she see him again? She wouldn't dare tell anyone what happened outside the other night. They might not let her see him again.

Listen to me, Katie thought. *I'm worried about what people will think about me in my dream.*

She thought about the kiss. It was just like in the fairytales when the heroine waited for the prince to kiss her, like Snow White or Sleeping Beauty. Only she didn't want the prince to wake her from her dreams.

Katie got out of bed. She knew the routine. She filled her pitcher with water and then visited the outhouse. She looked around almost hoping to see Drew. All she saw was miles and miles of blue sky. It seemed to go on forever. It was the most beautiful shade of blue she ever saw. She was overwhelmed by the beauty of it.

A voice broke through the moment. "Any day now. We'd all like to use the facilities." Lucinda laughed and waved at her.

Katie waved back, then hurried off. When she returned to her room, her uniform was lying on her bed. Katie slipped on the black dress, the black stockings and shoes. Finally the crisp white bib apron was tied on over the dress, and she was ready. She found a lovely gold-handled brush in her drawer, and fussed with her hair until she looked presentable. Then Katie headed to the kitchen for breakfast.

"Good morning, everyone," Everyone was already at the table

except her.

"God Morgon, Katie," said Mr. Johansson. Katie frowned.

"That was good morning in Swedish," Ruthie informed her. "Mr. Johansson tries to teach us a few phrases now and then."

"Oh, then *god morgon* to you, too, Mr. Johansson."

They ate breakfast quickly so they wouldn't be late for work. Lucinda told everyone about the pillow fight the night before and had everyone laughing. Katie could see why Lucinda was so much fun to be around. She decided to give her another chance.

After cleaning up breakfast, the four girls piled into the car and were ready for another day at work.

"Thank goodness it's Friday. Our last day of work for the week!" Lucinda clapped.

Katie almost laughed aloud when she heard the saying 'thank goodness it's Friday'. If Lucinda only knew what that simple phrase would turn into. As the old car rambled down the road, Katie found it hard to keep her eyes open. She felt like dozing but sat up straight because she did not want to fall asleep. She decided to close her eyes and rest until they got there. She heard the girls laughing and talking the whole way there and then the car suddenly came to a stop. They must be at the hotel. They all got out of the car and ran into the back door of the kitchen.

Miss Betsy was waiting for them. "Lucinda dear, you will be working in the dining room all day today. Ruthie, Anna and Kathryn, come with me."

She assigned tasks in the kitchen to each girl and then went into the dining room to watch over Lucinda.

Katie had the job of retrieving eggs from the hen house again. She did much better this time. Just as she opened the kitchen door to go inside, she heard a familiar voice.

"You do get a lunch break, don't you, Kate?"

She whirled around to see Drew standing behind her. She almost dropped the basket of eggs.

"Yes, of course I do," she said indignantly. She really didn't remember last time if she did or not.

"Well, then I would love to have lunch with you. I'd love to show you the park." Drew pointed past the hotel.

"The p-p-park?" She completely forgot she was at some sort of resort people in the 1920's vacationed at.

"Do you know where you're at?" Drew chuckled light-heartedly.

"Well, I know it's hot and dry here. Not too much grass. Lots of pine trees. The sky is always blue and the sun shines high in the sky," Katie tried to be factual. Too scared to look around the first day, she just gazed at the other girls' faces during the car ride to the hotel. This morning she had her eyes closed the whole time.

"Come here," Drew took Katie's hand. She almost dropped the basket again. He took it from her and set it on the step.

They walked to the end of the building and around the corner. Katie gasped. She put her hand over her mouth and then mumbled, "The Grand Canyon."

"Yes, that's right. You didn't know you were working at El Tovar at the Canyon?"

"Yes...yes of course I knew!" Kate fibbed. Her eyes were still as large as saucers. It was such an overwhelming sight. She looked at Drew. He was looking at the canyon with awe, too. "You love it, don't you?"

"Yes, that's why I'm here. To learn as much as I possibly can about it." He became very quiet.

"I need to get back, but I'll meet you later for lunch."

"Lunch it is."

The morning seemed to drag by. Katie thought it would never be lunchtime. Then the backdoor flew open and Drew walked in. He was greeted by everyone. He knew them all by name. "Cook, what's good for lunch today?" He slapped Cook on the back.

Cook's brown skin glistened from working over the hot stove. He wiped his brow and turned toward Drew. "Everything's good, Andrew. You know that. I *am* the Cook!" They laughed like they were the best of friends.

Katie loved when Cook laughed. His teeth were the whitest Katie ever saw. His face lit up the room and he put everyone in a good mood.

Cook handed Andrew a pail. "Have a good lunch. And don't fall into the canyon. I swear you get too close to that edge."

"You'll have to join me, Thomas, on a hike or maybe that mule ride down the trail," he teased. "I know you don't care to get too close to the canyon edge in any form. You'll have to get over that fear if you want to be a ranger someday." He slapped Thomas on the back. "Or you can stick to being the greatest cook here at the park."

Waiting for Dusk

Andrew headed for the door, but not before catching Katie's eye and pointing toward the canyon. Katie's heart skipped a beat. She wanted to gaze into that face for longer than a minute. She couldn't wait.

Cook broke Katie's thoughts. "Hello, Kate! It's time for a lunch break. Hey, that rhymes." He laughed at his own joke.

Katie jumped and came back to reality. "Thanks, Cook," she said as he handed her a little pail covered with one of the dining room's cloth napkins. She didn't realize he called her Kate.

Anna ran up to her. "You are on your own today. You can go into the lunchroom or there are tables outside in the back. Here's some sweet tea." She handed Katie a small jug.

"Thanks, Anna. I think I'll go outside today."

Anna's dark brown eyes seemed to have love and concern in them as Katie took the tea from her. Anna was lovely, even though her long hair was tied back in a bun and covered in netting like the other girls. Anna's dark blonde hair was done up so neatly. Katie didn't know if she'd ever get the hang of it.

"Have a good lunch then. See you in a half-hour."

Half-hour? That's all I get? Well, I better make the best of it. She hurried out the door.

Katie ran around to the front of the hotel. She didn't see Drew anywhere.

"Up here!" She looked back at the hotel. El Tovar was an amazing structure of dark timber and stone. She scanned the building from side to side. Then she spotted Drew on the front porch.

"Oh, I don't' think I'm allowed up there."

"It's fine. Come on!"

Katie sheepishly climbed the steps. It was a beautiful day, the porch was beautiful and he was beautiful. Cook gave them fresh turkey sandwiches on crusty rolls with lettuce and tomato. Katie shared her tea with him. As they ate, they talked about trivial things. Kate realized she wanted to know more about him but could wait.

Drew pulled out a pocket watch. "You still have fifteen minutes. I want to show you something."

He took Kate by the hands and pulled her up, stacked the pails and put the napkins inside. He set the pails under some brush, hidden from view. They went straight to the canyon from the porch. Drew walked out on a piece of rock that jutted out a little further than the rest of the land.

"Drew!" Katie felt butterflies in her stomach.

He held out his hand. "Come on. I won't let you fall."

She slowly stepped onto the rock, and inched towards him. Her heart pounded but she felt safe. He put both arms around her, holding her tight as they both faced the canyon. "There is nothing like it, is there?" He whispered softly in her ear.

Katie could have stayed like that for the rest of the day, but knew she had to get back to work. The magic had to end. "I have to go."

"Yes, I know."

They stepped back a few feet until they were on what Katie thought was more solid ground. She knew the rock was just an extension of the land but it felt as if she was miles from El Tovar. She turned to run back to the hotel, then stopped.

"Drew, I..." She looked into his eyes, his sparkling emerald eyes. Her heart flipped. "I hope to see you later."

"You will. You definitely will. Tomorrow is Saturday!"

Katie ran up to the brush next to the hotel, grabbed the pails and headed to the back of El Tovar. Saturday couldn't come soon enough. For now, she needed to finish her shift and then head to the boardinghouse and go to sleep. She knew the only way to get back here was through her dreams. *How confident am I? Will I be able to return? I'll just have to believe, like in all good fairytales.*

After the work day finished, Mr. Carl was waiting in his usual spot as the girls came out the back door. "Where to?" he joked.

"Home, my feet hurt." Lucinda answered for all of them.

"Sounds good to me." Kate nodded in agreement, although the girls would never know the real meaning of those words.

Waiting for Dusk

Chapter Six

Katie woke up in her own bed back in Ohio. Not as startled but still a little confused. How could she keep having the same dream? She needed to do some investigating. Maybe she saw those people on the family trip to the Grand Canyon. She sprang out of bed because a brilliant idea just came to her.

Her father always took a lot of pictures. He liked to take what he called 'people' pictures because it added to their memories of the vacation. He snapped pictures with the servers in the restaurants, and even the bellhops bringing in the luggage. He loved to get pictures of strangers doing interesting things, too. Of course, there were lots of Katie and her mom, too.

"Morning, Mom!" Katie glided into the kitchen.

"Mmm, you're in a good mood today, sweetie. And look at you! You have quite a tan after being at the beach."

"I've been working on this tan all summer. You just haven't noticed." Katie quickly changed the subject. "Mom, where are the pictures from the Grand Canyon vacation?"

Her mother's expression changed to one of surprise. "You want to look at vacation pictures?"

"Mom..." Katie was impatient.

"They're on the computer. You know that."

"Yeah, I do. Didn't you make an album, too?" Her mom had the habit of making a scrapbook of all their trips. Katie really wanted to study the pictures.

"Yep, I did. Guilty as charged. Don't make fun of me. It's relaxing and also a good hobby." Her mother laughed.

"I'm not making fun of you. I really want to see your album. I'm sure it's very well done, fun to look at and informative." Katie hoped she gave all the right answers.

Her mother disappeared for a minute and returned with the book. "Have fun! I'm going to the grocery store. Want anything?"

"Not that I can think of but I'll call you if I do!" Katie said as she headed outside and sat on the deck. She really wanted to concentrate on the photos.

Her mom did a nice job. The book began with their road trip. They stopped along the way to detour from their route and do extra sightseeing. Katie flipped the pages. *Come on! Get to the canyon already!* She thought and then stopped.

There was a beautiful scenic picture of the canyon with her father standing on the edge of what looked like a rock, a very familiar rock—like the one Drew and Katie had stood on. *So it does exist!* She probably remembered that spot and placed herself there in the dream. Next she scanned the faces of the people in the pictures, but did not recognize anyone.

Suddenly she realized her mother didn't use all the pictures, so Katie ran in the house and turned on the main computer. She sat down and waited, tapping her foot. They took over three hundred pictures on that vacation, so it would take some time to load.

The phone rang. Katie picked it up one the first ring since she was right at the computer desk in the kitchen.

"Katie? It's Mom. I'm going to have to go to the university. Got a call from a student. I'll grocery shop on my way home from there. Sorry to leave you home alone. I thought we could do something again today."

"Not a problem. I have things that will keep me busy."

She hung up the phone, then got back to studying the pictures. *Ooo! There are some pictures of our servers at the Grand Canyon,* she thought. One girl had blonde hair. *Anna?*

Katie clicked on the girl's face and zoomed in. Not a match. She continued doing that throughout the day and came up empty.

Her phone buzzed. Katie took it out of her pocket and looked at the screen. She got a new text message. It was from Ty. *Coming home tomorrow. Can't wait 2 c u.*

Wow! Is it August already? Ty had been at basketball camp for **the**

Waiting for Dusk

month of July. They would start school in a few weeks and be juniors together—Ty on the basketball team and Katie as a basketball cheerleader. That's what they always promised each other every summer since Ty moved in across the street from her. Had eight years gone that fast?

Well, Tyson would be on the basketball team but Katie would definitely not be a cheerleader because she didn't try out. Ty kept telling her that she was good enough to make the squad but that wasn't the point. It wasn't a top priority anymore. She'd have one more chance in the fall and wasn't sure if she was going to take it.

Katie's mind wandered. She thought about the girls from the boardinghouse and hoped Lucinda had a good day as a Harvey girl. She wondered what Drew was doing at that very moment. Katie clicked on the picture of her father standing on the rock by the canyon. She stared at it until she heard someone come in the door.

"Katie, are you still looking at pictures?" her mother asked.

"No" She clicked off the picture and closed the window.

"Look who I found in the driveway," Joanna's voice sounded light and happy.

Katie swung around. "Ty! Your text said you were coming home tomorrow!"

He just gave her one of those goofy, crooked grins that she loved.

Katie jumped up and flew into his arms after he set the groceries down.

"Thanks, Ty, for helping me bring the bags in. I'll let you two catch up. I'm glad Katie has one of her friends back in town." Katie's mom patted him on the arm.

They went into the family room to talk.

"I swear you grew another inch while you were gone!" Katie exclaimed.

"Six-foot-three now! I'm going to make the varsity team, I just know it!" Ty seemed so self-confident. The camp must have really helped him. His sandy blonde hair was tousled and his hazel eyes flashed brightly. "Our dream will finally come true!"

"Oh, Ty, that's just a kid's dream. I probably won't make the cheer squad. I don't think I will even try out."

"You have to! It will be a perfect junior year just as we planned. Remember the other part of our plan?"

Katie nodded. "When we turn sixteen we have our first beer together. How lame is that?" Katie laughed so hard she rolled onto the floor.

Ty laughed, too, and joined her on the floor. He was lying very close to her. "Gosh, Katie, you are so beautiful."

Where did that come from? Ty was one of her closest friends. He was not supposed to be calling her beautiful. He moved his face closer to hers.

Oh, no, he wants to kiss me, Katie thought. She pulled back and then jumped up. "Come on, Ty. Let's go for a swim before dinner."

The two teens entered the kitchen.

"Would you like to stay for dinner, Tyson?" her mother asked.

"Yes, I'd like to very much, Mrs. Roberts." Ty nodded his head. He turned to Katie and said, "I'll get my suit and be back."

"Ty is such a nice boy. He's grown so much and is more mature. By the way, have you cleaned the pool today?"

Her mom seemed to be playing matchmaker. "Yes," Katie lied as she ran upstairs to get her suit.

She sat on her bed. She didn't like that Ty tried to kiss her. The only person she wanted to kiss was Drew and he was just a dream. She needed to stop that. It was turning into an obsession, but she didn't care. The dream was almost becoming her real world, and she was going through the motions in this one.

Katie found a bathing suit, and slowly began putting it on. She couldn't wait for the day to end.

Chapter Seven

Katie heard a familiar voice. "Kathryn? Are you awake?"
"It's Saturday and we don't have to work."
She sat up in bed. "Come in, Anna."
Anna opened the door and smiled at Katie. "We don't have to work but Lucinda volunteered to go in today. So I thought it was a perfect day for us to be together. I asked Mr. Johansson to saddle up two horses for us."
"Horses?" Katie was still waking up and a little confused.
"Yes, silly, Mr. Johansson has a barn with two horses in it. He lets us use them whenever we want."
"Give me some time to get ready and I'll meet you outside," Katie said while she got out of bed.
"Fifteen minutes, Kathryn. That's all I am giving you. I packed some bread and cheese so don't worry about eating."
"Okay." Katie wondered what she would wear for horseback riding. She looked in a little closet in the hallway outside her room and found some clothes. She did the morning ritual in less than fifteen, and then headed out the door.
Anna was already on a beautiful dapple-gray horse, holding the reins to the second one. That horse was a silky brown with a black mane and tail. Luckily Katie took riding lessons when she was younger, her father made sure of it.
"This is Flicka. Flicka meet Kathryn." Anna handed the reins to her.
"Nice to meet you, Flicka," Katie bowed. "And who is this other lovely horse if I may ask?"
"Thunder!" Anna shouted out as she galloped away.

Katie mounted Flicka, then followed Anna and Thunder. After they rode for about a mile, Anna came to a stop. "This is the perfect place to talk." She slid gracefully from Thunder, looped the reins over a low branch and sat down in the shade of the tree. Katie did the same.

"Alright, Miss Anna. Now that we are alone, you're going to tell me everything!" Katie felt the excitement growing inside. She couldn't wait to hear the gossip.

"I will tell you everything. But first you have to tell me how you met Mr. Andrew Martin." Anna's eyes grew wide.

"You know...you know him?"

"Why, yes. Everyone does. He works at the park, you know. And, yes. I do know…about you and him. You don't think I pay attention?"

Katie decided to fill her in on everything that happened, except for the boardinghouse visit and the kiss.

Anna rolled in the grass laughing after Katie told her how she fell over the fence on that fateful day she met Drew. "So ladylike! I wonder if Andrew saw your britches. You think he's the bee's knees, don't you?"

"The what?" Katie thought that was the strangest saying she'd ever heard.

"The bee's knees. You know…you think he is great."

Katie rolled her eyes. "Enough of that. Now on to you. Tell me how and why you came to the Grand Canyon."

"Actually, Lucinda and I came together. We met at the Lake Forest Academy—a private high school for boys and girls. Lucinda was one of my roommates freshmen year and we became inseparable. Ferry Hall was the girls' school and the boys attended Lake Forest Academy. We would have outings together. The school took us to the beach and organized hikes. In the winter, we ice skated and went on sleigh rides. What fun we had. Lucinda and I were the best of friends."

"I don't believe I've ever heard of that school."

"It's a private school outside of Chicago. Both Lucinda and I lived at the school because it was pretty far from home."

Katie was taken aback by that information. Lucinda and Anna knew each other. If they went to a private school, their families obviously had money. So what were they doing at the canyon?

"Tell me how you ended up here," Katie asked again.

"Lucinda read an article in the paper about the Harvey girls. They

Waiting for Dusk

were young, single and liked adventure. Fred Harvey hired pretty, smart girls with good moral character and backgrounds to work at his restaurants out West. It said the girls were provided with room and board. There are also managers, like Mr. and Mrs. Johansson, to watch over the girls. Plus the girls were also given free railway passes. We figured we'd see the country together, maybe meet a rich rancher and settle down with our husbands in a new part of the country." Anna laughed. "I'm probably boring you."

"No, I find it quite interesting. Go on."

"We knew we had the qualifications so we wrote letters to the company. It would be hard to convince our families while we were still in high school so we didn't tell them until after graduation. They didn't like it at all. My family really wanted me to go to college and I tried a semester. I had to prove to them that I really wanted to do this."

"And what about Lucinda?"

"Lucinda's family finally just gave in. When she came home from Ferry, she did nothing. She went on strike. That's Lucinda for you. She got her way."

"And you did too," Katie finished for her.

"Yes, I did. We arrived here by train in April. No regrets. The money is good, plus we get time off whenever we want. Lucinda and I never did get to travel together…" Anna's voice trailed off.

"What happened? If you two were best friends for years, what could have happened?" Katie looked at Anna and saw sadness in her eyes.

"A boy. A rancher's son, named Daniel." Anna looked away.

"Go on," Katie prodded.

"Lucinda met Daniel first. He liked to come for lunch at El Tovar. We, of course, were just learning how to be waitresses and were working in the back kitchen. She caught a glimpse of Daniel out in the dining room and was determined to meet him. She charmed her way out there and then went over to their table asking if everything was alright. She started up a conversation with Daniel. The next thing you know they had a date to go riding."

"I can picture Lucinda doing something like that." Katie giggled.

"Of course, Daniel said he would come to the boardinghouse first. Mr. Carl had to meet him and approve the date. When he showed up the next day, I was grooming one of the horses. He came into the barn looking for Mr. Carl. I never meant for this to happen, I swear I didn't!"

Anna threw herself onto the ground, crying.

"It's okay, Anna. It's okay," Katie assured her. "How bad can it be?"

"It was love at first sight!" Anna wailed even louder.

"For you?"

"For both of us!"

Katie saw that it was quite a problem. You can't help who you fall in love with, and you can't make someone fall in love with you. Haven't all the fairy tales in the world proven that? Look at Cinderella. She fell in love with the prince and it was love at first sight. Her stepsisters tried and tried to gain his attention but he didn't notice them. In the end, the right girl ended up with the right guy. Katie guessed that Anna's story didn't have the same happy ending.

She waited for Anna to calm down.

Anna sat up and continued. "Lucinda was head over heels for Daniel. I couldn't react. I couldn't hurt her like that. Daniel went on the ride with Lucinda. He did like her. How could anyone not like her? She was fun, smart, pretty and charismatic. He liked her as a friend. Daniel decided to stop seeing her when he realized she thought it was more than that."

Anna was quiet for a moment. Katie reached for her hand to give her support.

"Daniel wanted to be truthful. He told her how he met me in the barn and that he would like to start seeing me, if it was alright with her. It wasn't, of course. There was a big blow up between them outside the boardinghouse. I never heard such screaming come out of Lucinda's mouth. Then she began to cry. I looked out of my window and saw Daniel holding her. He walked her to the door, got on his horse and rode away. The next thing I knew, my door flew open and there stood Lucinda. 'Don't ever talk to me again, you traitor,' she screamed. 'How could you?'"

"What did you do?"

"I tried to explain that I didn't do anything. I told her we talked in the barn one time and then I only saw Daniel was when he came to get Lucinda. She didn't seem to believe me."

"Wow," was all Katie could say.

They sat and stared up at the blue sky that seemed to go on forever. Finally Katie had to ask, "Did you ever start seeing Daniel?"

Waiting for Dusk

"Yes," Anna's voice was barely a whisper. "It was wonderful."

"So then, what happened? Where is he?" Katie couldn't stand the suspense.

"Gone," Anna said. "He's gone."

Chapter Eight

Anna turned to Katie. "Let's go. Let's ride!" She ran, jumped onto Thunder, then seemed to disappear over the horizon.

Katie gazed down the road watching the swirls of dust as she contemplated all she just heard. Another horse was coming down the trail. As it grew closer, Katie saw the rider was Drew.

"Kate!" he called out. "It looks like you've been left in the dust."

"Yes, it seems so," she called back.

Andrew stopped in front of the tree. "Well, it is your day off. I'd like to show you more of the Canyon. Are you up for it?"

Katie hopped up. She took Flicka's reins and mounted the horse gracefully. She was pleased with herself.

Thanks, Dad, for those lessons, she thought as they headed off toward the canyon.

It was a short ride, shorter than Katie remembered. She loved that she was following Andrew on her horse. She looked at his broad shoulders and smiled. She loved how his dark hair just covered the back of his collar. He was even handsome from behind. Speaking of behinds...she stopped herself. I'm being a little naughty now! She laughed aloud.

Andrew turned around, "Is everything alright?"

"Yes. Everything's fine."

Andrew stopped and dismounted. "We're here." He came back to help Katie off her horse.

"Thanks," she said as slid into his arms. "This is beautiful." She couldn't get enough of the Grand Canyon. The colors were dazzling in

Waiting for Dusk

the afternoon sun. They didn't speak. Drew took Katie's hand as they walked along.

"Summer's coming to an end. I'll be going back to school soon." Andrew broke the silence.

"Oh, me, too," Katie nodded in agreement.

"You're still in school? The girls here are usually done with school. I thought you'd be here on semester break when I come back."

Andrew's face changed to surprise or disappointment. Katie couldn't tell which. "Where do you go to school?"

"Back in Ohio. I'll be a Junior this year."

"I'll be a Senior. I can't wait to get done and get back here. My parents want me to go to college on the East coast but I'd rather be out here."

"You live on the East coast?"

"New York—New York City to be exact. I go to a private boarding school."

"Oh." Kate couldn't help thinking that New York was pretty far from the canyon and perhaps his parents wanted to keep him closer to home. "Have you thought about a major?"

"Biology for now. But let's not talk about the boring stuff. I want to hear more about you." Andrew spun her around and looked deep into her eyes. "Is it too early to say 'I love you'?"

Katie laughed and playfully pushed him away. "Drew, you have a great sense of humor." Her heart pounded. She wanted to say that it was not too early. She would love to hear him say it again and again. She chose to talk about herself instead because that seemed like a safer topic.

"I live in a small town outside of Oberlin, Ohio. My mother works at the college there. Have you heard of Oberlin College?"

"Of course, I have." Andrew nodded. "It is a liberal arts college that's very accepting of women and Negroes."

"What did you say?" Her eyes flashed, then she remembered this was a different century, a different time.

"I said that Oberlin is very accepting of women and..."

"...Blacks, African Americans," Katie interrupted.

"Alright then. If that is how they say it in Oberlin, so shall I. I'm progressive and open to new century ideas." Andrew smiled.

Katie returned his smile. She knew she better change the subject and fast. She just might give away what century she was really from. "School starts the last week of August. It will be here too soon. I only have three more weeks here."

"Sad to hear. My first term does not start until September. Hopefully we will meet up again."

Drew pulled Kate close to him and she did not resist. She wrapped her arms around his waist, then felt him rest his chin on her head. The sun was lower in the sky, and the canyon took on another mystical glow.

"I feel like it's close to suppertime," Andrew said. "If you would like, I will ride with you back to the boardinghouse."

"Yes, I would love that."

They rode side-by-side on the way back, chatting about the canyon, the weather, and the people they worked with. When they came close to the boardinghouse, Katie turned to Andrew and said, "I think I'll go the rest of the way on my own." She didn't want to get into trouble with the Johanssons. They didn't know she was with Andrew, plus she hadn't cleared it with them.

"I understand." Drew said as if he knew what she was thinking. "Ask the Johanssons if you can go hiking tomorrow. I'll be by to pick you up early." He turned and galloped away.

Katie sighed. What am I doing? Living a dream?

She was starting to like this life better than her real life. It was all so confusing. There was no guarantee she could be back here tomorrow but she let Drew think she'd be here. As she rode toward the boardinghouse, a voice called to her.

"Where have you been? I was starting to get worried about you!" As Katie came closer, she saw Anna standing on the front porch, arms on her hips. "Well, you don't have to tell me where you've been. Come on. Get down and help me take care of the horses. I have some news to tell you."

Katie and Anna walked into the barn with Flicka trailing slowly behind. Anna piled hay into the stalls while Katie removed Flicka's saddle. Then Anna blurted out, "Lucinda's getting married."

"What?" Katie thought she didn't hear that correctly.

"Lucinda is getting married," Anna repeated.

Katie dropped the saddle. "To who? I thought she was in love with Daniel."

Anna frowned. "I did, too. She met a local, a very rich rancher's son a few weeks ago. They've been seeing each other every day since. His name is Henry Hasting."

"Mmm." Katie thought for a moment. "So do you think this is a rebound thing?"

"Rebound?"

"You know, she's going to marry Henry to forget about Daniel. She's only known him a few weeks."

"Girls! Supper!" Mr. Carl called them.

The pair ran from the barn into the house. Lucinda was waiting for them. "Kathryn, look!" She held out her left hand. "I'm getting married! And I want you to be a bridesmaid!"

Chapter Nine

I'm not ready to get up, and certainly not ready to end this dream. Katie sat up in bed and saw her butterflies on the wall. She could see sunlight streaming in her windows, bouncing off her sky blue walls and moaned. She decided to go back to sleep for a few hours. She needed to tell Lucinda she couldn't be a bridesmaid. Her loyalties were with Anna and she should be in the wedding. Those two were friends for a long time and came on the adventure together.

Katie lay back on her pillow and dozed off. She woke an hour later and she was still in her room. *What happened? I should be in Arizona.* She pounded her mattress in frustration.

She propped up some pillows and grabbed her laptop. She went to a search engine and typed in 'Harvey girls'. She expected to see the search engine ask, 'Did you mean...' with another suggestion because there was no such thing as Harvey girls. Instead there was a list of websites. Katie quickly chose one, and waited for it to load. She was nervous and excited. She never heard of a 'Harvey girl', now she practically was one.

Katie read the history of the girls. It was just like Anna described. Fred Harvey, a real person, wanted pretty, smart girls with high morals to work at his restaurants that were located out west. She read on and on, absorbing all she could.

There was a knock at the door. Her mother opened it slightly. "Oh, you are awake. Lindsey's here. She's home from her aunt's ranch and couldn't wait to see you."

"Tell her to come up!" Katie sprang up from her bed as Lindsey ran in. The two jumped and hugged for what seemed like forever. "Tell me all about the ranch and what you did there!"

Waiting for Dusk

"Oh, you know. It was the same old, same old. Riding horses, working on the ranch, meeting boys…"

"You met someone?" Katie clasped Lindsey's hands, and they bounced up and down on the bed.

"He'll be there next summer when I go again. Until then, we're just going to text and be friends."

"Oh, no. You didn't just say that. I see that look in your eyes. There's more to tell." Katie was glad to be distracted by Lindsey's stories. They talked the rest of the morning about her stay at the ranch.

"Wait for me while I get dressed," Katie said as she headed into her bathroom.

After she came out of the shower, Katie heard Lindsey's voice call out. "Your mom said you had a boring summer. Is that true?"

Katie threw on shorts and a tank. She wrapped a towel around her just-shampooed hair and opened the door. "Yes and no. I got to drive the Mustang! Ty is home now. And I've had some good dreams…"

"Dreams? Ooo, tell me about them," Lindsey leaned forward placing her elbows on her knees.

Katie hesitated. Lindsey was her best friend. Would she understand? Would she think she was crazy? Katie flopped on her bed and decided to tell her about the dreams.

"Do you think that book your mom gave you has something to do with it? You did say it was historical fiction, a romance novel. Maybe you're just dreaming about what you read in the book." Lindsey gave good advice.

Katie suddenly realized she didn't have a clue what the book was about. She thought she read it through to the end but couldn't tell Lindsey who the main characters were or what the plot was about. She blinked and then stared into space.

"Katie? Katie? Are you alright?" Lindsey shook her shoulder. "I think you need to get out of this room, out of this house! Come on. Let's go."

Katie grabbed her purse and phone, then they were out the door.

"Later, Mom!" Katie called as they shut the door.

Lindsey was a few months older than Katie and already had her driver's license. They hopped in her car.

"Where are we going?" Katie asked as they drove away.

"Jordyn's."

"Jordyn's home?"

"Yes, haven't you been checking your phone?" Lindsey said with a loud sigh.

"I haven't gotten any messages in days!" Katie looked at her phone and saw twenty new messages. "Oh, maybe I have. Don't know where my head has been."

"I bet ten of them are from me. I let you know when I left the ranch, when I was boarding the plane, when I got off the plane…"

"Okay, I get it! I'm so glad you're home, Linds, really!" Katie made her mind up to get back into the real world and stay there. "Let's see if Jordyn wants to go shopping!"

Jordyn was happy to see her two friends. They laughed and talked for hours. Jordyn had many tales to tell from her trip to China. Her two moms were so excited to show her all the places they were on their first trip. The best thing on that trip was adopting her as they always told her.

"My moms were so embarrassing. They made me pose with everything, even a street sign." Jordyn smiled, and Katie could tell she was really pleased. "They just wanted me to soak in everything. I told them I really appreciated all they did with the trip, but this is my home…with them."

"Awww…" Katie and Lindsey both said at the same time.

Just then one of Jordyn's moms came home.

"Hi, Ms. Taylor," Katie said.

"Girls, good to see you. How was your summer? Want to stay for dinner?"

"Fine and yes, thanks!" Lindsey answered for them.

Katie's phone rang. She saw it was Erin, the head cheerleader of the basketball team at school. "Hi, Erin, what's up?"

"Just want to know if you are going to try out for basketball cheerleader. You weren't at camp this summer."

"Gee, Erin, I haven't thought about it yet." Katie wasn't completely truthful.

"Katie, you're really good and I'd love to have you on the team. Please think about it. I'll see you when school starts."

"I will. Thanks for thinking I'm good enough. I'll see you in school, too!"

"Well, what's up?" Jordyn prodded.

Katie told the girls about the conversation.

Waiting for Dusk

"Of course, you have to try out. Remember you and Tyson made a promise to each other." Lindsey teased.

"We were nine! Things change."

"I think Tyson likes you, Katie," Jordyn said.

"We're friends, that's all."

"I'd love to be 'friends' with a hot guy like that," Lindsey replied.

Ms. White came into the room. "Dinner, girls. We're dining outside."

The rest of the evening was very enjoyable. Katie liked Ms. Taylor and Ms. White. They were funny, told good stories and had a lot to share about their trip to China.

Katie was glad they sat outside. The sun set and dusk settled in. Katie was glad about that because they couldn't tell she was really daydreaming about another time, another place that was only real to her and no one else.

Chapter Ten

Lucinda's voice could be heard above all the others. "My dress has to be perfect. This is going to be one of the biggest weddings Arizona has ever seen. Where's Kathryn? She needs to be fitted for her bridesmaid dress. Kathryn? Kathryn?"

Katie threw her door open. "Lucinda! I'm right here. What time is it? I need to talk to you anyway." She pulled Lucinda into her room. "Lucinda, I don't think it's right that I should be a bridesmaid. You are friends with Ruthie and…Anna. It doesn't feel right."

"We are friends, Kathryn. We work together, live at the boardinghouse together, and you will be so beautiful in the wedding. You're going to look wonderful in your dress. Now I won't take 'no' for an answer. The ladies are here to do our fittings."

"They're here?" Katie was surprised. Her mind was on other things, like hiking with Drew.

"Henry says that I can have and do whatever I want for my wedding. Isn't he wonderful?" Lucinda clapped her hands.

Katie decided to go along with it. She got measured, fitted, pushed and prodded. Lucinda was next, so Katie escaped back to her room. She dressed for hiking, and headed down the hall to Anna's room.

"Anna, are you in there?"

"Is it safe to come out now?"

"Yes, but let me in," Katie said through the crack in the door. As she entered the room, Anna was sitting on the edge of her bed holding something.

"What do you have there?" Katie pointed and then said, "Oh, that's none of my business. Sorry."

Waiting for Dusk

"It's a letter from Daniel." Anna hugged it to her chest. "He's been on a cattle drive. He went with some of the ranch hands down to Mexico to bring cattle they purchased up to their ranch. Daniel decided to go on the drive when I told him I couldn't see him anymore. I told him it was hurting Lucinda too much to see us together. Now that she's getting married, things could be different." Her eyes pleaded with Katie. "What do you think?

"Go for it!" Katie threw her hand in the air. "I'm so happy for you! Now, on to even more serious things. Anna, I can't be in this wedding. It isn't right. You should be in it, not me."

"No, that's quite alright. Be in the wedding. Lucinda wants you to be in it."

"But what about Ruthie? She's more of a friend than me."

Anna shook her head. "I don't know how that girl thinks lately. You've been fitted, haven't you? You can't back out now."

Katie threw Anna a 'why me' look, and stomped out of the room. She heard Anna laughing. That was a good sign. Anna was happy. It was all because of Daniel.

I hope Daniel gets here soon, Katie thought.

Her thoughts were interrupted by Mr. Johansson. "Mr. Andrew is here to see you. He said he would like to take you hiking for the day. Would you like to do that?"

"Yes, I'd like that very much." Katie nodded in excitement.

"Then be on your way! Be home before dark!" he called as she skipped out the door.

Drew waited for her outside, sitting on his horse. He gently pulled her up behind him, and they trotted off. Katie wrapped her arms around his waist. She felt a warm wind on her face and the breeze in her hair. She wished she had her camera phone with her to take a picture --Drew and Kate frozen in time. When they reached the Canyon, Drew stopped. He let Katie slide down and then dismounted himself.

"Ready for some lessons?" He smiled at her.

"No! School doesn't start for a few weeks yet!" She playfully came back but then reconsidered. "Actually, Drew, you can be the teacher and I will be the student and not make a fuss." Katie wished all of her teachers looked like him.

They strolled along to the edge of the Canyon. "This is called Yavapai Point," Drew pointed out.

They stood in one spot as he showed Katie what to look for. "You get a good view from here. The canyon is more than a mile deep. You can hike down to the Colorado River using one of two trails. Can you see the river? There?" he pointed. Then he pointed to another area. "That's Bright Angel Canyon."

He seemed so excited to show her everything. "Come on, walk with me."

Drew took Kate's hand. "I really want you to see Kolb Studio. It was built by two brothers, Emery and Ellsworth Kolb. They are very famous. Have you read about them? Perhaps you've seen their work in National Geographic."

Katie seemed to recall going to Kolb Studio when she was on the trip with her mom and dad. She wished she paid better attention. "They made a trip down the Colorado River and filmed it. I think they showed the movieat this studio."

"Yes, exactly right. They were the first to make a moving picture of their trip down the Colorado through the Grand Canyon. They still show the movie. We can go see it if you like. Emery still lives here, shows the movie everyday and narrates it himself. Today he's having a guest lecturer, Jack Woods. He's very famous in his own right and won't be here long. I believe he's going back east to get married soon. Jack's a good friend of mine and I'd really like for you to meet him."

Kolb Studio was a very fascinating building. It looked like it could fall right into the canyon, but was really built on a sturdy piece of rock. As they passed by, Katie saw a sign posted for the guest lecturer.

Boring! she thought. Maybe she could distract Drew and he wouldn't want to go to the lecture.

"What about that hike?" Katie asked. "We still have time, don't we?"

"Yes, for a short hike. Bright Angel path is just ahead. We can have a short walk if you like." He had a canteen over his shoulder and patted it. "We'll need water in this heat."

Kate hadn't thought of that. It was a warm day, and she wore more clothes than when she had come with her parents. The khaki-color knickers, pants that billowed out and banded at the knee, were kind of cute in an old-fashioned way. The matching vest was worn over a white blouse. Finally, brown knee-high boots finished the look.

Haven't they heard of shorts and tanks in the twenties? Katie

Waiting for Dusk

chuckled.

"A penny for your thoughts."

"I was just thinking that a short hike would be just fine."

They started down the path. Drew took out his pocket watch. "Fifteen minutes down, then a half hour to return." Katie looked a little surprised. "That long? What about fifteen down, fifteen back?"

It was Drew's turn to laugh. "It's all uphill, Kate. All uphill."

Drew paid the gatekeeper a one dollar toll to use the trail. He explained he was not too fond of having to pay someone for the right to walk on a trail. The park service was working on having the path transferred over to them, but the owner was giving them quite a battle. The land was still part of a mining claim owned by Ralph Cameron, a U.S. Senator, who was making things extremely difficult. There was another trail, Kaibab Trail, built by the park service so people had a free alternative.

"Then let's use that one." Kate was all for supporting Drew's passion about the park and also longed to tell him that there was no longer a charge to use Angel Bright.

"That trail has no shade and I want you to be comfortable. Plus it's farther away. So as much as I object to the fee, we'll use this one." Drew shook his head. "I'm getting a little too serious, aren't I? This is supposed to be your day."

They laughed, took hold of each other's hand and headed off down the path. The trail was a pretty easy walk for her. There were plenty of switchbacks that were incorporated into the trail to make the descent easier, but also made the hike longer to the bottom. Drew explained if they went all the way to the bottom of the canyon, it would have been several miles of walking.

When they returned, Kate realized she really hadn't looked at the sights but was focused on Drew the whole time. She listened to his every word, his laugh, his breathing. She looked at his face, his emerald green eyes, and his lips with just a little fullness to them. She watched him walk, so sure-footed and athletic.

"I'm sure you're ready to sit down and relax." Drew passed the canteen to Katie so she could have a drink. They walked along the rim trail until they reached the Studio.

Drew went inside first, and Katie followed. There were many people already there. She strolled around looking at photos and books for sale. Then she searched the room to locate Drew, and found him talking to a group of people. One man came up, slapped Drew on the back and shook his hand. The man looked oddly familiar. In fact he looked like... her father! No, that couldn't be right. He looked younger but it was her father. Thankfully, he couldn't see her. What would she say to him? What would he say to her? She decided to leave, and quickly went out the door.

"Kate! Kate!" She heard Drew calling. "Where are you going?" He caught up to her.

"It was just a little stuffy in there. Would you mind taking me home? I hope you can get back in time for the lecture."

"Of course, I will." Drew was a perfect gentleman. Katie wouldn't mind if he was less of a gentleman.

Drew's horse was waiting for them at the barn behind El Tovar. Katie was surprised. "How did that happen?"

"I have friends..." he said mysteriously and then laughed.

The ride to the boardinghouse was too short. Katie wanted to stay with Drew but knew she didn't want to see her father even though it was a dream. Why couldn't she control the dream a little better?

Drew stopped at the far side of the barn. He slipped off the horse, and Kate jumped into his arms. He pulled her close and kissed her. Not like the first time when it was a short, gentle kiss. Right then he kissed her like he would never see her again, very unlike the kiss in the fairytales she knew as a child.

"I will see you for lunch tomorrow, my sweet Kate." He whispered.

"Yes, yes you will." Katie barely could stand.

Drew rode off, and Katie hurried into the house.

"Hello, you must be Kathryn," a lovely young woman greeted her at the door.

"Yes, yes I am." Katie held out her hand.

"I'm Loretta, Lucinda's sister." The woman turned and walked with Katie inside. "I came out early to help Lucinda and to get fitted for my dress."

Katie looked at Loretta and thought there was something familiar about her. She looked like Lucinda but was a softer, prettier version. Her hair was more of a light golden brown.

That must be it, she thought. *She seems familiar because she's*

Waiting for Dusk

Lucinda's sister. Katie felt comfortable in her company.

"Have you heard they set a date?" Loretta asked.

"No, no I haven't. When is the big day?"

"The first Saturday of September."

"Really?" Katie knew school would have started. Plus she told Drew she would be gone. Now she had to figure out how to come back.

Dreams! Who knew they could be so much work!

Chapter Eleven

Katie heard loud, muffled sounds. It almost sounded like a fight. The door to her bedroom was closed, so she tiptoed over to open it.

"I can't believe you let her do that, Joanna! She's too young, too irresponsible. She could get hurt!" It was her father's voice.

"She was bored, Jackson. I was trying to think of something she could do, something that would occupy her time," her mother answered.

"Bored? Now you're starting to sound just like Katie!" He still sounded angry. Katie thought she better get downstairs and help her mother out.

"She was only trying to make me feel better, Dad! I only drove the Mustang around a parking lot! Geesh!" Katie defended her mother as she bounded into the kitchen.

Jackson swung around. His expression changed when he saw his daughter. "Pumpkin, come and give your old dad a kiss."

Katie ran and hugged him. It was good to see him. On the other hand, she never heard her parents fight like that. She was a little disturbed. "So you guys aren't getting a divorce or anything like that, are you?"

Jackson laughed. "No, Katie my love. I just happened to see the mileage on the Mustang and knew it had been driven. I was surprised to find out it was you. That's all."

"It was just around a parking lot." Katie rolled her eyes.

"She needed a distraction. You had fun, didn't you, Katie?" Her mom looked at her with wide eyes. Katie knew she was looking for a diversion.

Waiting for Dusk

"Dad, school starts in less than two weeks. Do you think you can give me some more driving lessons now that you're home? I should have my driver's license by now." Katie wrapped her arms around his neck, jumped on his back and Jackson started running around the house with her, finally dumping her on the sofa. She looked at her mom and gave her the okay hand signal.

"My two girls, you know how to get the best of me," Jackson ran back in the kitchen and gave Joanna a kiss on the cheek. "Dinner's on the deck tonight, girls. I'm cooking."

Katie was happy things were back to normal. During dinner she planned on asking her parents some questions, being careful not to reveal too much about her dreams or who she had met. She ran back upstairs, found her phone and made plans for the day.

"Ty, I need something to do."

"Come over and we'll shoot some baskets."

"Don't really want to do that, how about the mall?" Katie really wanted to shop.

"Okay, but you owe me."

"Fine, see you in a bit." She would make it up to him. Maybe a quick game when they got back.

"I'll be home in time for dinner," Katie said as she ran down the stairs. "Ty is taking me shopping."

"That boy must really like you to take you shopping." Her father grinned as she ran by.

"Oh, Dad," was all she could say as she went out the door.

Tyson's mom sat in the car, waiting to drive them to the mall.

"Sorry about this," Tyson whispered. "I should have my license soon."

"Don't we all wish we had our licenses?" Katie whispered back as she climbed in the car, and to his mother she said, "Hi, Mrs. Gray. Thanks for taking us."

Ty and Katie were soon walking around the mall. Ty was helpful, carrying Katie's shopping bags and waiting for her to try on clothes.

"Aren't you going to buy anything, Ty?" Katie felt he should have some fun, too.

"No, I'm good. I would like a soda though, how about a break?"

They walked over to the food court, got something to drink and sat at a little table off in a corner.

"I want to ask you something, Katie. I know it's early, and school hasn't started yet, but I didn't want to take any chances. Will you go to Homecoming with me?"

Katie was taken aback. Ty was right. It was a little early. She hadn't even thought about school or Homecoming. She had a wedding to be in first. Plus she already had a boyfriend…what was she thinking? She nodded her head and then said, "Of course, I will, Ty. I'd love to go with you."

Tyson's mouth slowly grew into a large grin. He slapped the table and put his arms over his head like he won a race making Katie feel a little uncomfortable. Then he leaned over and kissed her cheek. "Thanks, Katie, you know I love you. Do you want to go dress shopping now?"

Katie assumed he was kidding and playfully punched him in the arm. His arm was solid. He got more muscle at basketball camp. She studied him carefully, and began to see him in a new light. Her girlfriends said he was hot. Maybe she never noticed because she always saw him as a ten-year-old boy that was her friend. She needed to start looking at him in a different way.

Boyfriend? Katie had trouble associating that word with Tyson. She thought she'd try it out again in her head but instead thought, Drew. Groaning, she put her head down on the table.

"Katie, are you alright?"

"Yes, sorry. Just tired. Can we go home now?" Katie sat up.

"Sure, I'll let my mom know." He pulled out his phone.

They walked to the middle of the mall by the fountain. Ty took Katie's hand and had all of her shopping bags in the other. It felt a little awkward, but she didn't resist. Her head was too cloudy, too confused.

"Sorry, kids. Didn't mean to keep you waiting." Mrs. Gray hurried up to them. "I got Tyson's text when I was in line."

"It's fine, Mom. No worries."

On the ride home, Katie made small talk with Mrs. Gray and tried to ignore Tyson moving closer to her in the backseat. Something didn't add up and she couldn't wait to get home. She wished his mother would drive faster. Kate let out a sigh of relief as they pulled into the Gray's drive. As soon as the car came to a stop, she hopped out.

Katie walked across the street to her house, waving to both Tyson and his mother. "See you tomorrow; I'll owe you a game, Ty!" and quickly went in the house.

Waiting for Dusk

No one was around so she ran up the stairs to her room. She threw her bags in the corner, and sat down in her overstuffed yellow chair to think. Leaning her head back and closing her eyes, Katie stated all the reasons why Tyson was a good guy and would make a good boyfriend. Then she debated with reasons to keep everything the same. The bottom line was that she liked him as a friend; she did not like him as a boyfriend.

What was she going to do? Definitely talk to Lindsey about everything, but it could wait till later. She was looking forward to dinner. Katie wanted to grill her parents on the past--their past and hers.

"Dinner," Katie heard her father call up the stairs. "We'll be outside!"

Katie jumped up and headed for the backyard. "Anything I can carry out?" she said as she slid back the screen door to go out.

"Take this lemonade." Her mother handed her a pitcher. "Homemade. Just how your father likes it."

They sat down at the table while Jackson adjusted the umbrella so no one would have sun in their eyes. "Great to be back with the family," he said.

"Speaking of family, why does the name Loretta sound so familiar to me?" Katie played with her salad.

Joanna and Jackson looked quizzically at each other. Her mom then answered, "That's the name of your great-grandmother. You probably forgot. When we did speak of her we called her Grandma Rett."

"I remember hearing about her." Katie tried not to be too interested. "Didn't she have a sister?"

"Yes, Lucinda, my Great Aunt Lucinda. I remember going to her ranch once when I was a young girl. Grandma Rett, my mom and I flew out there. It was my first time on a plane and I was so excited. Plus I couldn't wait to meet Uncle Henry. I had heard so many rumors about him. I remember hearing the adults talk about him when they thought the kids were in another room, not listening. We knew how to listen without getting caught." Her mother laughed.

"Well, what did they say about him?"

"He was a very sweet man. He was very attentive to Lucinda and did everything she wanted. He also was not very…ah…ah…" It seemed her mother was having a hard time choosing the right word. "…attractive."

"Oh," was all Katie could say.

They ate in silence for awhile.

"But they loved each other, didn't they" Katie broke the silence.

"Who are you talking about?" her mom seemed to have forgotten the earlier conversation.

"Henry and Lucinda."

"Um, I don't really know. They weren't talked about too much. When I saw them, they were old by then. I would say Henry really loved Lucinda. I think she loved him. They had three children, girls. Two of them never married and lived at home with Henry and Lucinda. The youngest got married and left the ranch. I think her family left Arizona entirely. I never met her. I only met my two older cousins, Lucy and Henrietta. We may have some pictures. There's a box that says 'Grandma Rett' somewhere in the attic and there's probably pictures in it. Not too many, I don't think, maybe none at all."

"Is it alright if I look after dinner?"

"Sure it is. I'm glad you're taking an interest in your roots." Her mom patted Katie's arm.

Katie's dad told them stories of his trip while they ate. She was used to him being gone. He always had stories to tell when he got back. She faded in and out of the conversation.

"Am I boring you?" Jackson looked intently at his daughter.

"Um, no, Dad. It's so-o-o interesting." Katie pushed her food around her plate.

"Well, Joanna, I think you are right about our daughter being bored this summer. I think I may go for an evening swim. You should join me, give you something to do." Her father laughed, pushed back his seat, then disappeared into the house.

Now that Katie had her mom alone, she decided to ask a few more questions. "Do you think that Lucinda was happy?"

"My goodness. All these questions about Lucinda. Where is this all coming from?" Her mother poured them some more lemonade.

"I was just thinking about her and how you said her husband wasn't too attractive. He was rich, wasn't he? Was that why she married him?"

"Maybe so. The family didn't talk about it too much. Lucinda was always known for her great personality. I heard she was very happy and bubbly as a young girl. Not so much as she grew older, according to Grandma Rett. She had a very good life, was a devoted mother and very

Waiting for Dusk

helpful running the ranch.

I think she had something to prove. Loretta was the pretty sister, and Lucinda was the personality sister. I think she wanted to one-up her sister."

"Grandma Rett stayed in Chicago her whole life, didn't she?"

"Yes. She met Grandpa Stan there and lived a very happy life. I just wish she would have lived to see you," Joanna sighed.

"Grandma Rett had Sandra and Richard, and Sandra was your mother." Katie tried to put all the pieces of the puzzle together in her mind.

"And my mom met Mitchell in college and ended up here." her mother continued. "You know the story."

"I love to hear you tell it." Katie leaned forward.

"Fine. Then I went to college here at Oberlin, met your father, traveled with him and then ended up back here. End of story."

"You left out your two older brothers. I don't think they would appreciate that. You moved back here because you missed them all, your mom, dad, and brothers."

"Guilty as charged. Now help me clean up."

After they cleaned up, Katie ran up to the attic. "Don't spill that lemonade on anything old." her mother hollered up the stairs. "I'm going to join your father in the pool."

"Okay. I won't bother you two lovebirds then." Katie teased.

"Stop it, Katie. You can join us." her mother teased back.

"Nope. I have plans."

She went up the next flight of stairs to the attic. Katie always loved it up there. She loved the way it smelled. She loved the coziness of it. Her mother had done some decorating so it didn't feel like a real attic. There was a blue and white pinstripe loveseat against the wall, and a pastel braided rug on the floor. Pictures of family hung in floral frames on the walls. Her mother had painted the walls a creamy white so it would feel bigger. Everything was neatly stacked or hung up, not your average attic. Katie turned on the ceiling fan, a couple lamps for light, set her lemonade on the small table next to the loveseat and then went to work.

She went to the shelves where the old photo albums were and was tempted to start looking through them but thought better of it. She was on a mission. Behind the albums was a stack of boxes. The bottom one said 'Grandma Rett'.

Katie was so excited her hands trembled as she reached for the box and carefully pulled it out as she tried to picture Grandma Rett. She had passed away before Katie was born, so all she ever saw were pictures of her grandmother. In most of the pictures, Rett was older and had white hair. That's how Katie remembered her. She always seemed lovely to Katie with her kind face, soft blue eyes and an endearing smile.

Katie slowly pulled the lid off the box. On top of the pile was one of those pictures Katie remembered seeing. It was of Katie's mom when she was a teenager, Joanna's mom Sandra, and Grandma Rett. She set the picture aside, making plans to frame it and put it in her room. Picture after picture were of the grandchildren, her mother and her brothers.

Where are the pictures of Loretta when she was younger? As Katie went through the pile, she came across older black and white pictures. There were pictures of Grandma Sandra and Great Uncle Richard from their school days. There were holiday pictures of Sandra and Richard as children. It made sense that Rett would have lots of pictures of her children, but there had to be more. The pile kept getting smaller and smaller. Katie felt frustration overwhelm her. Didn't they take any pictures back in the old days?

She sat on the floor with all the pictures spread out around her. She leaned back on the loveseat, reached for her lemonade and sipped, staring at all the history in front of her. There has to be something in this pile. I am not giving up.

Katie grabbed the last handful from the box. Bingo!

There was a picture of Loretta and Stan when they were young. That was the face Katie recognized from her dreams. Katie then saw a beautiful picture of Grandma Rett in her wedding dress. She set that one aside for herself, too. Loretta and Stan looked happy in all of the pictures. There were many pictures of them at the beach, posing with old cars (new cars to them, Katie laughed) and group shots with family and friends. No Lucinda in any of the pictures. Did she ever visit? Did she ever send pictures of her and her family? What's going on?

There was only one picture left. Katie slowly pulled it out from behind the one she was holding, and gasped. "That's it. The one I've been looking for."

She gazed in awe, Lucinda's wedding picture. It was a posed picture of her entire wedding party. Katie turned the picture over and on

Waiting for Dusk

the back was written September 3, 1927. Turning the picture back over, Katie looked at it again. She must have seen the picture before. Lucinda looked exactly the same as in Katie's dreams. No one was really smiling in the photo except for Henry. There was a slight gap between his two front teeth. He was a short stocky man, maybe an inch or two taller than Lucinda. Katie rated him as just average looking. From what she heard, he was a nice man. Her mother said he loved Lucinda very much. His face beamed. The more Katie looked at him, the more she liked him.

Then she moved on to the other two men in the picture. They looked very much like Henry. Brothers?

Lucinda looked beautiful in a traditional wedding dress. She had a long veil that wrapped around her and was draped on the floor in front of her. She wore a crown of flowers around her head. Then Katie looked at Grandma Rett. She was young and pretty, well stunningly beautiful actually. She had the short hairdo of the twenties–the bobbed look with those waves and short pin curls.

Katie looked at the other bridesmaid and a cold chill went up her back. She felt like she was looking in a mirror. This girl looked exactly like her. Her hair was long but pulled back. The front wisps of hair had been made into ringlets. She shook her head to focus because the more she looked at the girl; Katie thought it could really be her. Grabbing her lemonade, she took a few sips to cool down and face reality. It wasn't her; it was silly to think that.

Katie slowly traced her finger over the picture, looking carefully at the girls, trying to figure out why it all felt so familiar.

"Katie?" a voice broke the silence.

"Yes, Mom?"

"You've been up there a long time. I thought maybe you fell asleep. It's past midnight. Is it alright if I come up?"

"Sure."

Her mother came up the attic stairs. She was showered, and in a tank and pants pajama set.

"Mom, do you know who this girl is?" Katie pointed to the bridesmaid in the picture next to Grandma Rett.

"Why, yes I do. That's Kathryn."

Katie gasped, then she swallowed hard. "Kathryn?"

"Don't be so dramatic. My Grandma Rett gave me the box of pictures right before you were born. We knew you were going to be a girl. When we got to that picture, Grandma Rett told me the girl's name was Kathryn. I thought it was a beautiful name. I said I was going to name you Kathryn. Grandma Rett smiled and said 'She is a beautiful girl'. I was a little confused by the word 'is' about you but Grandma was getting old by then and did get her past and present mixed up sometimes. She was probably still talking about the other Kathryn. I only wished she would have lived a few more months and then she would have met you."

Maybe she already has, Katie thought. She was getting her past and present mixed up, too. Or should she say her dream world and reality?

Studying the picture once more, Kate noticed the two bridesmaids wore dresses that she guessed would be called flapper-style. It was hard to tell the color but they were beautiful. Intricate beading covered the sleeveless dress. It hung straight, no waistline, stopping at the knee with a handkerchief hem. The girls also wore headbands that wrapped around their heads. All three girls wore choker pearl necklaces, but Lucinda's was more ornate. It had a large rhinestone in the center, and the pearls were connected to it. Why did the picture have to be black and white…well, actually, brown and white? "These are beautiful dresses."

"Yes, they are."

Katie yawned, and stretched her arms. "Thanks for straightening that out. Look at these other photos I found. I'm going to frame them, and put them in my room." She grabbed the wedding party picture and included it with the other two.

"That's really nice." Her mom hugged her. "Maybe we can go shopping together and pick out some frames for them."

"Yeah, that'd be great," Katie hugged her back. "Good night!"

They turned off the lights, and left the attic. The house was quiet. Katie entered her bedroom and sat down on her bed. She was suddenly too tired to change. She slid into bed, picked up her book and opened to the next chapter. Her eyes felt so tired she could hardly stay awake.

"Kathryn! Kathryn! It's me, Lucinda. Are you awake?"

"I am now, Lucinda. Come in," Katie sat up in bed.

"Sorry to disturb you so early but I have so much to tell you. The dresses are going to be delivered this afternoon for out fittings. We only have to work the lunch shift today so we don't have to go in early or stay late. It works out perfectly."

Lucinda's cheeks were flushed with excitement. Katie wondered if she was more excited about the wedding plans than the actual marriage

itself.
 "Sit down, Lucinda. Let's talk."

Chapter Twelve

Katie patted her bed and Lucinda obeyed. "First, I really have to talk to you about me being in the wedding. What about Ruthie? Shouldn't she be in the wedding too?"

Lucinda nodded. "I did ask her. She said no. She said she would be too nervous in front of everyone. It will be a huge wedding. After all, Henry's father owns the largest ranch in Arizona. He wants his son to have a wedding that measures up to the family's wealth and social standing."

Lucinda jumped up and started for the door. Just then a small card fell out of her sleeve and fluttered to the floor.

"You dropped something, Lucinda." Katie slid off the bed, and picked it up.

"Give me that!" Lucinda said sharply.

"Whoa. I'm just picking up a piece of paper."

"I didn't mean it to sound like that. It's just the wedding jitters. That's a list of things I need to do for the wedding." Lucinda held out her hand.

Katie looked down at the blank side of the card. She couldn't resist and turned it over. It was not a wedding to-do list. It was a picture. It was a picture of Lucinda and a young man. It was definitely not Henry and looked like it was taken at the Grand Canyon outside of Kolb Studio. Katie looked up at Lucinda. Lucinda had tears in her eyes. She had her hand out. "May I have the picture, please?"

Katie felt sorry for Lucinda but wasn't going to let it go. "This isn't Henry, is it?"

"No." Lucinda collapsed on the bed. She began to cry. "It's

Waiting for Dusk

someone named Daniel. It's someone I used to love and Anna took him away from me!"

"Is that why you are mean to Anna?" Katie already knew the answer, but she would like to hear her Great-Great Aunt Lucinda's side to the story.

"Yes," Lucinda's face crumpled. "I know it's horrible of me. I can't stop myself. I don't know why I can't forgive her. Anna and I were best friends in high school."

"Lucinda, you seem to still have feelings for Daniel. How can you get married to Henry if you do?"

"I do love Henry. I really do. I just love him in a different way. There was so much passion with Daniel. I suppose that wasn't good. I wasn't thinking clearly when I was around him." Lucinda gazed out the window.

Katie knew just how she felt. She was a little like that whenever she saw Drew. Her feet didn't quite touch the ground. Her head spun with thoughts of being together forever. "So you are going to marry Henry no matter what?"

"Yes, no matter what. Let me tell you something about him. Henry calls me Cindy. No one ever called me Cindy except my father. He passed away when I was in high school. It's a fond memory I have of him. My father would sing to me, 'Lucinda, Cindy, Cindy' and pull me onto his lap. He would then sing to my sister, "Loretta, Rettie, Rettie and then pull her onto his lap, too. We would giggle and laugh and he would cover us with kisses. We were his Cindy and Rettie. How could I not love someone that reminded me of my father?" Her eyes shone with tears. She had lovely pale blue eyes that Katie never noticed before.

"Maybe you should just wait a little longer. Get to know Henry better." Katie was determined to do something about the situation.

"No, we go ahead as planned. I will be leaving the boardinghouse the end of the month and moving into the big house on the ranch. I will be a rancher's wife, not a Harvey girl anymore. That is what I want." Lucinda also seemed determined. She got up and left the room.

Katie hurried to get ready, and headed for the kitchen. "Good morning, Mrs. Johansson. God morgon, Mr. Johansson," She was proud of herself. She remembered what Mr. Johansson had taught her. "I guess I have a little time off this morning." She sat down at the table.

Mr. Johansson looked at her and said, "What's troubling you, flicka?"

He was calling her the horse's name?

"Flicka?"

Mrs. Johansson chimed in. "Girl in Swedish, Kathryn."

"Oh, so Flicka is not a horse?"

Mr. Johansson seemed to enjoy that. He let out a hardy laugh. "That made my morning. Let's see if we can solve your problem now."

"Well, Lucinda doesn't seem happy about the upcoming marriage. What I mean is…" Katie thought she said too much.

"What you mean is what will be, will be," Mrs. Johansson interrupted. "Lucinda is meant to marry Mr. Henry. She can grow to love him."

That was an old fashion thought—grow to love him! Lucinda loved Daniel, didn't they know that? It wasn't her place to tell, so Katie kept quiet. "Breakfast was wonderful as always, Mrs. Johansson. May I be excused?"

"You sure can. Tell the other girls to get in here or the kitchen will soon be closed." Mrs. Johansson smiled at her. It was MiMi's smile. Again Katie said nothing.

She went out into the hallway, and ran into Ruthie with another girl she never saw before. She looked a lot like Ruthie, only with redder hair.

"Kathryn." Ruthie ran up to her. "I want you meet my sister, Molly."

So that's why they look so much alike, she thought. "Nice to meet you, Molly." Katie put out her hand.

As Molly shook her hand she said, "You must be Loretta's sister. You two look so much alike."

"No, I'm no one's sister."

Ruthie turned to Molly. "Don't you remember I told you Loretta and Lucinda are sisters?"

"That's right. This is all so confusing." Molly smiled. "But they don't look very much like sisters. Kathryn, you and Loretta could definitely be sisters."

Or great-grandmother and great-granddaughter, Katie thought. "Are you here for the wedding, Molly?"

"Oh, no," Ruthie jumped in. "She's taking Lucinda's place at the restaurant. Molly has been waiting for an opening."

A voice called out from one of the rooms. "She's invited to the

Waiting for Dusk

wedding, too." Lucinda's head popped out of her door. Then she popped back in. They all laughed.

Mr. Johansson called to the girls that it was time to go. Lucinda ran up to him and said, "Your suit will be ready, too."

He made a face.

"Oh stop that." she giggled. "You will be so handsome!"

Katie looked at Lucinda. She was puzzled. Mr. Johansson had a suit made for the wedding. She didn't think he had that kind of money.

Lucinda must have guessed what she was thinking. "He's giving me away at the wedding."

"That's nice," Katie responded. "I'm happy for you." She really meant it this time.

Lucinda grabbed Katie's hand and squeezed lightly, "Thank you, friend. I felt like I knew you from the minute I saw you and knew we'd be good friends."

It was Katie's turn to have tears in her eyes. She wrapped her arms around Lucinda and hugged her tightly. She turned to get in the car and saw Anna coming. *I hope Anna doesn't think I'm a traitor or anything like that.*

But Anna's eyes said the opposite. They were warm and kind. They almost seemed to say 'thank you'.

Katie almost forgot about seeing Drew. She was so wrapped up in the drama at the boarding house. She would have to find him and tell him how the plans have changed. Drew was in the kitchen when the girls arrived. He was laughing and talking to Cook. It seemed Drew could go anywhere he wanted and no one seemed to mind. Everyone must love him as much as she did. *What did I just say? Love?*

No, she was too young to be in love. She just turned sixteen in June and it was what the adults liked to call an infatuation. That's all it was. He turned and looked directly at her. She melted when she saw those eyes. *Okay, it's love.*

Katie grabbed the egg basket and headed outside, hoping Drew would follow. And he did. She filled him in on all of the latest developments. She even told him how Lucinda loved Daniel.

"I remember when they had that picture taken this spring," he said when Katie was done with her summary. "I don't think Daniel realized how smitten Lucinda was with him. He enjoyed her company, that's all."

"You know Daniel?"

"We met last summer. I would go out to his ranch with him and go riding. He taught me how to herd cattle."

Katie pictured Daniel and Drew riding the range, herding the cattle. It was too much. She wanted to grab Drew right then and there and kiss him passionately. She snapped back to reality and said, "Then you knew he loved Anna?"

"Yes. He was deeply hurt by how everything turned out. He blamed himself. I got word to his family that Lucinda was engaged to Henry Hasting. I wanted them to let Daniel know he was free to contact Anna."

"He did and it was all because of you." Katie threw her arms around him. "Thank you, Drew!"

Drew lifted her off her feet and swung her around. "I didn't know that would make you so happy. Anything to make you happy." He lightly kissed her on the lips. "Come on. I'll help you with the eggs."

They talked about trivial things as they collected the eggs. Katie had named all the hens, and had Drew laughing from the choices she made. Little did he know she just borrowed a lot of those names. There was Buzz Lightyear, who looked like she was wearing a space helmet, the twins Blossom and Bubbles, the red hen she named Ariel, Miss America for the most beautiful one, and the three tough chicks–Buffy, Super Girl and Wonder Woman. The black chicken that always attacked her was named Darth Vader. She knew she'd always have a battle with that one. "Where did you come up with these names, with the exception of Miss America?" Drew breathed more calmly now.

"I'm just creative," Katie shrugged. Then she changed the subject. "Are you invited to the Hasting wedding?"

"Yes, I am. When I saw the date I was wondering how you could be in the wedding. You said you had to return to Ohio for school."

"My parents are letting me come back for the wedding. They're letting me miss a few days of school." Katie had to think fast on her feet.

"Then you'll be coming by train?"

"Yes…yes! I'll be returning by train." Katie was thankful he helped out on that one.

"Then I shall meet your train. Just let me know the day and time and I will be there."

"Um…yes, sure, as soon as I know." Katie was a little nervous about trying to figure out how she could arrive by train when she always woke up in the boardinghouse.

Waiting for Dusk

"Let's make the best of it until you leave. When you return, I may have a surprise for you," he whispered as he grabbed her closer.

Katie felt weak again. She could not fight him. He kissed the top of her head, then her cheek, then her mouth. She didn't want to leave for school and come back. She wanted to stay there.

"Kathryn! Are you in the henhouse?" They heard Anna's voice calling. They sheepishly stepped out into the late morning sun.

Anna laughed. "Oh, Andrew Martin. You are a cad, aren't you?"

Drew laughed and waved. "I hope to see you later, Kate. I'm off to work."

Katie ran to the back door of the kitchen. Anna stood, waiting. "I think you are smitten, Miss Kathryn." She shook her head, and they both went inside.

* * * *

Mr. Johansson waited in the Buick as they all came out after work.

"Are the dresses here? Did the tailors come too?" Lucinda bounded out to the car.

Mr. Johansson, a man of few words, nodded his head. Lucinda clapped, and hugged him. "Then let's get going!"

As they pulled into the boardinghouse driveway, there seemed to be a lot going on. People were going in and out of the house carrying garment bags, hat boxes and various other things.

"Lucinda, you must have an army of people here. What in the world are they all needed for?" Katie couldn't believe her eyes.

"There's the seamstress who worked on my wedding dress, the seamstresses who did the bridesmaid dresses and the tailors for the men's suits. There are people to help us with jewelry, shoes, undergarments, you name it!" Lucinda peered out the window at all the commotion in the yard.

Loretta came running out to greet them. Lucinda looked at Katie and said, "Did you meet my older sister?"

"Yes, I already have. We met yesterday. She's a very sweet girl."

Lucinda looked at her with a sly smile. "Until you get to know her!"

Then she ran as Loretta chased after her. Lucinda spun around, and grabbed Loretta at the waist. They twirled and chanted, "Cindy and Rettie, Cindy and Rettie!"

Katie enjoyed watching them. She could see the love between the sisters. They had their own way of communicating. It would be nice to have a sister, someone you could count on. *That's what I get for being an only child,* Katie thought.

They all went into the house. Mrs. Johansson had been baking and it smelled like bread and cookies all rolled into one. Katie popped into the kitchen.

"Ooo, these look so good! Do you mind...?"

At that moment Lucinda grabbed her by the arm. "Dresses first!"

Katie went into her room. There was a garment bag lying on her bed. She opened the flap, and saw the most beautiful dress. It was a dark sapphire blue. It had a striking pattern of matching color beads on it. It looked as if Tinker Bell had sprinkled pixie dust over the dress. She slipped it on and ran out into the hallway.

Ruthie was standing there. "Kathryn, you are stunning! Come in Lucinda's room. They have a large mirror set up in there."

Loretta was already in the room and trying on shoes. "Here is your headband, Kathryn." She handed a matching blue velvet band to Katie. It had a cluster of orange blossoms attached to it. She went to the mirror and put it on. Loretta came over, took it off and pulled Katie's hair back. She pulled a few wisps of hair forward. "We can curl these into ringlets around your face. I'll take these two front pieces and tie them back here." She touched the back of Katie's head. "The rest of your hair will just hang down your back in curls. Is that alright?"

Katie could only nod because she felt like she was staring at the girl in the wedding photo she found in the attic.

Lucinda turned to look at the girls. "What do you think?"

Katie thought that Lucinda was beautiful in her gorgeous wedding dress. It was an off the shoulder satin dress that went all the way to the floor. She wore a veil with yards of dreamy silk tulle, sprinkled with wax orange blossoms and velvet leaves.

"You are absolutely beautiful, Lucinda!" Loretta covered her mouth.

"And you all look beautiful, too!" Lucinda exclaimed. "The dresses are just right. My wedding is going to be all blue and white just like the Arizona sky. You know I ordered bright blue sky and those huge puffy white clouds for my wedding day."

Katie tried to picture it all. It would be quite a wedding. It might be the social event of the year, just like Lucinda wanted. Where does it go from there? Has Lucinda thought that far ahead?

Lucinda's voice interrupted her thoughts.

Waiting for Dusk

"There are going to be white flowers everywhere, orange blossoms and white roses. Father Hasting is having them shipped in. He's also putting up a huge tent on the property. Henry and I will be married outside in a white gazebo just at the edge of the garden. There will be white covered chairs for the guests inside a huge tent. Isn't it dreamy?"

Yeah, it's dreamy alright, Katie thought. *I don't even know what a dream is anymore and what isn't.*

The picture she recently saw explained a lot–the dresses, the veil– but she hadn't known the details of the wedding. She put her hand to her head.

Loretta ran over to Katie. "Are you alright?"

"I think it's just a headache. Too much excitement for one day," Katie lied.

"Then you should go rest," Lucinda chimed in. "But before you do, I have something for you. Kathryn… Loretta." She placed pearl chokers in their hands. "Please accept this gift from me and wear these on my wedding day."

"Thank you, Lucinda. They're lovely," Katie managed to say.

"Here's my gift from Henry." She took out another pearl choker from the box. It had a large blue sapphire in the center and the pearls were attached to it. It was just like in the picture.

Ruthie and Molly looked at each other, eyes opened wide. Kathryn realized that all this jewelry was the real thing. These Hastings didn't mess around. She left the room and headed for her own.

Anna was in the kitchen as Katie walked by. "You need any help?"

"Yes," was all Katie could say.

Anna came into Katie's room. "Now what's going on with you and Mr. Andrew? Is this serious? I really do like him. He would be a good catch."

A good catch? "Anna, what are you talking about?"

"Hasn't he told you?" Anna replied.

"Told me what?"

"His family owns a large men's clothing store in New York City. Haven't you heard of Martin's Menswear? Andrew's father, Nicolas, is a famous men's designer. His grandfather came to New York from Italy leaving his family business behind, a very famous Italian fashion house. He wanted to strike out on his own and break away from his brothers. Andrew's grandfather saw the talent in Nicolas at an early age and decided that the United States would be a great place to start over. They were the Martino family in Italy but his grandfather decided to drop the 'o' and become more Americanized."

Katie remembered her family talking about people who came from other countries at the turn of the century. They came through Ellis Island in New York. Sometimes their name would be changed right away to make it more familiar to Americans, like Johansson could be Johnson…

"Kathryn, are you still there?" Anna waved her hand in front of Katie's face. "I take it you didn't know any of this."

"How did you know?"

"Daniel and I spent time with Andrew earlier this summer. We rode together when we were out at the ranch. We all shared our stories. I knew Andrew worked at the park but seemed to do whatever he wanted. I teased him one day about it. He finally gave in and told me his family donated lots of money to the park so now it made sense. He didn't abuse the power, don't get me wrong. He truly cares about the environment. It's his life's passion."

Katie already knew Drew loved the park. It made sense why the help could sit on the porch that first day and eat their lunch, and why they found his horse in the barn after just leaving it tied to a post at Yavapai. She didn't care if he was rich or not. It didn't really matter since they were from two different centuries. What was she thinking? Drew was not real. It was time to enter the real world and stay there.

Waiting for Dusk

Chapter Thirteen

The next two weeks went by quickly. Katie was getting closer to the start of school. She hung out with Lindsey and Jordyn. Erin kept texting her to try out. Ty came over to swim and she'd go across the street to play basketball with him. Katie noticed he was getting a little more serious about the girlfriend thing. She didn't want to hurt his feelings, though, because they were friends for such a long time. She planned on going to Homecoming with him and would continue tell him she wanted to remain friends. She discussed her dilemma with Lindsey and Jordyn one day in her bedroom.

"Ty already asked you to Homecoming? How lucky can you be?" Jordyn bounced up and down on Katie's bed. "Let's start dress shopping, all of us. If Lindsey and I don't get dates, we'll go with each other."

"You're too funny, Jordyn. I can see you trying to get a date the first day of school," Lindsey laughed.

"Or Katie can ask Ty to fix us up with some basketball guys!" Jordyn stared off into space. Katie thought she was imagining all of them at the dance. "We can triple date then."

I was right. Katie patted herself on the back.

Jordyn grabbed Katie by the arms and said, "What do you think?"

"Um, I'll think about it." Little did Jordyn know that Katie had way more on her mind than a Homecoming dance.

Katie still went to the boardinghouse every night in her dreams. She saw Drew more and more every day. It was like he knew she'd be gone soon and didn't want to waste any time either. She also snuck off to the train station and looked at schedules, picking a day and time, Friday at 1:30 p.m., for her return. That would give her time to get up, dressed and run to the station. She wasn't sure what she'd do next. Hide until the train came? She laughed aloud.

"What's so funny, Kates?" Lindsey frowned.

"I was just picturing me hiding in a train station."

"What did you just say?" She held her hand to Katie's forehead. "I think you're coming down with something." She then flashed a knowing look. Katie was keeping her informed of the dreams.

Jordyn jumped up and said, "I've got to get going. I promised the moms they could take me school shopping."

The girls said their good-byes, then Katie and Lindsey went outside and sat on the deck. No one was home so they knew they could speak freely.

Lindsey went first. "I'm a little concerned that your dream life is overtaking your real life."

"I know you mean well, but don't worry about me. Don't you think this is all based on the pictures I saw of my family and the stories I heard my mom and dad tell?" Katie swung around in her chair. She convinced herself Drew was not real and the dream world was just for fun.

She sighed and looked around her. It was a beautiful day. The sky was almost like an Arizona sky, bright blue with white puffy clouds, reminding her of another place, another time.

"Then how do you explain Drew?" Lindsey broke into her thoughts. "Think about that, why don't you? I'm afraid you're falling in love with a dream, that's all. I'm your best friend and will always be here for you, support you no matter what."

"Thanks for that. The same goes for me, you know that don't you?" Katie turned back in her chair and threw her hand out. Lindsey slid her hand along Katie's and then they grasped hands. "Sisters till the end." It was their joke of a secret handshake. They laughed and sat in silence for awhile.

"School starts on Monday."

"Don't remind me! This is our last weekend to have fun. What shall we do?" Katie looked at Lindsey.

"You should have a pool party. Let's invite everyone we know!" Lindsey peeked at Katie from the corner of her eye.

"That might not be a bad idea," a familiar voice said. It was Katie's mom. She slid the screen door open and sat down with the girls.

"Really?" Katie couldn't believe it.

Waiting for Dusk

"Really."

Lindsey jumped up. "Come on! Let's go to your room and start inviting people!"

They stayed up very late calling and texting people. "Yes, this Saturday. Yep, two days away! Good! See you then!" Katie hung up the phone. "You may as well sleep over, Linds. It's really late. Ty's bringing the basketball team, he has so many friends on it. Gosh, I hope he makes the varsity team. His heart is set on making it."

"Katie, you're rambling. Calm down. Are you sure you want me to sleep over? I may interfere with your dream life."

Katie playfully pushed her and Lindsey screamed. Katie put her hand over Lindsey's mouth. "You don't want to wake the parents!"

They talked and planned until the wee hours of the morning, finally falling asleep, exhausted, on Katie's bed.

When morning came, Katie was the first to wake up. She looked over at Lindsey. She snored lightly. Wow, I must have been tired. No dreaming at all.

She gave Lindsey a little shove. "Come on, we have to go shopping for the party. New bathing suits!"

Lindsey popped up. "Sounds like a plan. Let me call my mom and tell her I'm never coming home. Then we can get going."

Katie looked forward to the party. She would see a lot of people she didn't see all summer. The weather was great so there were no worries for a rain out. She went into her bathroom to take a shower and looked in the mirror. She saw a 16-year-old girl who was going to start her junior year in high school. Why did she ever think she could live a glamorous life with Drew? Oops, there I go again, mixing up my worlds. Well, no more of that. This party will be the start of a very good school year.

When she came out of the bathroom, Lindsey was looking at the old pictures Katie found in the attic. "Is this Lucinda?" She pointed to the bride.

"Yeah."

"Wow. Henry could use some braces, couldn't he?" Lindsey teased.

"He's a very nice man. Don't make fun of him." Katie met him over these past few weeks. He was a gentleman, yet there was something very macho about him. He also loved Lucinda, his Cindy, very much. Katie could tell that much. It was a little harder to tell if Lucinda loved him back in the same way. There definitely was affection on her part.

"And this is your great-grandmother, Loretta?" Lindsey was still looking at the picture.

"Yep," Katie brushed her hair.

"She looks like you. Or you look like her, which is it?" Lindsey lay back on the bed, picture in hand. "This other girl is Kathryn? The one you're named after?"

"Yes, again." Katie kept brushing as she studied the picture with her friend.

"Spooky resemblance." Lindsey did a fake shiver.

Katie needed a distraction. "Let's go shopping. We'll eat something at the food court. Good thing your car is here." She grabbed Lindsey's hand and the two ran down the stairs and out the door.

* * * *

When she got home, Kate found her mother unloading the car and they walked into the house together. "Why is it you have one small bag and I have all the party supplies and groceries?" Katie's mom whined and then said, "Show me what you bought." Katie pulled a new swimsuit out of the bag. Her mother raised her eyebrows. "Don't show that to your father before the party starts." "Look, Mom. It has a cute skirt that goes with it. I'm going to wear that when everyone first gets here."

"Dad will be the chaperone and grill master, so I have everything covered." Her mom sat down on the sofa. "How many are we expecting?"

"Forty or so people."

"Forty?"

"You didn't give me a number. They probably won't all show up. There might be about thirty kids here. How's that?" Katie sat next to her mother, leaned her head on her mother's shoulder and looked up at her.

"When you give me those puppy dog eyes, Blue Eyes, I can't resist." Her mother squeezed her. "Just don't tell your father."

"Hey, there's been a lot of 'just don't tell your father', 'don't show your father' comments." Katie loved having secrets with her mother.

"And don't tell your father that either!" Joanna got up and started to head for the kitchen.

"What's this 'don't tell your father' business I'm hearing," Jackson walked in the door.

"Nothing," they both answered.

Waiting for Dusk

"My girls are at it again." Jackson shook his head.

Joanna gave Jackson a kiss on the cheek as she passed by. "We're letting Katie have a pool party tomorrow. Sort of a back-to-school party, you might say."

"Oh, we are, are we? Why am I always the last to know?" Jackson threw his hands up in mock disbelief.

"Because you are never home," Joanna and Katie answered in unison again.

They all laughed and Katie knew everything was a go.

* * * *

The sun shone brightly in the late afternoon sky. Katie helped her mom get things ready for the party. Lindsey and Jordyn both slept over and also helped set up until they went home to get ready. Katie had no dreams that she could recall. She thought about it a lot while she prepared for the party.

"Mom, is it alright if I go get ready now?" Katie was anxious to go upstairs to her bedroom for some reason. She saw her mother nod so she headed up.

She grabbed the bag that her new suit was in and looked for scissors in her drawer next to her bed so she could cut the tags. As she opened the drawer, she looked at the book lying there on her nightstand. She picked it up and turned it over and over in her hands, thinking, Every time I read this book, I have the dream. The nights I didn't read, I did not have it. That's it! The book and the dream must have some sort of connection. Well, I'll definitely read a chapter tonight because I need to say good-bye to everyone. They know I'll be back for the wedding but I definitely want to say my good-byes. It's the proper thing to do.

Katie smacked her forehead. Listen to me! I'm worried about being proper and polite. She learned some different life lessons at the canyon. Wouldn't her parents love that? Plus I have to see Drew one more time and firm up our plans. I need to make sure he stays away from the station until exactly one-thirty.

She had confided in Anna a little but did not say she was from the future. Anna would think she was crazy. Katie just explained she was coming earlier than she thought and still wanted to meet Drew at the station. Anna said she would come up with something to keep him away until the designated time. Katie hoped Drew would be agreeable.

Katie crossed her fingers, kissed them and raised the fingers to the

73

sky. "Here's to you, Anna," she said aloud.

"I'm starting to think Anna is your best friend instead of me," Lindsey teased as she came in the bedroom door. "You're not even ready. Go in that bathroom and get ready, girl."

When Katie came out in her bikini top and matching skirt, Lindsey whistled. "You are totally…I know we hate using this word…hot! What did you do to your hair?"

"I bought a wave iron. Do you really like it?" Katie twirled around.

"Yes, And these outfits are totally awesome!" Lindsey twirled, too.

"Oh, Lindsey you look great. You should definitely get a Homecoming date tonight!"

They went downstairs to find Jordyn talking to Katie's mom. She wore a tankini with a wrap-around skirt with a slit up to the waist, so the bottom of the suit was still visible. "You're rockin' it too!" Lindsey grabbed Jordyn's hand. They all went outside.

Jackson was already on the deck. The tiki torches were lit and Japanese lanterns, kept for special occasions, were strung around the deck.

"It looks great, Dad, thanks."

Just then, a group of boys rounded the corner of the house. "Is this where the party is?" Ty's voice was heard above the rest. Five boys jumped into the pool all at the same time. Water splashed over its sides.

"Let the party begin," Katie shouted to her girlfriends.

Waiting for Dusk

Chapter Fourteen

Katie never counted how many people showed up at the house that night. It probably was more than thirty. Her parents didn't seem to mind. They kept smiling at each other. Her dad was manning the grill, filling plates with hot dogs and hamburgers. Her mom had coolers filled with ice and kept replenishing them with soda pop and bottled water. There were the usual snacks of chips, pretzels and taco chips with an assortment of dips. Joanna made sure she had a platter of fruits and veggies, too. Everything was going well. People were in and out of the pool, but Katie didn't venture into the water.

Jordyn ran up to Katie, soaking wet. "Aren't you coming in?" She grabbed her hand.

"No, not yet. Give me some time." Katie was thinking of an excuse not to get her hair wet. She worked too hard on it.

"Guess what? I have a date for Homecoming," Jordyn lightly clapped her hands. "Matt Parker asked me! He threw me in the water three times. I told him if he did it once more, he'd have to ask me. He threw me in, jumped in and asked me to the dance."

"That's great, Jordyn." *And so high school,* Katie thought. *What's wrong with me? These are my friends. They seemed so immature at the moment.*

"Par! Ty!" someone yelled and then there was a loud splash.

Katie giggled. I'm being a little too serious. I should definitely party.

Ty came up on the deck, grabbed some food and sat on the step. Katie joined him. "Not swimming? It's the hair, right?" Ty pointed to her locks.

"How did you know?"

"Well, you have a new bathing suit and you did your hair in some fancy way. It wasn't too hard." He winked at her. "I brought something for us later."

Katie wrinkled her brow. *I guess I can wait and see,* she thought.

The evening turned from dusk to night. The torches reflected in the pool and gave a mystical glow to the party atmosphere. Someone plugged their MP3 player into the outdoor speakers. Music filled the air. Lindsey started to dance and many others joined her.

"Dance?" Ty cut in.

"Sure." Katie took his hand.

The night seemed to go on and on. It was magical for awhile. Katie let herself get lost in the music. She danced with all the girls, but Ty always managed to find her.

"Come on, I want to show you what I brought." He took her by the hand, guided her through the dancers and out to the side fence that led to a garden. The garden was a secluded place that really couldn't be seen too well at night. Solar lights lit the path and a few lanterns hung in various places in the garden. They walked to the glider and sat down. Ty leaned over the back of it, and pulled out a bag. He dug around in the bag, and turned around. In his hands, he had two beers. "Here's to us turning sixteen, Katie." He handed her a can.

"Ty, where'd you get those? What if my parents see?" Katie was a little nervous.

"From our refrigerator in the garage, it's stocked with everything and won't be missed. Your parents are busy." He quickly answered her questions. He popped open his can and reached over and did Katie's for her. "Drink up."

Katie didn't know if she really wanted to drink up. She had a few sips of wine on holiday occasions. Her parents always talked openly about drinking and being responsible. She took a sip. Yuk!

Ty seemed to be enjoying his. She would try again. Even though she didn't really like it, Katie decided the best way to drink it was fast. If she did that, it would be over and done with.

"Wow. You don't want this going to your head now, do you?" Ty gently touched her arm.

Katie felt warm and lightheaded. Maybe it was too late. "Did you bring anymore?"

Waiting for Dusk

Ty produced two more. Katie took it, popped the can and said, "Race you!"

Ty took the challenge. When they were done, they looked at each other and said, "Happy Birthday!" Ty grabbed Katie and kissed her. Not a friendly kiss, but a boyfriend's kiss. She kissed him back. She liked it. She curled her legs up on the cushion of the bench and leaned into him. Her skin touched his bare chest and he pulled her closer.

"You don't know how long I've waited to do this. Kiss your lips, feel you skin against mine. I could stay here forever." Ty whispered into her ear.

Forever. That word brought her back to her senses. "Drew," she said softly.

All of the sudden, Katie felt a little sick. She drank the beers too fast, plus she didn't even like it.

"What did you say?" Ty looked puzzled.

"I said...do you want to get something to eat? I'm starving," Katie stood up.

Ty stood up, too. "Okay, if that's what you want." He pulled her close again and she froze. His lips touched hers but they weren't Drew's. She wanted to cry and she wanted this party to be over.

"What's wrong, Kate? Did I do something wrong?"

"Don't ever call me Kate! Do you hear me? Don't ever call me that!" Katie started to cry. She ran up the path, through the fence and jumped into the pool. The water felt cool and soothing. She wanted to just sink to the bottom and stay there. The next thing she knew she felt arms around her, and someone pulling her to the top.

"Are you nuts? What are you doing?" Ty gazed at her with hurt eyes.

"I'm sorry, Ty. I can't do this. I can't be who you want me to be. Please, let's just stay friends. Promise me you're not mad at me," Katie's words tumbled out.

"I'm not mad at you. I can wait. I know you'll feel different eventually. I will be so irresistible that you won't be able to stop yourself." He swam away and joined his friends.

Katie swam to the side of the pool and got out. She grabbed a towel from the pile and sat on the side of the pool with her legs in the cooling water. She watched a group of people play volleyball. Ty was in the middle of it. The girls seemed to love him, Erin especially. She seemed to conveniently fall into him whenever she could.

Take him, Erin. He's all yours. Katie got up and dried off. She headed for the deck and sat on the step.

"Where have you been? I was looking for you. Did you hear about Jordyn?" Lindsey sat down next to her.

"Matt Parker asked her already. I know."

Lindsey put her head in her hands. "Now what about me?" She pouted.

"You'll be fine. School hasn't even started yet." Katie leaned forward, and lightly pinched Lindsey's pouty cheek.

The party guests started to depart. The music stopped. Her father put out the torches, and invited everyone up to the deck. A few people stayed and chatted for awhile, but finally they all headed for home. Katie went into the house. She looked at the clock. It was one a.m., time left to read.

Katie kissed both her parents. "Good night and thanks. Is it alright if I help clean up in the morning? I'm really tired."

Her mom nodded. "Your father will probably have it all done by then, but it's fine, honey. Go to bed."

When Katie got to her bedroom, she grabbed a tank and pajama shorts, and went into her bathroom. She decided to take a long, hot shower. She dried her hair and in the steamy mirror wrote 'Drew' with a heart under it.

She thought about Ty and what happened tonight. She really didn't want to hurt him. He'll be fine. Look how he rebounded when he was playing volleyball.

Katie padded over to her bed, looked at her nightstand, then opened the drawer. The book was gone. It was nowhere to be seen. She looked under the bed, in the closet and in all of her drawers. She even called Lindsey. Her heart began to pound. Finally, she went downstairs.

Her mom was still in the kitchen with a glass of wine in her hand. "I thought I deserved this after that wonderful party." She held the glass up to Katie.

"Mom, where's my book?"

"What book, sweetie?"

"You know, the one you gave me. The romantic historic fiction book, remember?" Katie was getting upset.

"Oh, I thought you finished it. I lent it to one of my college students. She has such an interest in those types of books. I told her I had the

Waiting for Dusk

perfect one for her."

"I wasn't done reading it!" Katie screamed. She wasn't sure how many times she read it. It was all a blur. "Plus it was just here this afternoon!"

"You weren't done? You've had that book since the beginning of July," her mom acted surprised. "She stopped by this evening, during the party, and I gave it to her then."

"I hope that girl in your class is a fast reader. Tell her I need it back in ten days." Katie breathed heavily.

"Ten days? What's the significance of ten days?" Her mother now seemed more interested.

Katie thought fast. "It will be Labor Day weekend and I'll have more time to read." She wasn't going to say it would be September third, Aunt Lucinda's wedding, and I'm in it. Katie wondered how she could tell her mother that.

"Yes, ma'am! Will do! Now go to bed."

"Sorry for yelling. Thanks again for everything, Mom. You too, Dad, wherever you are!" Katie called out as she went up to bed. She hesitated on the stairs for a moment, thinking she heard her father's voice.

"Good job, Joanna."

That was weird.

Chapter Fifteen

School started uneventfully. Katie counted down the days until the wedding, and seeing Drew again. She went from class to class in a fog.

"Hey, Katie! You walked right by me." Erin ran to catch up. "Ty told me he asked you to Homecoming. Are you two a couple?"

"No! We're just friends."

"Then you don't mind if…" Erin started to ask.

"Be my guest," Katie waved her hand. She was glad Ty would have a distraction.

"Tryouts tomorrow. Be there!" Erin waved as she headed off to class.

Katie decided she would go to tryouts just to keep everyone quiet. Ty kept reminding her about them. Even her mother got in on the act.

Katie spotted Matt and Jordyn holding hands in the hall. Wow, they are a couple! "Hi, Jordyn, Matt." Katie raised her eyebrows at Jordyn.

"Oh Katie, stop it! Everyone knows. And guess what? I'm going to try out for cheer squad, too!"

"Great. I hope you make it instead of me," Katie said almost under her breath.

"I hope we both make it. It will be so much fun. Talk to you later." She walked off with Matt down the hall.

When Katie got home later that day, she reminded her mother about the book. "That girl has less than a week to finish reading."

Her mother changed the subject. "Basketball cheerleading tryouts are tomorrow? I ran into Sheri Taylor at the grocery store. She said Jordyn was so excited. They're helping her practice at home. Want me to help you?"

Waiting for Dusk

"No thanks, I've got this." Katie would say anything at that point so her mom would leave her alone.

"Ty really wants to make the basketball team, doesn't he?" her mom continued. "Such a nice boy and so handsome too. Don't you think?"

"Mom, stop it! Are you trying to play matchmaker? First it's cheer coach, and now this?"

"I'm just trying to take an interest in your life, sweetie. We working moms have to try harder."

"Well, don't!" Katie thought that sounded a little harsh. "Sorry, I've had a long day. I'm going to my room to study."

"Before you go, I wanted to tell you that Dad made a reservation at the state park for Labor Day. He really wants to go fishing. Plus he'd love to have some more time with you. I'm even calling you off school on Friday so we can get there a little earlier."

"Great." Katie said as she went up the stairs. "I guess I better start practicing some cheers."

* * * *

Katie nervously rubbed her hands together. There was a part of her that wanted to make the cheer squad and another that didn't care. She watched the other girls warm up and decided to join them.

Jordyn ran onto the floor and stood next to Katie. "I'm so excited. Just want to make it through to the final round."

"Yeah, that'd be nice."

"There's Erin. I think it's time to start."

The girls were called in groups of four to perform a variety of school cheers. Katie barely watched the proceedings until it was Jordyn's turn. She did well and Katie was positive she made the call-back list. When her turn came, she mindlessly went through the routines and hoped for the best.

When tryouts were over, Jordyn grabbed Katie's hand. "Meet you first thing Monday and we'll check the list together."

"Sounds good, I'll see you then."

* * * *

The following Monday, Katie met up with Jordyn and headed to the gym. The results were posted on a bulletin board in the hallway. Both girls were on the list.

"We made it! One step closer." Jordyn clapped her hands together. "One more round and we're in."

"I'll practice with you tonight, if you want," Katie offered. She decided to make an effort if she made it through to the final round.

That night, after they practiced for a few hours, Katie got a call from Jordyn. "Hey, didn't I just see you?" she teased.

"I know, I'm sorry. I had to call and talk. This is going to be the longest two days of my life. I hope we both make it. I don't want to do this without you."

"Listen, whatever happens, you did great. If I don't make it, you'll be fine without me."

"I won't be fine without you. You're one of my best friends. Besides, you could make the team and I won't."

"You need to stop worrying so much. Whatever happens, it was meant to be. Hey, Jordyn? I just got another call. Gotta go." Katie switched over to the new call.

"Katie, do you have a minute? I need to go over something with you." Erin's voice sounded hesitant. "I know Jordyn's your friend. She was good enough to make the final callback but I'm not so sure about the team. She's just not as good as you." There was a silence.

"It's not my choice, Erin. It's yours and the other girls." Katie didn't know where this was going.

"Yes, but the other girls look up to me, being the senior captain."

"I think Jordyn would make a good addition to the team."

"You're better," Erin paused. "She could make the team…if…if…"

"If what?" Katie wasn't really into the conversation.

"If you'd put in a good word for me with Ty. There, I said it. I know it sounds terrible but I'd love if you would."

Katie was stunned. "Is this blackmail?"

Erin laughed. "Oh, no. Never mind that I said anything. I just hope Jordyn does well tomorrow. You never know what could happen."

Katie hung up. Her head pounded. She hated the idea. She would not do it, even for Jordyn. She'd have to make it on her own.

Her phone rang again. "What!" she answered with a huff.

"Well, hello to you too."

"Sorry, Ty. I thought you were someone else." Katie rubbed her forehead. Too much thinking for one day.

"That's okay. I know how that is. Just wanted to ask you something. You know that movie we've been waiting to see? It starts Labor Day weekend. Thought it would be fun for us to go. I really want to see it on

Waiting for Dusk

the first night. How about Friday?"

"That's nice, Ty, but I don't think I'll be here this weekend." Katie was glad her mom gave her an excuse. "My parents booked a cabin at Salt Fork. I'm not even going to school on Friday. Maybe you can ask someone else if you really want to see it. I'll go with you when I get back."

"I just may do that…"

"Which? Ask someone else or wait for me?"

"Both!"

They laughed together, like old times.

"See you tomorrow, Ty," Katie said, then hung up the phone.

Katie was glad to finally have some time alone to focus on her own problem. How would she go on a vacation with her parents and still go to the wedding? She needed to get her hands on that book so she could take it to the cabin. That college girl better return the book soon. She flopped back on her bed, and gazed at her ceiling hoping it would all work out.

She wished it was Wednesday and tryouts were over. Jordyn did pretty well today and Katie hadn't really put her heart into it. There was little chance she'd make the team. Besides, she had too much on her mind to give it the effort it deserved if she was chosen.

The next day, Katie had trouble concentrating on her school work. Her mind kept drifting to other places and the conversation with Erin kept popping in her head. If that wasn't blackmail I don't know what is.

She drifted through the day, barely paying attention to the teachers. She wanted to scream out "boring" a few times but promised herself she'd stop using that word. It drove her mother crazy.

Finally it was time to head for the gym and tryouts. Katie threw on her workout clothes in the locker room and ran out to join the others. Erin was organizing them in groups. She winked at Katie as she passed by. It made her stomach churn and confirmed she was right. This made her more determined to do her best. No more I-don't-care attitude. Katie ran out to the middle of the floor when her group was called and put on the show of a lifetime.

After it was over, Jordyn and Katie left the locker room together.

"You were on fire," Jordyn slapped hands with Katie. "There's a spot for you on the team for sure."

"You weren't bad yourself."

"Thanks, now we just have to get through the next twenty-four hours and we'll be golden!" Jordyn waved as she went out the building.

Chapter Sixteen

"Let's get this day over with," Katie never thought she'd dislike the word Wednesday as much as she did today.

"Come on, it's not that bad." Lindsey tried to cheer her friend up. "I could've tried out. Me and my two left feet."

"Now that I'd love to see."

Jordyn ran up to Katie. "Come on, I heard they're posting the new members for the team!"

They headed for the gym. Erin was closing the glass to the case where all the physical education messages were posted. She turned, and winked at Katie. "I didn't know you had it in you," she said as she walked away.

Jordyn was busy looking at the list. She didn't hear what Erin said. "I made it! I made it! Katie I don't believe it."

She turned to Katie jumping up and down. "Oh, sorry, I didn't even look for your name."

Both girls looked at the list again and Katie's name was not on it. She didn't really care, but tried pretending to be disappointed. "Maybe next year."

"How could I make it and not you? That's just too hard to believe. I think we should talk to Erin."

"No, that's alright." Katie didn't want her doing that. Maybe that was Erin's way of keeping her away from Ty. Erin was on the basketball cheer squad, Katie would not be. Still, thinking back, it was strange what Erin said on the phone and so was the wink she just gave her now. She acted like Katie would make the team and Jordyn would not if Katie didn't give into her blackmail. Well, it didn't work. Jordyn made the team on her own just as Katie thought.

Ty came up to the girls who were still standing by the case. "Well, ladies? What's the verdict?"

"I made it and Katie didn't," Jordyn glowed with excitement. Katie shrugged her shoulders as Jordyn put her arm around her. "Sorry, Katie. I really mean that."

"Do you mind, Jordyn, if I talk to Katie alone?" Ty asked.

"Sure, I'm going to find Matt and tell him the good news!"

"I just want to check out something with you. Is it okay that I asked Erin to the movies on the Friday? She was nice to me at your pool party and I thought she'd like to go. I don't like her as a girlfriend or anything like that. I don't want you to get jealous…or maybe I do." Tyson's eyes twinkled as he teased her.

Katie was a little shocked. Now it all made sense. Erin thought Katie had Tyson ask her out to the movie. That's why she winked and said what she did. That's why Jordyn made the team. Erin planned all along for Katie not to make the team. Now she wasn't sure she liked Ty taking Erin to the movies.

"Just be careful of that one," Katie answered.

* * * *

Thursday finally arrived. Katie got through the day somehow. All her friends were consoling her for not making the cheer team, and she tried to go along with them, but underneath she didn't care. She got the assignments she would miss on Friday, looking forward to the day off. If only she had the special book in her possession she could be happy about missing a day. Katie hoped it would be waiting for her when she returned home. At last the final bell rang.

Lindsey came running up to Katie. "Kates, have fun at Salt Fork. Catch a lot of fish. I'll be thinking of you."

She turned to Lindsey and said, "Can I tell you something?"

"Uh, oh. I can tell by that look on your face this isn't going to be good."

"I have to get out of going to the state park with my parents. It's the wedding weekend and I need to get the book back."

"Tell them you don't want to go and you can stay with me. We'll look for the book together."

"I don't want to hurt their feelings. I have to think of something really good."

Waiting for Dusk

"We have a project due next week, and have to work on it."

"That's pretty good. I'll let you know what happens." Katie hugged her friend. "What would I do without you?" She ran to catch the bus.

When Katie walked into the kitchen her mom was packing a cooler. "Wow, you are getting a head start, aren't you?"

"We're leaving tonight instead. Aren't you excited?" Her mom continued to pack.

"Did you get the book?"

"Oh, no. She wasn't finished yet." Her mom peered into the refrigerator.

"What?" Katie felt her cheeks turning red.

Her father came out of the family room. "No need to get upset, Katie. I'm sure you'll get the book back in a few days."

"A few days? I need it now!" Katie started to cry.

"There are other books you can take, honey."

"No, there aren't! I want that book. Don't you understand?"

"I don't see the big deal." Her father crossed his arms.

She couldn't explain to her parents what the big deal was. It was not a good idea to say her dream world and her friends and the boy she loved were more important than going on this trip.

"You don't? Well, I know who will!" Katie stormed out the patio door. She went down the deck steps and onto the 'Katie' path. It was a small path that Maya built when Katie was small so she could get back and forth between the houses easily and safely. There was a picket fence on the side of the path facing the street. On the other side was a small garden. Katie and Maya had planted perennials and annuals along that path for years.

Maya usually had her back door open during the day so Katie was able to get into the house. "MiMi!" Katie was hysterical when she came in the door. She stopped in her tracks. There, standing at the mantel looking at photos, was a handsome young man. He turned around and looked at Katie. "You seem upset, little sis!"

"Carl Jr.!" Katie flew into his arms. Everything seemed a little better now that he was home. Carl started college when the Roberts moved in. He came home for the summer and on holidays. Even though he was much older than Katie, they bonded like sister and brother, and she hated it when he moved to the west coast. He teased her that he couldn't be a marine biologist in Ohio.

They sat down on the couch.

"Now tell me what's bothering you?"

Katie gave him a shortened version of the dreams she had after reading the book, the connection she made between her family, the old photos and the dreams. She told him she was supposed to be in her great-great Aunt Lucinda's wedding this weekend and he didn't even laugh. She left out Drew, though, because she didn't want him to think it was all about a boy. Katie put her head on his shoulder and let out a deep breath.

"Carl! Carl Jr.!" Maya was calling his name.

"In here, Ma, with li'l sis."

Maya entered the room. "Ooo, you look like you have been crying."

"I think she's okay now."

"I didn't know Carl Jr. was coming home." Katie looked at her intently. Then she looked at Carl and smiled. "He looks more and more like Carl Sr. every day."

Then both Carl and Katie said, "God rest his soul."

"You two stop making fun of me. I can't help how I talk." Maya gave them a huge grin.

"Oh, and Carl? Are you still the only Swedish-African American in California?" Katie turned back to Carl, and they both high-fived.

"Yes, the one and only. There better never be another."

"Then your joke won't work anymore." Katie laughed with Carl.

"I didn't know you were here, Katie. Let me go and get something for us to drink. Iced tea okay with you?" Maya walked out of the family room.

"I'll help." Carl jumped off the sofa.

Katie wandered around the room while they were gone. She looked at the pictures on the mantle. There were many pictures of Carl Jr. in different phases of his life. Maya sure loved him. There were some pictures of Katie, too, as well as a portrait of Katie and Carl Jr. they took for Maya one Christmas. Katie was lost in her thoughts until she heard Carl's voice coming from the kitchen.

"It wouldn't hurt, Mom. Talk to her. Feel her out. Don't give too much away, that's all."

Maya came back in carrying a tray with glasses and a picture of iced tea. "Sweet tea, just the way you like it. Carl tells me you've had some reoccurring dreams, is that right?"

Waiting for Dusk

Katie nodded. She looked gratefully at Carl. She wouldn't have to tell her story all over again. She took her glass of tea and sipped slowly. "I need to get my hands on that book. You have to help me. That's the only way I can have the dream. Can you call my mom and talk to her?"

"I can do better than that."

Mrs. Johnson walked over to an antique bookcase. Her house was an eclectic mix of old and modern. It worked well, and suited her to a tee. Maya took out a chain that hung around her neck with a key dangling from it. She used the key to open the bottom shelves, swung open the doors and there was a set of old books that Katie recognized.

"Oh!" Katie put her hand over her mouth. "You mean there's more than one?"

"Yes. As you see, I have a set. Mr. Johnson bought them at an antique store on one of our trips."

"One of those books will take me to the Grand Canyon on September 3, 1927?" Katie couldn't believe she was saying that. "So, this is real?"

Carl and Mrs. Johnson looked at each other. "Let's just say it's a realistic dream," Mrs. Johnson answered.

"Do you use the books too, MiMi? Do you go and visit Mr. Johnson before he…" she couldn't finish. She thought it was too cruel to say the word 'died'.

She looked at Mrs. Johnson again. "Wait a minute, you look an awfully lot like a Mrs. Johansson I know in my dreams. Only Mrs. Johansson is younger than you."

"This is all I will tell you, Katie. Yes, I do use the books. When I miss Mr. Johnson and that Swedish accent of his, I go back in time in my dreams and there he is. He's working at the boardinghouse and tending his horses. His dream was to have a stable of horses and teach people to ride."

Katie was confused. "So how did you end up in the exact place in 1927 that I do?"

"Too many questions, child. I told you I would help you and I will this one time only. Do not ask again. I don't want to go up against your mother and father."

"They know about this, too?" Katie was still trying to make sense out of all the new information. "Did you give my mom that book? Is that how she came to have it?"

"Slow down, Katie. I will try to answer what I can. Yes, your parents know that the books cause realistic dreams. I gave your mother a book to read once when your father was out of town. I thought it would occupy her thoughts and help her pass the time. Just like I thought it would for you this summer."

Katie was taken aback. "You're the one that told my mom to give me the book to read this summer?"

"You did say you were bored, didn't you?" Mrs. Johnson chuckled.

"Yes, I did. I knew you could tell when you came over for dinner, right after you got home from California." Katie smiled at Carl. She forgot he was still in the room.

"Mom, why don't you call Joanna and tell her that Katie can stay here for the weekend. She's too upset to go camping and won't have fun. She'll just make her parents miserable." Carl winked at Katie. "Besides she has a big project due next week, don't you?"

Carl was a good listener. He heard everything she told him up to the little white lie she wanted to tell her parents.

"Fine, if that's what she wants. Your parents may feel I'm spoiling you, but do you want to stay here for the weekend?"

"Yes, I do!" Katie began to feel better.

Mrs. Johnson disappeared, and didn't return for quite awhile. When she did, she said, "Everything is set. I don't like lying to your mother. This is the only time I will ever do this. You do understand that?" She looked hard at Katie.

"Yes, ma'am. Now may I have the book?"

She put out her hand giving Maya one of her best little girl looks. Katie already knew which bedroom to use because Maya had decorated it just for her. Mrs. Johnson liked decorating and really enjoyed doing a girl's room since she only had Carl. The room was done in pinks and sea green with a quilt of those same colors on the bed. The antique dresser was painted in distressed white. The walls were a cool, calming sea green. Katie loved going to her room. She was ready for her dream to start.

"You have to wait for dusk."

Katie was confused. "Wait for dusk to do what?"

Carl stood up. "What my mother means is that the book doesn't work until dusk. You have to wait till the sun starts setting. Reading the book doesn't work during the day."

Waiting for Dusk

Katie thought back to the day she tried to go back to sleep because she didn't want the dream to end. It was late morning and the sun was shining. Nothing happened. It was starting to make sense.

"There is one more thing. I want to stay there for three days in a row without coming back. How do I do that?"

Carl and Mrs. Johnson looked at each other again. Mrs. Johnson seemed to be struggling with an answer.

"You may as well tell her, Mom," Carl said softly.

"After you read the book, do not put it next to your bed on a table or nightstand. Leave it in the bed with you. The book will be in the bed when you wake up at the boardinghouse. Don't put it on a nightstand or next to you while you're there. Hide it in a drawer with some personal effects. On the last day, take it out and put it next to you in the bed before you go to sleep." Maya fidgeted. "That's enough. Now you can enjoy Lucinda's wedding. I'm sure it will be the finest wedding the state has ever seen."

That sounded so familiar. "Then you'll be there, Mrs. Johansson?" Katie was sure now that Mrs. Johnson was Mrs. Johansson. She just quoted Lucinda's words about her wedding.

"Mrs. Johansson will be there, I'm sure," Maya got up and walked into the kitchen. "I guess it's dinner for three tonight, isn't it?"

Katie was outgoing and bubbly for the rest of the day. She helped Maya in the kitchen and bantered with Carl. She loved being with her second family. She knew they would help her and they did.

While they were eating dinner outside, Katie's parents came over. They walked up on the deck.

"We just wanted to say good-bye and to tell Katie to behave for Mrs. Johnson," her mother told them and then turned to Katie, "You stay here at her house and no long nights at Lindsey's."

They bought the lie, Katie thought. Mrs. Johnson must have been very convincing.

Joanna patted Carl on the shoulder. "I heard you'd be here for the long weekend. Good to see you!"

Katie's dad didn't look as calm as her mom did. "I hope we're doing the right thing, letting you stay here." He gave her a quick hug. He shook Carl's hand and then saluted Maya. "It's all in your hands now."

"Don't worry about a thing. We'll be here when you get back all safe and sound," Mrs. Johnson said.

91

* * * *

After dinner, Katie ran back to her house and got some things to have at Maya's for the weekend. She decided to sit on the Johnson deck and wait for the sun to set. Waiting for dusk, she thought.

Excitement pumped through her. Katie planned over and over in her head how to get to the train station. It just had to work. How could she explain any of this to Drew if he caught her lying? Katie closed her eyes for a few seconds. When she opened them, the sun was finally starting to set. When it reached the horizon, she held her breath. Only a minute to dusk. Katie forgot how beautiful and peaceful that time of day was. It was not quite dark and everything seemed to have a natural glow about it. When it was finally dark, and the first star appeared in the sky, Katie went inside. Maya sat on the sofa knitting while classical music played softly in the background. Carl was reading the newspaper in a corner chair.

"Good night, everyone," she said quietly.

"Such an early bedtime. I couldn't get you to bed this early when you were little," Maya teased. "Good night, Katie. Book is on the nightstand."

Katie leaned over, and kissed her on the cheek. "Thanks, MiMi. I love you."

Maya patted Katie's hand as if almost to say 'enjoy the weekend'.

Carl looked over the top of the newspaper and said, "Hey, sis, be careful out there."

"I will. Love you too, Carl." Katie thought that was an odd thing for him to say.

She didn't really care or give it much more thought as she ran up the stairs, two at a time, and into her bedroom. She grabbed her bag of clothes, went into the bathroom and got ready for bed.

Katie came out and carefully folded the comforter placing it on its stand. Then she fluffed up the pillows, slid under the cool, crisp pink sheets and reached for the book. The cover looked the same as the book her mother gave her. She wondered what the story would be about and laughed. There would be no way to compare the stories because she didn't know what the first book was about. She opened to the first chapter hoping and praying this would work.

Waiting for Dusk

Chapter Seventeen

Her heart pounded as she slowly opened her eyes. Relief flowed through her as she gazed around her boardinghouse room. Katie got up, put the book in the drawer and hurried to get ready. She tiptoed into the kitchen and grabbed a piece of banana bread from the table, not wanting anyone to know she was there.

"Where do you think you're sneaking off to?" a loud whisper came from behind her. Katie jumped, and whirled around to see Anna. "You've been gone for two weeks, Kathryn. It's seemed like forever. Why didn't you say good-bye before you left?" Anna's shoulders drooped.

"No time to get into details now. I am very sorry about that. Two weeks was a lifetime for me. I want to get started walking to the train station. So please forgive me."

Anna handed her a small bag. "Tell Drew you left most of your things here since you knew you were coming back. I packed a few things for you." She gave Katie a hug.

"Wish me luck!" Katie was out the door.

She ran along the road toward the park and train station being careful to stay hidden. As she walked along, Katie hoped Anna got a message to Drew and he would be meeting with her when the train came. Knowing Drew, he would come early to meet the train so it had to work. Her head hurt trying to sort all the details.

Katie arrived at the station. She looked at the large clock and saw she still had an hour to wait. It would be best to stay undercover while waiting for the train. At last she heard a whistle. The train was coming. Katie ran into the station. The clock said one-fifteen so it was early. She couldn't believe her good fortune. If only Drew would be late, things would work out for her.

She sat on a bench in the station as Drew walked in right on time. "I am so sorry I'm late! I planned on being here early but got a message from Anna to meet her in the kitchen of the restaurant. Let me take your bags." Drew looked around.

"I only have this one. I left most of my things here. Please don't be sorry about being late. I was early." Katie looked longingly at him. Two weeks was a long time, and she realized how much she had missed him.

As the two left the station, Drew picked Katie up and swung her around. "I was worried you might not come back with the way you left!" He set her down and kissed her lightly on the lips.

"Not my fault. Blame my parents!"

Before she knew it she was on the horse holding onto Drew, and heading back to the boardinghouse. Drew slowed to a stop before they reached the house. Gently lowering her to the ground, he continued on to the barn and then came back to join her.

"I know this will be a busy weekend for you. I wish I could have you all to myself. So if you don't mind, I would like that time now." He took her hand. They strolled awhile, not really going anywhere in particular, and finally sat down under a tree. Drew reached into his pocket. "I have something for you, my darling Kate." He handed her a little velvet box.

Katie took the box carefully, not knowing what to expect. She opened it slowly and let out a light gasp. "Drew, how did you know the bridesmaids' dresses were blue?" She was staring down at a gold chain with a blue sapphire enclosed in a tear drop setting. "I already have something to wear on the wedding day. It's beautiful though."

"I didn't know about the dresses. This isn't for the wedding. It's for you. The gemstone reminded me of the color of your eyes when I saw it. The tear drop symbolizes how I feel when I am away from you." Drew pulled her close, kissing the top of her head.

Katie never heard anything so romantic. Kids her age just didn't talk that way. Even in the lyrics of most of the songs she liked, she never heard anything like it.

"Put it on for me." Katie pulled her hair back and up. She felt the necklace slid down her neck and she touched it with her fingers. Then Drew's lips were on the back of her neck and she shivered. She leaned

Waiting for Dusk

back into his lap and stared up at his handsome face. He pulled her up toward him and kissed her for a very long time. She ran her hands up into his hair and around the back of his neck. That was the passion Lucinda was talking about. She didn't want it to ever end.

Finally, Katie was able to take a breath and said, "This is too much, really." She touched the necklace.

"It's only one of many that I would love to give you."

"Oh, this is plenty. I don't need any more," Kate laughed. "I probably won't ever take this off."

"I'm glad to hear that." He kissed her again.

Katie had no idea how much time passed. She knew she needed to get to the boardinghouse because they all planned to drive out to the ranch for the wedding rehearsal later that afternoon. "I have to get back," she said sadly.

They walked slowly to the house. "Drew, thank you, I…I…lo…" Katie was interrupted by Anna.

"Finally! I was getting a little worried. We have to get ready to go. See you tomorrow, Andrew!" Anna pulled Katie into the house.

"Anna, you're hurting my arm." Katie struggled to get away.

"You're lucky I'm the only one who saw the two of you out there. Loretta, Ruthie and Molly already went to the ranch with Lucinda. She will be staying at the ranch for good, and never come back here," Anna sighed. She looked a little sad at the thought. "Mr. and Mrs. Johansson are packing the Buick with things for the wedding. Now we have to get ready, and out to the car."

The ride to the ranch took awhile, maybe an hour or so by Katie's guess. When they arrived there were many cars already parked by the house—which was more like a mansion than a house. Katie was surprised the house was so big, with everything painted white making it look even more majestic. Plus there was a new section being added onto the house. She couldn't believe they would need any more room.

They walked up to a large staircase leading to a beautiful front porch that swept across the front of the house. There were six large, white columns two stories high around the front door. The pillars went straight up and connected to a large piece of roof that jutted out over the front porch. Below that overhang were ornate French doors that led out to a beautiful second floor balcony. Those doors flew open and Lucinda rushed out. "Oh, good, you are all here. I'll be right down."

So that's what those balconies are used for. To announce you'll be right down. So useful! Katie thought sarcastically. She giggled, amused by her own humor.

The door was opened by a maid from the way she was dressed. Her outfit was very close to Katie's Harvey girl uniform–black dress, white apron, and black stockings. Lucinda was still coming down the stairs and what a staircase it was! It curved around from the second floor down to the first. The banister was polished gleaming redwood with white painted spindles.

"Thank you, Frieda. I'll take my friends to the dining hall." Lucinda spoke sweetly to her.

Then Katie saw Mr. Carl kiss Frieda on the cheek. Katie gave Lucinda a questioning look.

"That's his younger sister. Carl asked the Hastings if Frieda could work for them. She didn't speak much English at the time. She came from Sweden last year. She traveled all the way from New York City—after landing at Ellis Island—to Arizona to be with him. It's been quite a change for her. We all try to help her as much as we can. Mother Hasting helps her by giving her English lessons."

As Katie walked through the house, she couldn't believe the size of it. The floors were hardwood with a glimmering reddish tone. Beautiful Persian rugs were in each room and the colors matched each room perfectly. They walked down the hallway on Persian rug runners. Katie couldn't stop looking around, trying to peek in all the rooms. As they entered the dining room, Mr. Hasting, Henry's father, poured champagne into tall crystal flutes. A huge buffet was being set up on a long table by more servants.

Henry went up to Lucinda. "I'm glad everyone is here now and we can get underway." He looked around. "Well…it seems everyone is here except for Gilbert and his wife." He raised his eyebrows. He turned to Katie and said, "Arlene is notorious for being late."

"I'll go get them, Henry. You keep everyone entertained." Lucinda grabbed Katie's hand and took her along.

They walked back to the front of the house and then turned right, continuing through a short hallway with floor to ceiling glass windows. It led to another whole living area. "Gil, Arlene, are you two ready? We're all waiting," Lucinda called out in the empty room.

That part of the house was decorated much differently from the rest

Waiting for Dusk

being more modern and sleek in design. Lucinda took Katie's hand and had her sit down on the sofa with her.

"This is Gilbert and Arlene's house. They have their own separate living quarters, even though this wing is attached right to the main house. Did you see the builders when you came in? They're adding on to the other side of the house for Henry and me. I can decorate any way I want. Isn't that wonderful?" Lucinda looked off into the distance, as if she envisioned the new place.

Katie thought Lucinda looked especially beautiful that night. She was wearing a fashionable soft, flowing floral blouse and skirt with gold jewelry. Her fine hair seemed to have bleached out to almost blonde. Katie touched Lucinda's hair lightly.

"Oh, this, can you believe it? The Arizona sun has given me a new look. I've been riding and learning all I can about the ranch. I intend to help with it, Kathryn. I'm not just going to sit in this big house and sip lemonade and sew. Not me."

Katie believed her. She also thought it would be the perfect time to bring up the marriage and thought she'd start off with something not too controversial.

"Lucinda, do you know Andrew Martin?"

"Yes, I do. He's invited to the wedding. I did that for you," Lucinda teased.

"You know, too?" Katie hit her forehead.

"We all have eyes at the restaurant. We could see he's in love with you, and you with him."

"Love?" Katie had to think about that. Yes, she was in love with Drew. She fought it as hard as she could, but she knew it was true. "Since I don't have to explain the situation to you, as you already know about it, I can get to the point. Remember when you told me about passion? I felt...feel it...with Andrew. I just want to make sure you're doing the right thing in marrying Henry when you don't feel the passion."

A tear fell from Lucinda's eye. "I am so happy for you, Kathryn. I know I told you about passion in a weak moment. I also told you that Henry is a good man who loves me. It will all be fine in the end."

Katie still wanted her aunt to think about what she was doing before it was too late. Maybe she could fix all of it. Maybe Lucinda could go on to have a happy life with someone else, someone she truly loved.

"Lucinda, you know you don't have to …"

"There you two are. We thought you got lost," a familiar voice said from the connecting hallway. Katie turned and saw Mrs. Johansson. "Lucinda, why don't you go see what's taking Miss Arlene so long? And Kathryn, you come back to the dining hall with me."

Both girls did as they were told. Mrs. Johansson put her arm around Katie. "You need to leave well enough alone. Didn't I tell you what will be, will be?" She pulled Katie closer and hugged her. "It will all work out."

The afternoon was filled with food, drink and laughter. Katie learned that Gil was Henry's oldest brother, and Clifford was the middle brother. Cliff was not married. He would be her partner in the wedding. The wedding would take place outside. They would exit from the house through the backdoor, and down the stairs into the garden. From there it was a walk up the garden path to the gazebo at the end of the garden. Katie stood on the back porch and looked around at the beauty of the garden. It was not a formal garden or very large for that matter. It was more natural. She wasn't a flower expert, but Drew had pointed out some of the native flowers on their walks and she recognized the desert marigold, aster, sunflower, paperflower shrub, morning glories, four o'clocks and evening primrose. The colors were all whites, yellows and purples.

The instructions to the bridal party continued throughout the afternoon. The bridesmaids and groomsmen would stand outside the gazebo, and Lucinda and Henry would walk up the steps where the minister would be waiting. A large white tent was set up in the backyard. Inside chairs were set up for the guests so they would be protected from the sun. The sides of the tent entrance were pulled back and tied open with sapphire blue ribbon. It was like a fairytale.

There I go thinking of fairytales again, Katie thought. She just couldn't think of one specific story that matched the scene.

Dusk set in. Katie began to panic. What if she did not wake up here? What if she ended up in her bed back at Maya's house in the present? It could be over in an instant.

"Are you okay, Kathryn?" Loretta's hand touched hers.

"It's starting to get dark. I think we should be heading back."

"Oh, we're staying here for the night. Didn't anyone tell you?" Loretta seemed relieved. "Plus indoor plumbing," she laughed.

Waiting for Dusk

Katie pretended to laugh with her. It had been quite a day but she was worried about getting through the night.

They were all shown to their rooms. Katie was impressed there were enough rooms for everyone. Her bathroom was across the hall from her bedroom. Mrs. Johansson had packed her bags which meant that she could have seen the book in her boardinghouse dresser drawer. Katie dug around in the bag. No book. She prayed it was safely back in the drawer where she put it. After she was ready, Katie slid into the huge, oversized bed. There was no time to worry or think about anything because before she knew it, she was asleep.

* * * *

The next morning, Katie woke to voices in the hallway, and someone knocked on the door. "Kathryn? Are you awake? We have to get ready."

Katie looked around and realized she was still at the Hasting house. She threw off the covers, jumped out of the bed and twirled around the room. She was thrilled to still be there.

There was a knock again at her door. This time it was Frieda. She had breakfast on a tray.

"Thank you, Frieda." Katie wanted to say more but was afraid Frieda wouldn't understand her. She just watched as the girl put the tray on a corner table.

"Du är välkomen," Frieda said softly and left the room. Katie assumed she said 'You're welcome'.

She ate her breakfast slowly. She did not want this day to go too quickly but it didn't seem to be the case. Again, there was a light tap at her door.

"I thought I would help you get ready. I have your dress." It was Mrs. Johansson's voice. Katie opened the door and motioned for her to come in. "Loretta will do your hair. She'll be here in a minute."

Before Katie knew it, she was in her sapphire blue dress, had her hair done and curled, pearl choker clipped on and headband in place. They all had their makeup done by someone who came to the ranch for that specific purpose.

"How could you not love this life?" Katie said to no one in particular.

Then it was time. The girls all assembled in the upstairs hall. Katie looked for Anna, but she was nowhere to be seen. She figured Anna must have gone down to get a seat. Molly and Ruthie fussed over Lucinda. They were going to help carry the train of her dress and get it placed correctly for the walk down the aisle. Mr. and Mrs. Johansson came out of their room. Mr. Johansson wore a white suit, and Mrs. Johansson fixed his tie. She then turned and kissed Lucinda. "I'll see you downstairs."

All that was left was the wedding party, Molly, Ruthie and Mr. Johansson.

"Go ahead." Lucinda took a deep breath, and motioned for Katie and Loretta to head down the stairs. The rest of the party then followed.

When Katie and Loretta got to the bottom of the stairs, the front door flew open. They heard laughing and someone say, "I hope I'm not too late." In walked Anna and following right behind her was Daniel.

Everyone stopped right where they were, as if frozen in time.

Waiting for Dusk

Chapter Eighteen

Lucinda was still on the staircase. Katie thought she heard a gasp come from her. Anna looked up and their eyes meet. Lucinda's eyes seemed to burn right through Anna. Anna's were apologetic.

Daniel broke the ice. "Good to see you, Lucinda. Best wishes on your wedding day. I'm sorry for intruding last minute. I just got in last night. Took me longer to clean up for your wedding than I thought!" he smiled sheepishly.

Lucinda continued staring. Anna turned to Daniel, grabbed his hand and said, "We best get a seat, looks like the wedding is about to start."

When Katie finally gained her composure, she turned to look at Lucinda again and saw her sitting on the stair with a blank look on her face. Mr. Johansson tried to help her up but she held her hand up as a signal for him to wait. Then she stood up, smoothed out her skirt, and continued on down the stairs as if nothing was wrong.

Katie heard music drifting in through the back door. As they continued down the hallway, she saw Henry, Gil and Cliff all standing to the side of the gazebo.

Katie was first. It helped that she couldn't really see the people in the tent as she walked down the path. A hand went up in the sea of people sitting out there, as Katie rounded the gazebo. She had to laugh as Drew continued to wave. Loretta came next and stood closer to the steps of the gazebo. Then Mr. Johansson and Lucinda came around and stopped in front of the stairs. Henry walked up to the couple and stood on the other side of Lucinda. She handed her flowers to Loretta, then Henry and Lucinda walked up the two steps to the minister. Everything was just as lovely as planned. There was a brilliant blue sky and white puffy clouds. The white tent shone in the afternoon sun. The gazebo was laced with white orange blossoms and roses.

Too perfect, Katie thought, and not like a fairytale at all.

The ceremony was short, Lucinda promised to love, honor and obey like many brides do and Henry beamed as he placed the ring on her finger. They had a quick kiss at the conclusion of the service and Henry held two fists up, shaking them like he just won first prize. Tears filled Katie's eyes as she watched her aunt's wedding first hand. The feeling was indescribable.

Afterward, everyone headed for the house. The wedding party stood on the large back porch, greeting guests as they headed inside. A late afternoon supper was served in the dining hall. The tent was cleared out so a wooden floor could be installed for dancing later in the evening. Katie's head spun from all the new people she met. Finally some friendly faces reached her.

"Kate, this is Daniel," Drew introduced her to his friend.

"I have heard so much about you." Katie shook his hand.

"And I, you, lovely Kate. Andrew, you didn't do her justice." Daniel slapped his friend on the back.

Anna hugged Katie and whispered in her ear, "I'm so happy. Is Lucinda alright?"

Katie nodded. "She seems to be. Plus she went through with the wedding, didn't she?"

"We'll see you inside." Drew lightly squeezed her arm.

The wedding party sat at a long table in the front of the dining hall. There were round tables of eight scattered around the rest of the massive room. Servers circulated the room with plates of food, pitchers of lemonade and water plus bottles of wine. It was all very festive.

Katie noticed one of the servers approaching Henry and then heard him say, "There's a Mr. Jack Woods here to see you, Mr. Henry. He just wants to wish you well and tell you he's sorry he missed the wedding. He didn't want to come in since he wasn't dressed for the occasion. He said something about fishing."

"Nonsense! Tell him to come in and at least share a toast with us." Henry was always so kind to everyone.

Jack Woods! The same Jack Woods I almost met at Kolb Studio. The one who looks like my father. Katie thought she better leave the room for some reason. She got up, excused herself and headed for the

Waiting for Dusk

stairs.

When she was safely in her room, she looked out the window that overlooked the back porch and garden. There, standing talking to Henry, was her father...or Jack Woods. Katie sat on her bed and wondered how long she should wait.

She must have dozed off for a few minutes and was startled awake by voices outside her door.

"I don't care what you say, Maya. That girl needs to go home now. This isn't right. I was never for it and now I'm definitely not! It was just for the summer, I was told."

There was silence and then it seemed someone else was talking. Katie couldn't make out what the person was saying. Then she heard Jack's voice again.

"I love her but I don't think she takes this as seriously as I do. She never did!"

That voice definitely sounded like her father. He said Maya. That was Mrs. Johnson's first name. Then silence again.

Katie cracked the door open to look around. Seeing no one, she walked quietly to the top of the stairs. Mrs. Johansson was just at the bottom of the stairs so Katie quickly stepped back until she was gone.

She was talking to my father or Mr. Woods. Katie planned on getting to the bottom of this but not now. She intended to enjoy every moment of this wedding and this day. She ran down the stairs, around the corner and back to the dining room.

"There you are!" Drew came walking toward her. "Would you care to take a stroll in the garden?"

Katie took Drew's arm and they walked out of the house and into the evening air. The band started to play and music floated into the evening sky. Torches were lit throughout the backyard. Guests mingled in the garden and headed for the tent. Strings of lights hung inside giving it a magical glow. Katie wanted to distance herself from the wedding theme of the night and just pretend she was at a really great party, with a really great guy.

"A penny for your thought," Drew said.

"A what...? Oh, um, nothing. I was just thinking this was a magical night."

"Kate, I hope we get married on a night just like this, a magical night." Drew pulled her close. She took a step back. "Am I scaring you again? Too fast?" he said with an impish grin on his face.

"No, you are not scaring me. Just slow down a bit and let me at least tell you…"

"…that you love me," he finished for her.

Katie playfully pushed him and he pretended to fall down bringing her with him. They landed on a little wrought iron bench. "You knew that was there all along, didn't you?" Katie couldn't stop laughing.

Drew kissed her and said, "Would you like to dance?"

"Here? In the garden?" Katie saw that everyone was gone.

Drew took her in his arms and they swayed to the music. Soon they were joined by another couple.

"Aren't you two ever coming down to the tent? We are so alone done there. Kathryn, I need you for support," Anna's voice traveled through the night air.

"If I must!" Katie said as dramatically as she could. Then she giggled, took Drew's and Anna's hands and headed for the tent.

It turned out to be a very enjoyable evening. Katie danced with Cliff, her partner, and then they cut in on the wedding couple. She was thrilled to be dancing with her Uncle Henry. She even danced with Mr. Johansson. She noticed Cliff slipped away and thought she saw him dancing with Frieda on the back porch. How romantic. It was like Frieda was Cinderella. Why was she seeing everything through the eyes of a fairytale? She needed to remind herself to be more tough and independent like Mulan or Pocahontas. Yet, didn't even they fall in love?

Lucinda came up to her. "Kathryn, did you know that you are all staying again tonight? We will serve a big breakfast in the morning. Then Henry and I will be on our way. We leave Monday for our honeymoon in San Francisco and then the shore. I've never seen the Pacific Ocean before."

"How are you doing?" Katie was dying to ask her that all night.

"Fine. I'm fine. I'm a married woman now with responsibilities." Lucinda crossed her arms almost defiantly.

"Know that I'm always here for you and when I am not, you are in my heart. I love you, Lucinda."

"I love you, too. You know, there is something special about you that I just can't place my finger on. I feel like I've known you forever."

"And I, you."

The girls hugged and Lucinda wiped tears from her eyes. "Stop it

Waiting for Dusk

now. See what you've done to my make-up." She half-heartily laughed.

The guests began to leave and Lucinda was called to say good-bye. Katie walked away from the tent. She stood alone looking up at the evening sky.

"Are you looking at the man in the moon? If you are, I'm jealous." Drew came up behind her. He pointed up in the sky. "Let's say when you see him, that's me, smiling down on you…wherever you are."

"Why? Are you going somewhere?"

"Not tonight but we are both heading back to school. We need to make plans to write to each other."

Katie didn't know how she would do that. She tried to think of a way to get out of it without hurting his feelings. "Can we just make plans to meet back here? I'm not very good at writing. I don't want you to be disappointed."

"Whatever you wish," he whispered in her ear.

"I wish to have you take this necklace off. It feels like it is choking me." Katie touched the pearls that were around her neck as Drew undid the clasp.

"There, all safe and sound." He patted his pocket as they walked around the side of the house. They were alone. Katie stopped, and turned to him. "Don't leave tonight, Andrew."

"This must be serious. You called me Andrew." He took Katie in his arms and kissed her. He kissed the front of her neck and down to the top of her dress.

"Don't stop," she breathed. Right then and there she made up her mind that if this was going to be her last night with Drew, then it would be a special night. "Stay with me in my room."

He stopped kissing her and took her by the arms. "How could I do that?"

"We'll sneak you in. You're invited for breakfast, aren't you?"

"Wearing the same clothes?"

"We'll roll up the sleeves of your shirt and you don't have to wear the jacket, no tie. It will work."

"Are you sure about this?" Drew looked very solemn.

Then it dawned on Katie it was not the 21st century but the 1920's. Good girls didn't do these kinds of things. Well, neither did she. What was she thinking? She just decided that Drew would be her first and hopefully her one and only. She was not thinking rationally. Plus how did they have safe sex in this day and age? Her head spun and she took a step back. Andrew grabbed her, breaking her fall.

"Would it be alright if you just stayed with me in my room, nothing else?" Katie decided to clarify. "I don't want to spend a moment away from you."

"I think I can do that." Drew pulled her to him. "Or at least try."

They rounded the corner to the back of the house. Most of the guests were gone. No one seemed to miss them. Katie looked around for Mr. or Mrs. Johansson. They would be the hardest to fool, but didn't see them. She looked at Drew in the moonlight, and wished he wasn't a dream. She hoped she would wake up, and see him next to her in bed tomorrow.

They waited until the servers cleaned up and put out the torches. Then they both said good night to the newlyweds, then Loretta and Anna. Katie pointed to the window of her bedroom.

"I think I can get up there from out here," Drew said.

There was a roof over the back porch. The plan was to climb up to it, then over to her window. They kissed and acted like they were parting ways for the night.

Katie ran up to her room. She quickly took off her dress and hung it away in the closet. She rummaged through the bag that Mrs. Johansson packed for her. She found something that was appropriate and casual to wear. No nightwear, not a good idea. Then she heard a light tap at her window. She ran over and opened the window. Drew slid into the room.

They stayed up talking for most of the night making plans on when and how they would meet again. Drew was determined to come to the canyon as much as he could his senior year. He was trying to get permission to do a field study here and receive credit for it.

"My parents aren't too happy that I will miss Thanksgiving with them," Drew stated. "I offered for them to come out here with me. I don't think my brother and sister would like that very much. They are younger and their friends are in New York. I'm sure they have plans for the holiday week. My sister loves to shop. There really is no shopping here, is there?"

"No," Katie laughed, "There's not." She couldn't believe what a gentleman Drew was. She decided this is what it felt like to really be loved. That's what Lucinda got, too. Love from a man that would do anything for her.

"Kate? Kate?" Drew waved his hand in front of her face. "I think I

Waiting for Dusk

lost you for a moment."

"I'm so sorry. What were you saying?"

"I asked you if you thought you could come here for Thanksgiving holiday."

"Yes, most definitely. I will be here." Katie really didn't mean that because she knew she had to get her hands on a book. She wanted a book she could keep, not depending on anyone else, so she could come and go as she pleased.

They both fell asleep right where they were—Drew in the overstuffed chair and Kate on the bed.

* * * *

Katie woke with a start. Sun streamed in her window, and Drew was asleep in the chair. She was thrilled he was still there. She tiptoed out of the room to the bathroom, splashed water on her face, then gazed in the mirror. She still had some remnants of yesterday's makeup so she scrubbed until it was gone, fluffed her hair and snuck back to her room. When Katie opened the door, she saw the chair was empty. Drew was gone.

She got ready for breakfast wondering how Drew woke up and disappeared so quickly. She looked out her window and saw guests in the garden. She decided to go down and join the others. Drew was already mingling with the other guests. He and Daniel were in a discussion with some men she recognized from the wedding. Drew had his white shirt on with the sleeves rolled up, just like she suggested.

Anna came up from behind her. "This time we are all sitting together!"

She took Katie over to where Drew and Daniel stood.

"Kate! Good to see you again." Daniel called out. Katie realized that all of Drew's friends would be calling her Kate. That's how he referred to her so it made sense they would also.

The couples sat together and waited for the bride and groom to enter. The best man announced them. Everyone clapped as Lucinda and Henry came in. Henry had a large grin on his face. He beamed. Lucinda seemed a little more subdued but was smiling, too. Katie hoped they were happy and things worked out.

After breakfast, Anna told Katie they had to pack and get ready to go back to the boardinghouse. Katie couldn't believe it was time already. Everything was over. The dream was over. She had to go back to reality, but not before she told Drew she loved him. That was on her list and nothing was going to stop her. She tried many times to tell him but something or someone always got in the way of the moment. She touched the necklace Drew gave her. Kate would never take it off. She would wear it every day.

"I will see you later back at the boardinghouse before I leave." Drew told her.

"Before you leave?"

"I'm afraid I leave before you this time."

Kate hoped to make him feel better. "Then I will come to the train station with you."

"Sounds good. I will pick you up." Drew squeezed her hand.

The Johanssons were packing the Buick when Katie came to the front of the house to go upstairs. Molly and Ruthie were already in the car. Anna ran down the stairs. "We got your things, sweetie. Let's go."

Everyone was pretty quiet on the ride home. Katie thought of all the events that led up to that point. It wasn't over yet and she planned to make the best of it.

"I'm going to see Drew off at the train station when we get home," Katie announced.

"He's finally going back to New York. Good for him. He's a nice young man, but his life is there." Mrs. Johansson seemed to know more about him than she let on.

"He's planning on coming back here. He wants to study here and even find a college close by."

"Really?" Then Mrs. Johansson got very quiet.

When they got back to the house, everyone helped unpack the car. Katie couldn't wait to get to the room to see if her book was still there. She slid open the drawer and there it was. She took it out and hugged it to her chest. "I wish I could make you all mine," she said to the book. Now I'm talking to a book, she thought, I must be going crazy!

She gazed out of her window until Drew came for her. As soon as she saw his horse she ran outside.

"Now it's time for me to ask you where your bags are," Katie teased.

"I had them sent ahead to the train station." He pulled her up behind him.

She hugged him tightly. Tears rolled down her cheeks. She was glad

Waiting for Dusk

Drew couldn't see her crying. They arrived at the station and the train was ready to go. It was all so final.

"Don't forget all our plans. Don't forget everything we said to each other and everything we have felt. Keep it here." He pointed to her heart. "I know I will. I love you more each day. It's painful to leave."

Katie flung her arms around him. They kissed for one last time. Then they heard the call, "All Aboard!"

The train started up, and people hurried to get on.

It was hard to talk after she was crying but Kate knew she must. "Drew..."

"There's Thomas," Drew pointed. "He will take you home."

Thomas smiled at her. Kate was glad to see a friendly face but how could she tell Drew she loved him in front of Thomas? That would be a little awkward. She walked with him to the steps of the train. Thomas walked right with them. Thomas and Drew shook hands.

"I will see you soon, Thomas." Drew then turned to Katie. "And you, too." He quickly stepped onto the train.

"I love you," Kate said softly, knowing he didn't hear her.

Thomas and Katie stayed until the train pulled away. Katie ran beside it until she couldn't keep up. She saw Drew's face in the window, hoping it wouldn't be the last time she'd ever see him.

Back at the boardinghouse, Mrs. Johansson was busy making dinner and everything seemed to be business as usual. Anna, Ruthie and Molly said their good-byes to Katie.

Anna had tears in her eyes. "You've been a good friend to me and to Lucinda. I don't know how I can ever thank you."

"I hope you don't think I was trying to take your place as Lucinda's friend. It just happened." Katie wanted Anna to know. "You're my best friend here. The person I trust the most."

The two girls hugged. "You're so special to me, Kathryn. You'll never know how much. Now I better let you get ready to go." Anna left her at the bedroom door.

Katie went into her room. She looked out her window and knew she had to wait for dusk. She also wouldn't have any problem sleeping. It had been quite a weekend. Katie walked over to the drawer, took out the book and placed it in the bed. Then she slipped on her nightgown and touched her necklace. I will never take this off. She promised herself as she drifted to sleep.

The first thing Katie did when she woke up was to reach for her necklace. It's gone! Where is it? She searched around in the bed, lifting the pink sheets and looking on the nightstand. She screamed and then cried.

Mrs. Johnson flew into the room with Carl Jr. right behind her. "Katie! What's wrong?"

"I was wearing a necklace. It's a gold chain with a sapphire…oh, please help me find it!"

Chapter Nineteen

They looked around the room and the necklace was nowhere to be found. Katie was so upset it took awhile for them to calm her down.

"So it's all just a dream. That's all it was. I know it now. How could I have been so stupid?" Katie flung herself back onto the bed.

Carl paced back and forth, not even searching for the necklace. "I've had enough of this! Katie, it's Monday. Make of that what you will." He stormed out of the room.

"What did he just say? It's Monday?" Katie sat up. The last time she remembered being at the Johnson house was Thursday night.

"Remember, I'm not answering any more questions. How was your weekend?" Maya tidied up the room.

"Wait, I'm not supposed to ask any questions but you get to?" Katie chuckled as she wiped her tears. "It was fine. It was beautiful and I'm in love."

Mrs. Johnson stared at her. "No, you're not. It's probably just an infatuation."

"That's what all adults say. Don't they know teenagers can be in love?" Katie was defensive. She thought it was real and just had to prove it. The proof would be when she found her necklace. She'd spend the whole day searching this house if she had to.

"Lindsey called yesterday. She wants you to call her." Mrs. Johnson looked away.

"You answered my phone?"

"No, Carl did."

"Oh, okay. Where is it? I'll call her back." Katie was a little aggravated with Maya's vague answers and felt bad about that. Maya was always in her corner. She was the one person Katie could talk to and tell her anything. "We'll talk later. Okay?"

"Fine, darlin'. Now go have fun and enjoy your real life. Summer's over and school has started. No more time for dreaming."

Katie decided not to debate Mrs. Johnson on realistic dreams and what was real for the time being. She got up and ran downstairs finding her phone in the family room on a table.

"Where have you been? I thought you'd be staying here for the weekend." Lindsey's voice had a worried tone to it. "Then Carl tells me you're out with Mrs. Johnson but he has your phone?"

"Yeah, I forgot it when we left. Mrs. Johnson gave me a good alibi and let me stay here. She's on my side too, you know."

"You're lucky to have her. Now, guess what? I got asked to Homecoming! Ty's friend, Brian, called and asked me. We have to go dress shopping. I'm going to pick you up and we'll meet Jordyn at the mall. We are going to shop till we drop!"

"Sounds good. I'm happy for you, Linds. Brian is a good guy."

Katie hung up and decided she would get ready to go even though she wasn't up for it. She told Mrs. Johnson about the shopping trip and she seemed extra happy about it.

"Go have fun," she said, putting two twenties in Katie's hand.

"She's here," Carl called out from the front door. "Tell her I said hi." He called to Katie as she ran by.

She hopped in the car with Lindsey. It was a bright, sunny day. Lindsey had the sunroof open and the music blasting. They didn't talk, just enjoyed the ride. When they got to the mall, Lindsey did not get out of the car.

"Can you believe this? We're going to meet Jordyn in a few minutes. Everything great has happened for that girl. She has a boyfriend now, we're all going to Homecoming together and she's a basketball cheerleader. How did that all happen?"

"Luck?" Katie said blankly. Then they burst out laughing, got out of the car and raced each other to the door of the mall. It felt good to just be a teenager again.

Jordyn waited at the entrance with her moms. Katie could tell she was trying to get rid of them but they were not budging.

"They want to help us shop for dresses." Jordyn rolled her eyes.

Waiting for Dusk

"That's fine, Jordyn. They can be our gophers!"

Lindsey grabbed Ms. White by the arm. Katie took Ms. Taylor and they were off.

The moms turned out to be a big help. They helped Lindsey find the perfect dress. They ooed and ahhed at the right moments and didn't complain when Jordyn tried on at least twenty dresses. They were up for shopping for shoes and accessories after the dresses were picked out. Each girl had a dress, except for Katie.

"I just didn't like anything I saw. I'll keep looking."

When Lindsey dropped Katie off at Mrs. Johnson's house, Katie saw that the garage door was open at her house. Her parents must be home. They were sitting in Mrs. Johnson's family room when Katie walked in.

"Mom, Dad, you're home." Katie hugged them both.

"No luck with a dress?" her mother asked. "Maya told us you were shopping for Homecoming."

"No, but that's alright. I still have time."

Her father stood up. "Are you ready to go home with your mean old parents?"

"Dad!" Katie felt like that fight was so long ago.

The family walked home on the Katie path. It felt good to be going home. Katie's mom offered to shop with her the next time she was up for it. Her dad announced there would be fish for dinner. No surprise there.

Katie decided to go up to the attic while dinner was cooking. She wanted to look around plus it felt like a safe refuge. Plopping on the sofa, Katie looked around. She noticed the long closets and decided it was time to explore what was inside of them.

Slowly, she opened the doors. Her mom's wedding dress was in a protective bag and so was Katie's christening gown. There were old shirts of her dad's that he wouldn't give up, some old winter coats, and dresses that were dry-cleaned and stored away. At the very end of the closet was a white bag. It looked vaguely familiar. Katie pulled it closer to her. She took it out of the closet and over to the loveseat. Peeking inside, Katie caught sight of a beautiful sapphire blue dress just like the bridesmaid dress she wore this weekend. She quickly ran down to her bedroom and closed the door. Immediately she slipped on the dress and turned to look in her mirror.

Oh my gosh, this is the proof. My dress is here. Sitting on the edge of the bed she opened her nightstand drawer looking for the book, hoping it was there. She gasped. My necklace! How did it get there?

Katie grabbed it and quickly put it on. It went perfectly with the dress—the dress she would wear for Homecoming.

"Dinner!" Her father knocked on her door. He slowly opened it and saw Katie admiring herself in the full-length mirror. "You like it?"

"Yes, I love it all! Where did it come from?"

"The dress, I believe, belonged to your Great-Grandma Rett and the necklace is from me. I'm glad you found it."

Katie turned to her father. "From you? The necklace is from you?"

"Yes, pumpkin, it is. I put the necklace in the drawer hoping you would find it. Happy back-to-school." Jackson kissed her lightly on the cheek. "See you downstairs."

She couldn't believe it. There was an answer for everything. She slowly changed back into her own clothes to go down for dinner, but could not stop thinking about the whole weekend.

Katie knew she had to talk to Carl before he went back to California. Reaching for her phone, she dialed Carl's number. "We have to have one of our secret talks."

"Ooo, a secret talk. You really mean business, don't you?"

"Outside. After dinner. Give me a half hour." Katie hung up and ran downstairs.

After dinner Carl and Katie met at the glider in Maya's garden. They slowly pushed back and forth not saying much.

"What do you want to know?" Carl finally broke the tension.

"Everything! Why is everyone lying to me? I know this is real. I can feel it. You can't have the same reoccurring dream time after time in such chronological order. Everything makes sense too. Usually dreams start out making sense but then something bizarre happens. You wake up and tell yourself that was quite a dream."

Carl laughed a hearty laugh. "You can say that again. Why just last night…"

"Carl, not to be mean or anything but I didn't come over here to listen to a silly dream. Let's get back to what this meeting is all about. You're going to spill it. Tell me all you know. Start talking!"

Katie tried to be forceful but it was hard after looking at Carl and the slight smile on his face. They both burst out laughing. Finally Carl calmed down, and became serious.

Waiting for Dusk

"I think you're old enough to know. If my mom and your parents are going to expose you to something, you should be told the facts. It's real, Katie. Reading that book is as real as it gets. That book has the magical powers of time travel. My mom checked in on you when you returned, saw you were still sleeping and removed your necklace. She gave it to your father after your parents returned from Salt Fork. He was going to destroy it but my mom insisted you get to keep it in some way. She told your dad how upset you were about losing it. He then decided to tell you the necklace was from him."

"Then Drew did give me this necklace." Katie touched it with love.

"Yes he did, and don't tell anyone I told you so." Carl patted her shoulder. "There is so much you don't know and so much you need to know. I'll be here for a couple more days. I'll let this sink in and will tell you more tomorrow."

"Thanks, I knew I could count on you," Katie said, then she walked back home. She tried to wrap her head around everything Carl had just told her. Time travel? It sounded so science fiction.

With every step she took, the madder she got. My father wanted to destroy the necklace. What if Maya didn't stop him? But she did, thank goodness.

Katie stopped in her tracks. She couldn't let on that she knew anything and would have to be the good daughter until she had all the facts. Katie breathed slowly through her mouth until she was calmer. Her parents were sitting on the deck when she got back.

"Have fun with Carl?" her mom asked. "It's so good to have him home."

"Yeah, we had a great talk. The weather's so nice; I think I'll stay out awhile longer."

Her parents got up, hugged her and went inside. "School night, don't stay out here too long," Her father said as he slid the door shut.

Katie curled up on the chaise lounge and stared at the night sky. There was a full moon and many stars out. Her eyes went back to the moon. There he was, the man in the moon. Her Drew was looking down on her. She didn't know how she would get back to him but she knew she would some way, somehow, even if she had to break into Maya's antique bookcase.

Katie's phone buzzed. She picked it up, and read a text message.

How was the wedding. That Lindsey!

Katie answered back. Awesome. Then added I luv Drew.
How immature is that? She thought but didn't care and hit 'send'.
Lindsey answered with—fill me in 2moro.

Waiting for Dusk

Chapter Twenty

The next day at school Katie and Lindsey decided to find a quiet place to have lunch. Since students were allowed to go to the outdoor courtyard for lunch hour, they chose to go there. They picked a grassy place away from the crowds to have their private conversation. Katie filled Lindsey in on the whole weekend. Lindsey stared with her mouth open the whole time.

"You haven't eaten yet," Katie told her.

"Neither have you! I can't believe this is real. I'm trying to grasp it all but can't. I'm still going with a realistic dream otherwise you're caught up in two different worlds. How do you pick which one you want to be in? I don't want to lose my best friend."

Katie never thought about it that way. She didn't think about choosing the world she wanted to live in. If she had to choose right now, she knew which one she'd pick. There would be no debate about it. She would live in Drew's world forever.

When Katie got home from school, she called Carl. "Hey, big bro. I'm home from school. Let's go to the walking trail and talk."

"Meet you out front. You have to see the car I rented this time." Carl sounded excited. Every time he came home he liked to rent a convertible or a sports car or a combination of both. She hung up and ran out the front door. Carl was pulling a silver sports car out of the garage.

"Wow, Carl! That's some car!" Katie wasn't a car fanatic but she knew he would fill her in.

"It's a beauty," Carl told her as she hopped in. "Do you mind if we go for a drive first? I just want to test this out on the freeway."

"Sure, go for it. I don't have homework or anything important like that," Katie teased.

"So where do you want me to start?" Carl asked her once they were on the highway.

"Anywhere, tell me what you know." Katie just wanted him to get started.

"I will tell you what I know about you and my family. That's all I will tell. If your parents want you to know any more, they will have to tell you their own history. Agreed?"

Katie nodded vigorously. She just wanted Carl to get on with the story.

"It was July, if I'm right, when all this started for you. My mom just got back from visiting me in California. She went over to see you and your mom. She could tell by the look on your face that something was wrong. After you went up to your bedroom, my mom and yours talked. Mine thought it would be a fun diversion to have you read the book, thinking it would be this great summer adventure. She never expected you to fall in love."

Katie was quiet for a moment and then said, "She knows I fell in love with Drew?"

"Yes, and now she regrets giving you the book. She pictured you riding horses, having fun with the girls and getting to be at the Grand Canyon. Plus she'd be there to chaperone you. That's the truth. Your mom, who never took all of this too seriously, went along with the idea and gave the final approval. She was also the one who decided that once school started, the book would disappear. She never dreamt you would like that world so much. She just thought you'd have fun, too. Your mom got a little nervous when you started asking a lot of questions about your family, your Aunt Lucinda in particular. She believes the past should stay the past. With our families that's not the case." Carl turned and winked at Katie.

"When your mom comes to visit you in California, does she bring the book?"

"Yep. She only goes back to visit when she knows someone is aware that she's gone. She always lets your mother know. When she misses my dad and can't stand it anymore, she goes. This summer she went back a lot because of you. She wanted to keep an eye on you."

Katie was still puzzled. "She was so much younger. How do you explain that?"

Waiting for Dusk

"There are some things we can't explain. I think it's because whatever age my dad was during that time, she compliments that. Although, as she likes to remind me, she was seven years younger than him. I believe he was thirty or thirty-one at that time, so she would be a young girl of twenty-four. Another theory is you stay the age you were when you first visited the Canyon."

"So if your mom misses him so much, why doesn't she stay there or just bring him back here?"

"You have to remember, my dad passed away in the 1990's. She can't bring him back here, although she did try. My mom's a spitfire! She was determined to figure out a way to get him back here but nothing worked. It took her awhile to accept that dad has passed on and that his spirit lives at the boardinghouse. Plus when she's there, he doesn't remember the future. Dad is just working on his plans to build a riding stable where he can give people lessons. He works at the boardinghouse to make money to put toward it and is just in the moment. He doesn't remember me or even know I exist although he talks about one day they'll have a Carl Jr." Carl paused for a moment. He wiped the corner of his eye. "I wish I could see him, too," he whispered.

"Then why doesn't she just stay?" Katie reminded him of her other question.

"She knows if she stays that she will have to live through his illness and death again. She will know exactly when he will die and how. She can't take that and I don't want her to. Something else holds her back from doing that…me."

"I just realized something…your dad…he's from the past."

"Yeah."

Katie wanted to hear more. "Why don't you just go back with your mom some time to visit?"

"I'll save that for tomorrow. Let's get back to you. My mom saw how much the wedding meant to you and decided to lie to your parents. They don't know you were gone the whole weekend."

"I was gone, literally gone. Not in the bed…gone." Katie kept repeating.

"Yep, gone. For some reason when you go for one day there is no interruption in the time continuum. You place the book on your nightstand, fall asleep and…Bam! You wake up to the next day here none the wiser. You still leave, or as you just said 'are not in the bed'.

You're gone for the night and are really time traveling. You just didn't know it. When you place the book in the bed you can stay as long as you like and not come back, if you keep the book away from you and with personal effects just like my mother instructed you to do. You are then in a different time zone, as I like to say. There's no explaining it."

"So that is why it was already Monday when I got back."

"Exactly. I was trying to explain to my mom that if she let you go for all that time, she would have to tell you why it was Monday and not Saturday when you woke up. She thought she had it all under control."

"Until you spilled the beans." It was all starting to make sense to Katie. That was why Carl was so upset when she couldn't find her necklace. "You are the best brother anyone could have. Did you know that?"

Katie turned the radio on in the car and played with the stations. An old song came on that she liked when she was younger. Carl and Katie sang at the top of their lungs as they traveled down the highway. Katie felt freer than she had in a long while. The clouds and confusion were clearing from her head.

Carl got off an exit, drove around and got back on the freeway. As he was driving down the entrance ramp to head back home he told Katie they would continue their talk the next day. She nodded in agreement. She did need to process all of it anyway. When they pulled in the Johnson driveway, Katie got out and ran across to her house.

"I promise we'll walk tomorrow!" Carl called out as he pulled the car into the garage.

Katie gave him a thumb's up, and called out to him, "Next time get a convertible!" She entered the house to find her parents talking to Tyson.

"Hi everyone!"

"Katie, Tyson came over to borrow something. Notes? Book?" Jackson shrugged his shoulders. "Where have you been by the way?"

"Carl wanted to take me for a drive in his rented sports car. Thing is really fast!" Katie ran up the stairs. "Come on, Ty!"

She was so used to having Ty in the house, and in her bedroom, she hadn't thought about what it would be like now that he thought of her as his girlfriend. Ty stopped in the doorway.

"Ty! Come in!" Katie was a little annoyed at how he was acting.

Ty sat on the floor while Katie found her schoolbag and rummaged

Waiting for Dusk

through it. "What exactly do you need?" She wasn't sure if she brought the right thing home.

"Actually, I really don't need anything. I just wanted to see you. I told your parents that so I had an excuse to stay until you got home. I heard you have a dress for Homecoming. What color? So I know what kind of flowers to get."

"Wow, Tyson. You are on top of things. Most guys wouldn't even know or care about stuff like that." Katie teased.

"Well, my mom sort of told me to find out or ask you what you like."

"How about white roses with a sapphire blue ribbon?" Katie wanted to settle that quickly plus it would remind her of Lucinda's wedding.

"Sure, whatever you want." He got up and sat next to her on the bed.

"How was your date on Friday?" Katie decided to distract him.

"Date?"

"You know, you took Erin to the movies."

"Oh, that. Fine."

Katie wanted a little more information than that. "Tyson Gray!"

"The movie was good. I want to take you to see it now. Erin is a fun girl. She can't wait for basketball season. She's positive that I will make the varsity team."

"As positive as she was that I'd make the cheer team," Katie said under her breath.

"What did you say?" Ty threw her back on the bed.

The next thing she knew he was almost on top of her, trying to kiss her. Her heart raced but for all the wrong reasons. She felt like she was betraying Drew and did not want to hurt Ty again. She decided she would just let him kiss her and get it over with. While he was kissing her all she could think about was that he smelled like a sixteen-year-old boy who, maybe, just got out of bed and hurried to school. Not that it was bad or offensive or anything like that. Katie started to laugh about having a mock debate in her head over the hygiene habits of sixteen-year-old boys.

Ty leaned back. "What's so funny?"

"You! Are you trying to take advantage of me in my bedroom?" She tried keeping it light. "If you were ten, you'd be saying 'ew, gross'."

"I'm not ten anymore," he said grabbing her once again.

As he kissed her again the comparisons continued. That time Katie compared him to Drew. Shouldn't she be concentrating on Ty and thinking only of him? When Drew kissed her she never wanted it to stop.

Ty could stop any time he wanted and she wouldn't be bothered that he did. When Drew just touched her she felt chills or tingles through her body, and with Ty there wasn't much of anything. Ty was meant to be a friend. She didn't have feelings for him. Katie knew it had to stop, especially when she felt his hand go up under the back of her top and come around to the side.

"Ty!" Katie quickly sat up.

"Oh. I know your door is open. Sorry." He wasn't getting the message, and she was giving the wrong one. She did like kissing him. She did like being around him. She didn't like him taking Erin to the movies. It was getting too confusing again.

Katie's mom called up the stairs, "Dinner's ready! I hope Ty got his homework done."

Yeah, right, he did his homework. They stood up and Ty pulled her close to him. He was taller than Drew. She had to get up on her tiptoes to barely reach his mouth.

Drew was just right, tall but not too tall. Before she knew what was happening Ty bent down and kissed her again. It wasn't bad. She liked it. It wasn't fairytale romantic, though. Maybe that's how it's supposed to be—two high school kids making out in a bedroom.

Katie pulled away. "I've got to get down there."

"Sure, I understand. I missed you. We could've hung out all weekend. Maybe this weekend?"

"Um, let's wait and see. May have a big project coming up." Katie used that excuse once too often this week. She ran down the stairs with Ty right behind her, walked him to the front door and let him out. She then leaned against the door and breathed a sigh of relief.

Waiting for Dusk

Chapter Twenty-One

Katie sent Carl a text message to meet her at the walking trail right after school. She didn't want to get on the bus or even get close to the bus stop because she knew Ty would be waiting for her. Lindsey drove to school most days and was supposed to drive directly there and back home, no detours. Katie pleaded with her to be dropped at the park knowing it would add extra driving time.

"I'll just tell my mom I was stuck in traffic." Lindsey put her arm around Katie. "And you can fill me in on the latest! Your life is much more exciting than mine."

Katie wanted to make her friend feel better. "Your life is fine. Hasn't Brian been calling you and meeting you between classes? Things are looking up for you."

"Yeah, but remember he's just a friend! Brian's quite the talker, Kates. Seems like Ty tells him a lot. It's like he's in love with you or something."

"No, no, that can't be. He's complicating my life!" Katie screamed.

"Calm down, girl! I'll see what I can find out." Lindsey pulled into the parking lot.

"Thanks for the ride. I don't know what I'd do without you. You're the best." Katie jumped out of the car.

Carl was already there, leaning on his sports car. Katie waved and ran toward him.

"Ready for that walk?" She couldn't wait to get started.

They set off down the trail as Carl began to tell his parents' story.

"First I want to tell you how my dad found the set of books. That's really how this all began." He took a deep breath. "This may be long so bear with me."

Katie remained quiet not wanting to distract his thoughts and wished he'd just get started.

"When dad was hired to run the boardinghouse, he had to fix it up first. It was an old, rundown place. No one had lived there for years. It was a good solid structure and my dad was a talented carpenter. He could fix or make anything, as you know. He worked on the house for months living out there alone.

One day Dad was pulling out some old rotted wood in the kitchen and behind the boards was a shelf. On the shelf was this set of old books. Dad liked to read and was thrilled he had something to occupy his time when he wasn't working. Little did he know what he got himself into!"

Carl came to the first resting bench and sat down.

"So your dad found the books. Your dad and mom didn't go antiquing and find them in a quaint little old shop?" Katie remembered the story Mrs. Johnson told her.

"That's right, although there's some truth to it. My dad did give the books to my mother for safekeeping," Carl continued. "Dad decided to read the first book that night before he turned in, placing the book on his nightstand when he was done. When he woke up, to his amazement, he was in a dormitory, a college dormitory for men. He thought he was dreaming, of course, so he set out to explore this alien territory. Everything seemed a little strange to him. People were dressed differently and he didn't recognize a lot of things. That's when he convinced himself that it was a dream and to just go along with it.

Dad found his way outside and discovered he was on a college campus. One building he could relate to was the library, so he headed there. He thought he could at least research and figure out where he was and why he was there. The first person he encountered was my mother, who had just graduated from the college and worked in the library. She was a free spirit and a liberal thinker, so maybe it was fate that the first person he would come across would be her. Plus it was the sixties. My mom came up to him and asked if he needed any help because he definitely looked like he needed it. It was love at first sight, for Dad anyway. Mom said that he had this bewildered look on his face, guess she couldn't tell it was love!"

Carl stood and stretched, then motioned to Katie to start their walk again. "Since he thought it was still a dream, he told her everything. He

Waiting for Dusk

kept on insisting it was 1927. Mom thought he was on some type of drug, not the prescription kind if you know what I mean."

"So your dad ended up here at Oberlin College, if I understand this correctly."

"Yep, you are correct. My dad ended up staying the day at the college library. My mom took him to lunch and explained what a lot of things were, especially television. At the end of the day she helped him find the dorm room he woke up in, and they parted ways. Mom thought she'd never see this guy with a Swedish accent again. She felt a little sad about that. He was so kind and sincere and was such a gentleman. They had exchanged first names and that was about all. When dad woke up, he was back at the boardinghouse. It didn't take him long to figure out that reading the book had something to do with the dream he had. He decided he would read again that night. He was determined to go back to figure this out, plus see that beautiful woman again. The motivation was love."

Katie gasped. Carl looked at her. "Are you okay?"

"Yes. It's just when you said that it sounded so familiar. I was determined to go back for the very same reason, love."

"Love can be a powerful thing. It's what kept my dad here. I'm getting ahead of myself though. You wanted to hear everything as it happened. You probably can guess where my dad headed first when he came back to the university."

"The library."

"Mom was shocked to see him and had to convince him this wasn't a dream. It was really happening. They decided to put their heads together and figure the entire thing out. My mom agreed the book definitely had something to do with the time travel. She told my dad to bring the book with him the next time he came and she would wait for him in the library as usual. He showed up the next day with two books, one for her. Mom said she would read it and maybe find some sort of clue. Dad said he'd let her do the reading now. She read the book that night and put it on her nightstand after finishing. You can probably guess what happened next."

"She woke up in the boardinghouse."

"Exactly right. Imagine their surprise when mom entered the kitchen that morning. Dad was making some coffee and dropped the pot when he saw her. Mom said that was the day she knew she was falling in love with him. He showed her the house and the property. He was building his barn for the horses he wanted to get. Mom could tell he really loved the place. She said his eyes lit up whenever he talked about his true passion, to own the property and make it a horse ranch."

Carl paused and opened his water bottle. He took a drink and then pointed down the path. "Which trail do you want to take?"

"This one." Kate didn't care. She just wanted him to keep telling the story.

"That's when my parents realized they were torn between two worlds. She didn't want him to leave his, and he didn't want her to leave hers. They went on this way for a few weeks, visiting back and forth. Finally Dad decided he wanted Mom to keep all the books with her, feeling that was safer. He brought all the books with him, and stored them in her apartment under lock and key. Since Dad left the books at her apartment, he didn't know he had no way of getting back. He originally thought if he read from the book to get to the present he'd just automatically go back. That's how they discovered the magic was not in the reading but the book itself. Dad went back to the dorm to sleep, unaware he would not go back in time."

"Let me guess," Katie broke in. "He was still in the dorm when he woke up the next day."

"Right again. You're getting good at this. When Dad woke up in the dorm the next day, without ever returning to the boardinghouse, he realized he needed at least one book to get him back to 1927 otherwise he would be staying in Oberlin forever. That's when they understood the power of the books. They did a lot of experimenting with the books until they understood how they worked."

This time it was Katie's turn to stop and look around. She thought she heard something, but didn't want to distract Carl. She pretended to check her shoe and ran to catch up with him.

"Then one day, Dad popped the question. They decided to marry at the college where they met. That's also when they decided to change his last name to Johnson. They didn't want him to have the same last name as he did in 1927. All they really did was Americanize his name. Dad was comfortable with that. He then wanted to introduce his new bride to everyone back at the boardinghouse because it was almost up and running and he had to be there. Little did he know they would encounter the racial prejudice that they did. Mom tried to prepare him but he kept saying everything would be alright. Eventually everyone accepted they

Waiting for Dusk

were a couple in both decades. When everyone got to know Mom and Dad as a couple, things were good. They went back and forth through time living an interesting life until I came along."

"Aw, Carl, that can't be true." Katie patted him on the shoulder.

"They both tried to convince me it wasn't true but I still believe it. They were having quite the life doing what they wanted for many years until I showed up. My mom and dad decided I would never travel back in time. They felt that having me grow up in the time period I was born was the right thing to do. I have respected their wish. My mother never went back when I was a small boy. My dad did once in awhile."

"Why, Carl? Why wouldn't they let you go? Didn't you want to see the boardinghouse and the barn? Meet Flicka and Thunder?"

Carl gave a quick laugh. "Even you have met the horses. That's alright. My parents were only protecting me. After I was born, they had a serious discussion. They wanted me to have the best life possible and decided I would grow up in the eighties and nineties, not the twenties. There would be less prejudice, they hoped. I would have it a little easier in the here and now, although that wasn't always the case. People can be cruel and judgmental in any time, any place. I guess my parents made the right decision. Dad stayed here with us, again out of love. They raised me together and took me all over the country.

The first time I went to Grand Canyon with them, it was if they were home. It is a special place, a wondrous place. I did get to see the boardinghouse and the horse ranch, only it was the nineties. Someone else owns it now. Then, as you know, Dad got cancer. I was in high school during that time. Mom still had her job at the library. She went to part-time when dad got sick. She just couldn't give that job up. It was a part of who she was and Dad didn't want her to. He passed the year before you moved in next door. You know the rest, Katie."

Katie was overwhelmed. It was a beautiful and romantic story. She loved the whole thing. She loved how Carl and Maya protected Carl Jr. and made sacrifices for him.

Katie and Carl walked along for a time in silence. They entered the wooded section of the path, and seemed to be the only ones walking the trail. They walked in rhythm, their feet hitting the gravel path in unison.

"You're getting off the beat," Katie teased.

"No, it's not me. Listen." They looked around but saw no one. "When I say 'run', you run as fast as you can."

Katie didn't like the tone of his voice. Carl was going into protective mode. He took her hand.

"This is ridiculous. It has to be an animal or something." Katie heart was beating a little too fast. She didn't really believe her own words. "This path isn't exactly straight. Maybe someone is just behind us and we don't see them yet. Let's stop and see what happens."

Carl's eyes narrowed but he nodded in agreement. They stopped and listened. The footsteps they thought they heard stopped too. Then they started up again, faster.

"Run, Katie, run!" Carl pushed her ahead of him.

"Hey, guys. No need to run. It's just me." Tyson came around the corner.

Katie felt a little odd. *He knew I was here. Did he follow me? Is he stalking me?*

"Ty! Long time no see." Carl shook his hand. "Boy, you have shot up. How tall are you?"

"Six feet three." Ty said. "Didn't know you guys were ahead of me. We could have walked together. I should actually be jogging for my workout. I've been running on and off here at the park. Had to stop for a rest back there. Do you mind, Carl, if Katie goes home with me?" He turned and faced her. "I got my license just in time for Homecoming."

She shot Carl a 'help me' look.

"You know, Ty, I promised Katie's dad I would bring her home after our walk. I have to stick to my promise."

"Oh, sure. I understand. I'll see you later." Ty jogged away.

"That was strange," said Katie.

"It's like he was stalking you," Carl repeated what Katie was thinking. "I don't like it. I leave tomorrow and now I wish I wasn't."

"It was probably coincidence."

They finished their walk and came out on the other side of the parking lot. Katie noticed the Gray's car in one of the spots. Ty was still there. She decided she was making way too much of what just happened. Ty had been her friend forever. He'd never acted strangely before. She just didn't like Carl's reaction to it all. He was acting like she was in danger.

"I want you to text or call me daily. I want updates about what's happening here in Ohio."

"Or you're just being the Carl police. I'll be fine. Didn't you ever stalk a girl when you were a teenager?"

"No, I didn't."

Katie thought it best to change the subject. "Speaking of girlfriends, do you have one?"

"Yes, back in California, I do. Nothing serious, so don't tell my mom."

Katie was happy that Carl was confiding in her. "Scouts honor." She held up two fingers, then three and then started laughing. "Whatever!"

They hopped in his car and headed home. Katie thought she saw another car close behind in her side mirror but said nothing. She wasn't going to let anything ruin the day. She, Carl and their families had a secret that was beyond all the high school stuff. It was important to protect it. What kept them all together was more powerful than anything she had ever experienced. It was the gift of love and she would do anything to protect that.

Chapter Twenty-Two

It was hard to believe it was the first week of October. The leaves were beginning to turn their fall colors. When Katie looked at the reds and oranges of the leaves, it reminded her of the colors of the canyon and took comfort in that for some reason. To occupy her time until Thanksgiving, she decided to write Drew some letters even though she couldn't mail them. Katie planned to tuck them in the book and take them to him in November. It was a great day to write about those changing leaves.

Katie pulled open her desk drawer and retrieved a flat, lavender box. She went to a stationery store to purchase what she needed to write letters to Drew. It was fun trying to pick out what would be acceptable as old-fashion paper. She was tempted to buy an ink well and pen, but found out that fountain pens had been around a long time already. At the very least Katie was learning some history.

"Katie! Ty is here!" Her mother called up the stairs.

"I'll be right down."

"I've already sent him up!"

Katie was trying to avoid having Ty in her bedroom or being alone with him anywhere. It made things much simpler. She tried to make sure she gave him enough attention so he didn't feel neglected because she didn't want him following her again. Throughout the first month of school she thought she caught him behind her in the hallways or saw him at the mall when she was there with Lindsey and Jordyn. Still those were typical places that teens would be or hangout so maybe she was being too suspicious. Katie also kept Carl updated on everything like he asked. Just what she needed, a paranoid brother and a stalker boyfriend.

Waiting for Dusk

"Hey, Katie. It's been a long time since I've been alone with you." Ty sat on the bed.

Katie was glad she was at her desk. She slid the stationery box back in the drawer, closed it and turned in the chair to face him.

Tyson continued. "Homecoming's Saturday. Football game is Friday night. Jordyn made all the plans for us. We'll meet at the game, but we're on our own getting there and coming home. On Saturday we'll meet here since I just live across the street, then carpool from here to the restaurant and dance."

"Sounds good. Jordyn is great at these things, remembering all the details. Hard to believe it's October and time for Homecoming."

Katie's phone buzzed. She looked down and saw it was Carl. She quickly looked at the message and all it said was, Update!!!

"Hey, Ty, can we do something quick tonight. I need to get back here and touch base with Carl and then Lindsey."

"Sure, whatever you want to do." Ty pulled Katie over to her bed as she stood up. "I could just stay right here with you." He kissed her cheek and moved down to her neck.

Katie was still having a hard time with that. In one way, she liked it but really wished he was someone else. Katie decided that she would stick to the plan. Go to Homecoming with Ty, gradually let him down and tell him being friends was what she wanted. She hoped Erin was waiting in the wings for him. Katie was pretty sure she was. Erin gave her the evil eye whenever she saw Katie and Ty together at school.

"You seem distracted." He got up and shut her bedroom door. "I want all of your attention."

"Ty, the rule is the door stays open."

"I don't think your parents would mind at all. They like me. Plus hear that lawnmower? I think your dad is cutting the grass. I heard your mom tell him she was going over to Maya's for a bit. The timing's perfect." Ty smiled at her. He took off his shirt and lay back down on the bed. "Well, what do you think?"

Katie was shocked. "Think? About what?"

"I've been really working out. Come on, give me a break!"

"Oh, you look great, Ty. You always do," Katie couldn't help but notice.

"And so do you." He took her hand and pulled her next to him. Katie couldn't help herself. Ty was so cute, and he did look good with his shirt off. She put her hand on his chest and could feel his heart pounding. She let him kiss her until she felt like she was drowning.

"I love you, Katie. I really do." Ty's voice sounded like it was far away. She needed to come up for air.

"Ty, I'm sorry..." How could she say she wanted to be friends after he professed his love for her? She was caught in something that really confused her. For a moment she had felt something too. Or was it just the feelings for Drew surfacing, now that she knew he was real? All she knew was that she wanted Tyson to leave. "I have a lot of homework."

"Only if you promise to say you love me, too."

The shock of hearing Ty say he loved her was overwhelming, but now he needed to hear it back. This was too much to handle and she felt pressured.

"Ty, you know I've loved you since we were eight. That will never change." Katie thought she found a good solution to answering his question.

"Not that kind of love. You know what I mean."

"I don't think you should be telling me I have to say it to you. That isn't how it works, is it?" Katie felt cornered.

"You're right as usual." Ty got up. "I'll wait for Friday night. Just teasing." Tyson grabbed his shirt and pulled it on. He brushed past her as he went to open her door and left.

Katie paced back and forth. What had she gotten herself into? Ty loved her! That was ridiculous. When did that happen? She grabbed her phone and sent a message to Carl.

He says he loves me. She wrote it as 'love' not 'l-u-v' so he would get the point.

I'm coming home

No you're not.

Then Katie's phone rang.

"Okay, maybe I'm not coming home. But I think that boy is getting serious too fast. I also think he's a little pushy and is good at making you do what he wants. He doesn't let you give any opinions or even give you a chance to make your thoughts known. He just assumes. I don't like it."

"Take a breath, Carl. Give me some credit." Katie told him of her plan of what would happen after Homecoming.

Before he hung up, Carl got very serious. "Katie, you're young. This is all new to you. Ty isn't from the 1920's. Just be careful."

Waiting for Dusk

Chapter Twenty-Three

Friday was a beautiful autumn day. The air was cool and crisp, perfect football weather. When Katie got home from school, she spent time in her room deciding what to wear to the game. She tried on a few outfits and then finally collapsed on her bed. She felt like she was a million miles and light years away from Drew. She wanted to see his face because it was fading from her memory. She concentrated until she pictured him again. Katie closed her eyes and then opened them again quickly. Sitting in her desk chair, gazing at her with a little smile on his face, was Drew.

"Come back to me, Kate. I'll be there."

She blinked, and he was gone. Tears filled her eyes. I will be there too, she thought.

Katie had the confidence to get ready. She decided she would have fun, and enjoy the weekend.

Tyson showed up at Katie's front door with car keys dangling from his hand. "I'm driving…no more mom." As they drove to the game, the sun was setting and glowing through the autumn leaves on the trees.

"Do you know how you glow in this light?" Tyson grabbed Katie's hand. "You're beautiful." He kissed her hand.

Ty and Katie joined Matt and Jordyn and Brian and Lindsey at the game. There was so much going on, Katie was relieved she didn't have to talk to anyone. She was still concerned over Tyson's comments and this wasn't the place to talk to her girlfriends about them. They watched the festivities and cheered for everything. Homecoming queen and her court were announced before the game and there was a wonderful marching band performance at halftime.

The guys left for a short time and Katie was finally about to talk to Lindsey. "Ty wants me to tell him I love him," she whispered.

Lindsey looked at her and said, "You are so not doing that. Do you want me to talk to him?"

"No, I can handle it. Let's just keep busy tonight."

After the game they went for burgers, and sat in the restaurant for a long time.

"I think Katie should run for Homecoming queen next year." Ty put his arm around her.

"I think I'll let the Erins of the world do that."

Erin was part of the Homecoming court and was in her element. She seemed to love all the eyes on her and the special attention that came with it. Maybe it was a good thing Katie didn't make the cheer team. She could do without all that.

"Oh, come on, Katie. Can't you picture you, me and Lindsey in the convertibles waving to the crowd?" Jordyn joked.

The rest of the evening was light and everyone was in a good mood as they left the restaurant. When Ty pulled into the Roberts' driveway, Katie jumped out of the car.

"See you tomorrow, Ty." She waved and smiled as she ran into the house. One down, one to go, she thought.

It was late and her parents were reading in their bedroom when Katie went upstairs.

"Have fun?" her mom called out to her.

"Yes, Mom. Good night you two." Katie stood outside their door.

"Close our door now that you're home, sweetie," her mom blew her a kiss.

Katie went down the hall to her room. As she got ready for bed, she thought she heard voices coming from her parents' room. Her parents sounded like they were fighting again. She tiptoed down the hall to see what she could hear. By then the voices had calmed down but it still seemed like a serious discussion.

"Shhh! She's going to hear us! I told you everything would work out. Katie has a boyfriend. In the here and now. She's distracted. Isn't that what you wanted, Jackson?"

"I just want to make sure it stays that way. You have that book under lock and key, don't you?"

"Yes, I do. You are such a worrywart, although I wouldn't have it

Waiting for Dusk

any other way."

"Joanna, as I have said before, and I will say again, you don't take all this seriously enough. I don't understand that book at times. I don't want to expose Katie to something I'm not completely sure about."

There was silence for awhile and then the light went out under the door. Katie slowly walked back to her room. Little do they know that I know what they are talking about.

That fight they had in the summer was not over the Mustang. It was over the trip she took back in time. Her mother must have told her dad about it when he first got home. Or maybe Jack Woods did see her and was really her father. She would find out all the answers eventually. For now, she decided she would work on worrying about the dance the next day.

When she got back to her room, her phone buzzed. It was a message from Lindsey to call if she was still up.

"Of course I'm still awake," Katie said after Lindsey answered. "What's up? Must be important if it can't wait until tomorrow."

"I know this is short notice but do you think you'll be allowed to go to my aunt's ranch in Arizona next weekend? It will be Columbus Day weekend and we'll get an extra day off from school. Plus my mom is going to let me miss an extra day of school, too. I have been begging to go back because it will be my great-grandmother's 100th birthday. I promised her I would come back for it. The rest of my family can't go because my brother is in a soccer tournament. My mom really didn't want me to go by myself, even though I go in the summer alone. I asked her if she would let me go if you came too, and she agreed. So?"

"Wow, I'd love to go. I'm sure my parents will let me. I'll ask them in the morning. Everyone is meeting here at five, right?" Katie was more excited about going to Arizona than the dance.

"Yes, I'll see you then."

Chapter Twenty-Four

The next day was filled with a flurry of activities revolving around the dance. Katie set out her jewelry. She'd be wearing Drew's necklace. She found some gold dangling earrings with imitation blue stones that matched the necklace pretty well. Katie decided to wear her hair as she always did with just a little more curl to it so she plugged in the curling iron to start working on it. Her mother told her to splurge on shoes since she didn't have to buy a dress so she practiced walking in them all day. Everything was set.

Katie's mom knocked on the door. "Need any help?"

"Sure, you can help me with the dress."

"You know, you and Ty make such a cute couple," her mom said as she removed the hanger from the dress. "You two could get married one day and live on this street with your parents and in-laws. Wouldn't that be great?"

"Mom! I'm only sixteen. Give me a break!"

"I didn't mean now. I was thinking more down the line, like after you graduate from college."

Katie's stomach flipped over. "I'm only going to a dance with Ty. After college I may not even be here. Who knows where I'll live or who I will be dating."

Katie knew her mom loved having her family close by. That's why she moved back to Ohio after Katie was born. Her mom, dad, and brother Michael were close by. Her other brother, Will, only lived an hour away. Plus, she had Maya next door.

Katie just hadn't thought that far into her future or wanted to. She thought it best to change the subject.

Waiting for Dusk

"Mom, Lindsey invited me to go to her aunt's ranch next weekend. Is it alright if I go?"

"The ranch in Arizona?"

"That's the one. Please, can I? Or may I?" Katie so wanted her mom to say yes. She needed the distraction. It would make her feel closer to Drew. It would help her get through the weekend.

"You'll be flying? You need a last minute plane ticket."

"It can be my Christmas present. Oh, please!"

"I'm sure it will be okay. I'll talk to your dad later. Make the final arrangements with Lindsey."

"Mom, you're the best."

"You're hard to say no to."

They finally had Katie dressed and ready. Her mom had tears in her eyes. "Katie, you are so grown up. When did that happen?" She eyed the framed picture of Aunt Lucinda's wedding. "You sure do look like this Kathryn in the wedding party. It's unreal. But you also look like Grandma Rett. Those two girls look like sisters more than Lucinda and Loretta do in this picture."

"That's what Ru..." Katie caught herself. She was going to say that Ruthie's sister, Molly, had said the same thing.

"Are you alright?"

"Yeah, look at my shoes!" Again, Katie thought of a diversion. She was getting good at it. She'd have to get better by Thanksgiving if she wanted to be gone for a few days.

She took her shoes out of the designer shoebox and held them up. They were polished gold leather dress sandals with four-inch heels. Good thing that Tyson was tall.

"Those are great! I hope you didn't spend too much of my money on them." Katie's mom took a shoe from her hand.

Downstairs, they heard her dad letting Lindsey, Brian, Jordyn, Matt and Tyson into the house. The Roberts had planned a pre-party for them. Champagne glasses were waiting to be filled with sparkling cider, plus Katie's mom had made appetizers. The parents of all the kids were invited too. Suddenly there were many voices drifting up the stairs.

"We better get down there!" Katie's mother left her room.

Katie took one last look in the mirror. She had a quick flashback to Lucinda's wedding day. She was so excited to be in that wedding. She couldn't wait for Drew to see her in the dress. She felt like she was betraying them all. She would be going to a dance in a dress that Lucinda chose for her wedding. Katie would dance with the wrong partner. She stared into the mirror, wishing she could step through it to her other life. Touching the mirror, it just felt cold and hard.

I'm still here. I'm a sixteen-year-old girl who's going to a dance with her friends. That's how it should be. I need to stay focused and get my life together. Tonight I break up with Ty.

Katie headed down the stairs and saw a large group of people. The other parents took her mother's offer to come over and enjoy the festivities. Everyone snapped pictures, talked and ate. No one noticed she came downstairs, except Ty.

"Katie! You look beautiful." He kissed her on the cheek. "This is for you." Ty handed her a clear container with her flowers inside.

"They're nice." She smiled at Ty and took them out. He tied them on her wrist.

Lindsey and Jordyn came up to Katie and grabbed her hands. "Pictures!" They said in unison and pulled her away from Tyson.

Before Katie realized, she was in the car with Ty, driving to the restaurant. The other two couples went together in Matt's car. They rode in silence for awhile and then Ty turned on some music. He took Katie's hand. "This is a perfect evening. You and me, alone. I don't want to share you with anyone. I know that sounds selfish but that's how I feel."

Katie stayed quiet because she had no idea what to say in return.

After dinner they headed for the school where the dance was to be held. Tyson parked the car in the school parking lot and ran around to let Katie out. "Just wait till all our friends see us as a couple. Can't wait. Erin will have to accept it. We're going to be together forever. This is just the start." He patted his jacket pocket as if he was checking something.

The entrance to the gymnasium was decorated with fall colored balloons, bales of hay, autumn leaves and a few friendly scarecrows. There were moons and stars hanging from the ceiling. The theme of the dance was 'Harvest Moon'. Everyone agreed to meet before going into the dance and Katie and Tyson waited patiently for their friends to arrive.

Formal pictures were taken and then the three couples entered the gym which was transformed into a twinkling nighttime dance floor. Katie had to admit they did a very good job. She especially loved the

Waiting for Dusk

moons. She danced with her girlfriends and Ty throughout the night.

Later in the evening, Jordyn brought Erin and some other basketball cheerleaders over to their table.

"Having a good time?" Erin looked directly at Katie.

"Why, yes we are," Ty answered as he put his arm around Katie. "Who'd you come with, Erin? Didn't I see you with Joe Donovan?"

"Yeah, we came as friends, though. That's all." She sat down next to him. "Do you mind if I steal him for the next dance, Katie?"

"No, not at all. Go right ahead."

While Erin and Ty danced, Lindsey and Katie had time to talk. Lindsey looked at Katie very seriously. "What are you planning on doing about the Tyson situation?"

"I'm breaking up with him tonight after the dance. I know that sounds mean but it just can't go on anymore. I feel like he's not hearing me when I say I just want to be friends. He has all these plans for us and he thinks I'm going right along with them. I know I have been giving him mixed signals but it stops now. Even my mom is getting in on this! She has me married with children!"

Katie didn't realize how serious it all was until she said it aloud. Ty was serious, she was not. She was letting him believe otherwise and wanted to end things before it went any further.

"Well," Lindsey leaned in closely. "If you are going to break up with him, do it before he starts to sound serious."

Katie looked at her suspiciously. "Do you know something I don't?" Tyson sounded pretty serious already tonight.

"Just heed the warning." Lindsey smiled with her attempt at humor.

Ty came back to the table and for the rest of the night didn't leave Katie's side. He made sure he danced the rest of the dances with her. He tried to kiss her on the dance floor but she managed to avoid it. Katie knew she wouldn't have to kiss him again if all went as planned.

"Would you like to leave?" Ty said before the dance was over.

Katie shrugged, "Sure, that's fine. If you want to."

They walked out into the wonderful night air. The sky was full of stars and the full moon was glowing brightly. Katie stopped and looked up. She sighed as she looked at the moon with a half-broken heart. She didn't realize that Ty had put his arm around her.

"Cold?" he asked as she shivered. He took off his suit jacket and put it around her shoulders. "Katie, I was going to wait until we got home but the night has been so great, I can't wait." He reached over to take something out of his jacket pocket. He put a small box in her hand.

Heed the warning, Katie heard in her head.

"Wait!" she didn't mean to sound as harsh as she did. "Ty, we need to talk and this is as good a time as any. Since you're not hearing me about just being friends, I feel like I have to break this off. I want to be friends forever, just like we said when we were eight. If this means we can't even be friends, so be it. You don't seem to get it. I like you, it was fun dating you, but that is all it was."

Katie looked at Ty. He seemed to be in shock. Good. He heard me, she thought.

"Is there someone else?" he said softly.

Katie didn't answer right away. She just looked up at the moon and thought of her Drew.

"There is, isn't there?" Ty's tone changed to anger. "Did you ever like me, Katie? Or were you just using me to go to Homecoming? That's what Erin said and I guess she was right!"

He stormed back into the building. Katie didn't know quite what to do. She slowly opened the door and went back inside. There was still a good crowd and the music was playing loudly. No one was sitting at their table. She just stood there, wondering what to do.

Through the crowd of dancers, Ty emerged with Erin in tow. He was holding her hand and pulling her through the dancers. She seemed to be asking him to slow down but he kept going. They whizzed right past Katie, with Erin giving her a slight grin as they went out the door.

Katie stood there, unable to move. What had she done? Ty was so angry. Now he was with Erin? She hoped they would be alright.

Lindsey came running up to her. "What happened? Brian and I were dancing and the next thing we see is Ty grabbing Erin off the dance floor and disappearing into the crowd." She looked at Katie. "Are you okay?"

Katie had been holding back the tears. "No, no I'm not. Do you think you guys could take me home?"

"Sure, sweetie. Just let me find the rest of the gang."

Katie sat in the back seat of the car with Jordyn on one side and Lindsey on the other. She cried the whole way home. No one spoke or asked her any questions. Lindsey made sure of that.

The girlfriends walked her to the door and made sure she got inside. Katie's parents were in the family room, waiting up for all the details.

Waiting for Dusk

When they saw her face with tears and mascara running down it, they panicked.

"What happened? Where's Tyson? Are you alright?"

"I'm fine," Katie answered. "I broke up with Ty and he went home with another girl. Jordyn's date brought me home."

"That irresponsible kid! I trusted him with you! Tomorrow I'm going over to their house and giving him a piece of my mind!" Her father paced the floor.

"No, dad, it's my fault. I shouldn't have let it go on so long. Ty and I were friends and it got complicated. I thought we were friends and he thought I was his girlfriend." Katie barely choked the words out.

Katie's mom wrapped her arm around her. "Let's sit down, shall we?"

Just then the phone rang. Katie's dad answered it, all the while looking over at his two girls.

"No, Janet, Katie's right here. We don't know the whole story yet. Please keep us informed." He quietly hung up the phone. "Tyson has been in a car accident. It seems he had some girl in the car with him and Janet thought it was Katie. She was calling to tell us she got a call from the hospital. When I told her you were here, she got a little freaked out. She's going to the hospital now."

Katie rocked back and forth on the sofa. She couldn't believe how the night ended. She pictured it differently. She wanted to wait until they were safely home and could talk quietly with Tyson. It was not supposed to end like that, not like that. Suddenly Katie realized she still had Ty's jacket wrapped around her and was clutching the small box in her hand. Slowly she opened it. There was a tiny heart ring with a very small diamond in the center. Ty had put a little note in the top of the box, 'Step One of the many steps to come'. She snapped the box shut and leaned back, closing her eyes and that was the last thing she remembered.

Chapter Twenty-Five

Katie heard her mom talking softly when she awoke the next morning. It was difficult to hear what was being said. She could only make out a few words here and there. Katie knew she would just have to wait for her mother to get off the phone and give her the details. Someone had put a very soft blanket over her and it felt so good. She would love to hide under it and make everything go away. Instead, Katie sat up and looked down at her dress. It was wrinkled from sleeping on the couch all night.

Lucinda wouldn't be too happy about that, she thought. Either would Grandma Rett.

She felt for her necklace…still there. On the floor in front of her was the little black velvet box from the night before. Katie picked it up, and opened it. The ring was still in there with the note. She removed it from the box and placed it on her left ring finger. It fit perfectly. How did he know her size? It was frustrating all Tyson seemed to know.

Well, he should! They knew each other for eight years. They went to toy stores together to spend their birthday and holiday money and swam the summer days away in her pool. He would follow her around the mall for hours as she tried on many outfits. She played video games with him for hours. He beat her at basketball; she out rode him on their bikes. Katie felt a twinge of nostalgia, for the simpler days. She wished she could have loved Tyson like he wanted, she really did. She took off the ring, snapped the box shut, and set it on the table. Her mom was done with the phone call and Katie wanted to know if it was about Ty.

"That was Janet Gray. Tyson is home now. He just got a few bruises here and there. It was a one car accident. He drove into a stop sign."

Waiting for Dusk

"What about Erin?"

"She has a few bumps and bruises, too, plus a sprained wrist." Her mother folded her arms and her brows crossed. "Want to tell me what happened now?"

"There isn't much to tell. I broke up with Ty on the way out of the dance. He went back inside, grabbed Erin and that's the last I saw of him." Katie wanted to stop talking about it.

Her mom picked up the ring box as Katie finished her story. "And this?"

"You can open it. And do me a big favor by giving it to Mrs. Gray."

Her mom opened the box and sat quietly for a moment. "He was getting a little too serious for you, wasn't he? You know that you have to give this back to him yourself, don't you?"

"Yes, I guess I do. I'm glad you finally get it." Katie looked away. Tears filled in her eyes. She didn't want to hurt Ty anymore.

"Oh, and Mrs. Gray said something else. She said Tyson said you like someone else, not him."

Katie was done talking. "Yes, that's right." She got up and went toward the stairs. "I'm going to take a shower and may never come out."

* * * *

She wasn't looking forward to going to school on Monday. Once the rumors from the dance settled down, she hoped things would get back to normal. She would do or say whatever Ty wanted about Saturday night. Katie would take the blame and make Ty look good. Slowly, brushing her hair, she'd do anything to delay getting on the school bus today.

"Katie, you're going to be late." Her father's voice drifted up the stairs.

"I'm coming."

"Looks like I'll have to drive you. You missed the bus." Her father grabbed his keys and they went out the door.

The plan was to find Tyson and talked to him before they entered the building. If she'd been on the bus, they might have already talked. She spotted him sitting under a tree and ran over. Tyson got up when he saw her. He had a bump on his forehead and a few scratches on his arm.

"Ty, I hope you're alright. I heard about the accident. Whatever you want to say about Homecoming night, I'll go along with. Plus, I need to give something back to you." She held out the velvet box.

"You keep it, Katie. I bought it for you. What will I do with it?" Ty said coldly. "We broke up, end of story. You don't have to make anything up for me."

"Ty, I'm sor…" Before she could finish, Erin came running up.

"You waited for me just where we planned!" Erin looked at Katie with a triumphant grin. She was wearing a brace on her left arm. Tyson put his arm around Erin and walked away from Katie. She was stunned. He bounced back really fast. She wouldn't worry about him anymore.

Jordyn came running up to Katie. "Did you hear how Ty and Erin got in the accident? They were kissing! Do you believe it?"

No, Katie could not believe it. If that was high school, she wanted out. The sooner the better. She was counting the days till she and Lindsey left for Arizona. She couldn't wait to meet Lindsey's family and get away for just awhile.

Waiting for Dusk

Chapter Twenty-Six

Lindsey and Katie were excited to be at the airport instead of school. Their parents came with them but could only go so far because of security. Now they were completely on their own.

"You never told me your aunt's ranch was so close to the Grand Canyon."

"You never asked," laughed Lindsey. "You'll love it there! We can even go to the Grand Canyon if you like."

Katie thought about it. She didn't know if she could handle going if Drew wasn't there. She'd probably look for him the whole time. Yet, it might make her feel closer to him and help her digest all that Carl told her. Yes, she wanted to go. She'd wait to tell Lindsey later. Right then, Katie wanted to hear all about Lindsey's family and who she would be meeting. It seemed like there were a few generations living at the ranch.

"You already told me about your great-grandmother so let's continue from there." Katie buckled her seatbelt to get ready for the long plane ride.

"You can call her Grandma J. That's what everyone calls her. She and Great-Grandpa had only one son who married and moved away for awhile. He lives there now with his mother and his daughter, my Aunt Sue. His wife, my grandmother, has passed away. I would have loved for you to have met her. She was the sweetest, funniest person I've ever met, besides you! Well, anyway, Grandma and Grandpa had Aunt Sue, my mom Beth, and twins, Steve and Scott. Uncle Steve and Uncle Scott live right on the ranch. Each kid was given a piece of property to build on. My mom is the only one who moved far away."

"So what do I call your Grandfather?"

"Grandpa!" Lindsey laughed again. Katie could tell she was in a good mood. "Just call everyone what I call them. They would want you to. You will love everyone, believe me. They are happy you're coming. They know you're my best friend and that we always have each other's backs."

Katie and Lindsey did their handshake again. "Sisters till the end!"

The time seemed to go quickly. Before Katie knew it, they transferred planes in Phoenix and landed in Flagstaff. Lindsey seemed to know the airport pretty well. Katie followed her out from the gate and into the concourse. They walked toward baggage claim and there Katie saw a large group of people, yelling and waving their arms.

"They're a little shy as you can see." Lindsey giggled. "Aunt Sue, this is Katie. Katie, this is everybody!"

She looked at all the smiling faces, and knew she liked them immediately. "I guess we'll all get to know one another soon enough."

The family drove in a large caravan of Jeeps, trucks and SUVs to the ranch. Katie felt like she was in a parade. "Do they always come out to meet you like this?"

"Yes, they're very demonstrative. Be ready for lots of hugs and questions." Lindsey patted Katie's knee. "We're almost there."

The caravan pulled into a long driveway. It was still light outside so Katie was able to see everything. The house and surrounding area were outlined with split rail fence. The white house with black shutters was very large, two stories high in the middle with one story levels on each side. It was not what she expected at all. Off in the distance, Katie saw another house. Lindsey pointed at it and said, "That's my Uncle Steve's house. Grandpa divided the land among the four kids. My mom never built on her piece of land. I'm thinking one day I may build something there. Uncle Scott's is on the other side of Steve. It's farther down from here. You can't really see it."

"I'd love to see your piece of land." Katie was truly excited about her stay.

They parked in front of the house and before Katie knew it she was sitting in a guest bedroom.

"Take all the time you need and come down when you're ready," Aunt Sue said. "Just walk through the kitchen out back to the deck. We'll all be there. Barbeque for dinner. Make yourself at home. We're so glad you came!"

Waiting for Dusk

Aunt Sue left and closed the door behind her. Katie looked at herself in the mirror. She was so happy to be there and away from the high school drama. It suddenly felt like her second home. She realized she better not daydream too long and get downstairs to join the others. She ran down the stairs and rounded the corner. There was a large kitchen, larger than any kitchen she'd ever seen. It seemed to take up the whole back of the house. Katie walked to the back door but noticed a hallway to her right.

Curiosity got the better of her and she headed off down the short hallway. The first doorway led to a bathroom, which made sense. The next doorway opened up into a small sitting room. The room was filled with overstuffed furniture and antique tables. Everything was the color of peach and sand with a touch of aqua, making it inviting and comfortable. Katie felt a twinge of guilt for snooping around the house and turned to go back to the kitchen.

"Kathryn? Kathryn, is that you?" Katie thought she heard Anna's voice. She shook her head to knock the cobwebs from her brain.

"Kathryn, Please!" Katie's heart pounded. It felt as if it could jump out of her chest any minute. She so wanted it to be Anna, but how could it be?

Katie had to look into the room. Seated on a peach striped loveseat was a lovely older woman. Her pure white hair was swept back in a bun that reminded Katie of the Harvey girl style they wore at the restaurant.

"Anna?" Katie couldn't believe that came out of her mouth.

"Yes, yes, Kathryn. Please come here!" The older lady sounded so excited. She put down the book she was reading.

Tears flowed down Katie's face. She couldn't talk or barely breathe. She ran over to the place where the woman sat and knelt on the floor in front of her. Katie put her head in the old woman's lap and hugged her legs. She sobbed. All the while, the woman stroked Katie's hair. Katie gulped for air, and finally calmed down. It seemed like all the tension, all the confusion left her. She looked into the old woman's face and saw her friend. She saw the kindly brown eyes of Anna. Those eyes were always filled with compassion and never contempt. They were the eyes of her best friend. "Oh, Anna, I can't believe it's you. And you know me!"

"Of course, I know you." Anna patted the seat next to her. "Come up here, sit beside me and dry those eyes." Katie did as she was told.

"Let me look at you. Oh, Kathryn, whatever happened to you? You disappeared and never came back. You never knew I got married or got to be a part of my life. I never got to be a part of yours. I missed you so much. I always prayed we would meet again some day."

"Anna, please tell me what happened in your life. I want to know everything." Katie was prepared to listen until the wee hours of the morning if she had to. Her heart felt like it could burst she was so happy.

"We waited, you know. For a long time, we waited," Anna started off.

Katie was confused. She realized Anna was very old. It was going to be her 100th birthday. She probably mixed things up as old people do.

"We? As in you and Daniel?"

"Yes. Daniel Jenkins and I waited for almost two years until we married. I made him wait. He wanted to marry much sooner. I wanted to make sure Lucinda was settled in her life. When she got back from her honeymoon she found out she was pregnant. Little Henrietta was born in June of the following year. Lucinda was a very good mother. She was so proud of her children. She taught them to be independent and rely on themselves.

About a year after Henrietta, Lucy was born. When I heard about the second pregnancy, I thought it was safe to finally go ahead and plan my wedding. We invited Henry and Lucinda. Henry came but said Lucinda was not feeling well. She just had little Lucy so I knew it might be too much for her. I was so hoping she would come. We always invited them over but Henry would come alone most of the time. When they both came, Lucinda found a way to cut the visit short. I tried, Kathryn, I really did. I thought after she had two children with Henry and was living on one of the largest, richest ranches in Arizona, she would be happy. It was like she could never forgive me. She couldn't see that what was meant to be will be."

Where had Katie heard that before? Mrs. Johansson had said that many times to her. From that experience, Katie realized love was meant to be and couldn't be forced. She had a good example of that in her own life. Tyson tried to make them a couple, and it didn't work just like Daniel and Lucinda were not meant to be together. That made Katie stronger in her will to see Drew again. It was meant to be.

She noticed Anna had stopped talking and her eyes were closed. Katie thought it would be a good time to leave and then something dawned on her. Anna was Lindsey's great-grandmother! She stared at

Waiting for Dusk

the sleeping Anna with tears running down her face.

"Thank you, Anna. Thank you for Lindsey," she whispered.

Katie got up as quietly as she could. Anna jumped and her eyes opened.

"No, don't go yet, Kathryn." She held onto Katie's arm. "There is one more thing I want to tell you. Daniel and I always wanted lots of children but we only had Daniel Jr. It took five long years before Dan was born and we were blessed to have him. He lives here now, did you know that? He's come home to his mother.

Dan is now the head of the household, the head of the ranch. He married Lucinda's youngest, Amy. Everything went well for awhile but Lucinda tried to control Amy and her life with Dan. It was like she was reliving a life she had wanted through her daughter. Amy couldn't take it anymore and begged Dan to move the family far away from here. They only came back when my Daniel passed away. All of Dan and Amy's kids were teenagers at the time and not too thrilled about moving west from their life in New York. Then to top it off, Amy never told her mother they were moving back. I was always trying to get her to call or go over there. It took more than a year before she finally did. Lucinda was much older and had mellowed. They had a few good years together before Lucinda left us."

"And what about you? Did Lucinda ever make amends with you?" Katie had to know.

"Yes, we would do lunch or tea once a week. Amy insisted on it. I let bygones be bygones. Lucinda apologized a few times but we didn't talk about the past too much. So much time had passed, so many wasted years..."

Anna's eyes were closed again. Katie flopped back on the loveseat and took it all in.

Oh my gosh, Lindsey is my long lost cousin! Katie gently hit her head with her hand. My Great-Great Aunt Lucinda's daughter, Amy, married Anna's son, Dan. We are connected. We are family.

Then Katie thought long and hard about Lucinda's wedding day. Katie wanted to talk Lucinda out of marrying Henry Hasting. She was positive she could have done it if Maya had not interrupted. That's why Maya stopped her from having the conversation with Lucinda. She knew if Katie talked Lucinda out of marrying Henry, there would be no Lindsey. Her best friend would not exist. Katie cried again, holding her head in her hands. When she looked up, Katie saw Lindsey standing at the door—beautiful, understanding Lindsey with her compassionate brown eyes and long blonde hair—looking so much like Anna.

"Are you okay? Get a little lost?" Lindsey seemed confused. "Is my Grandma J boring you with all her stories from the past?"

"No, not at all." Katie stood up. She walked over to her friend and hugged her for a very long time.

Waiting for Dusk

Chapter Twenty-Seven

Lindsey and Katie enjoyed the evening with the family, Katie's family. Katie didn't know where to begin to tell them that they were related, cousins of some kind, because of Amy. She was sure that cousins got naturally separated over time and distance and some of that helped seal the fate of this family. Katie's mom was not really friends with Beth, Lindsey's mom. They were more like acquaintances never talking about anything more than the weather, the kids or what happened at school. They wouldn't compare notes on family. Katie held the key to everything. She knew that because of her dream, she brought two families together like they were supposed to be. She couldn't wait to tell Lindsey. They made plans to go to the Grand Canyon the next day so that would be the perfect time.

"Brandon? Megan? Would you two please take this to Grandma J?" Aunt Sue handed her children a plate of food and a beverage. Brandon was about Katie's age, and Megan appeared to be about ten. They both obeyed their mother and went inside the house with the food.

"Brandon told me he invited Charlie to go with us tomorrow." Lindsey filled Katie in on the plans.

"Charlie? Mmm, could that be the boy you met this summer?" Katie teased.

"I told you it wasn't a big deal. But yes, it is the boy I met here this summer. He's...nice," Lindsey got a faraway look in her eye.

"Then, great! I'm happy for you." Katie looked at her newfound cousin and couldn't stop smiling.

Megan bounded out on the deck. "Grandma J said that Kathryn was her friend. I told Grandma that her name was Katie. She kept saying

Kathryn was here and Kathryn was an old friend."

Katie jumped up. She put her arm around Megan. "That's okay, Megan. Grandma J can call me anything she likes. My name really is Kathryn. Did you know that?"

She walked with Megan and took her over to a bench where she continued to talk to the little girl and get to know her. They laughed and told knock-knock jokes by the end of their conversation.

The evening ended too quickly for Katie. She loved Grandpa Dan. He was so much like Daniel. Happiness overflowed inside of her knowing Anna had her family at the ranch—four generations of Jenkins. Sue, Scott, and Steve were fun to be around too. Their spouses and children completed the mix. There were even three golden retrievers running around the property, one belonging to each family.

"We so need to get a dog," Lindsey whispered to Katie. "All my aunts and uncles have one and my mom keeps saying no. That's why she's the black sheep of the family."

"No, she isn't!"

"Okay, she's not. But why does she have to be the different one? I could be living here with all of my family."

"Then you wouldn't have me." Katie put her arm around her.

The two girls headed up to their rooms for the night. Katie was tempted to tell Lindsey what happened with Grandma J but decided to wait. She would call Carl instead. He would know what to do.

Carl answered on the first ring. Katie knew he always tried to answer, never letting it go to voicemail, if he could. "Are you okay?"

"Yes, Carl, I'm here at Lindsey's family ranch." Katie then proceeded to tell him what happened to her that day.

"Wow! That's quite a story! Let me think about it for awhile while we talk. I heard about Homecoming and Tyson from my mother. How are you holding up?"

"I'm fine. There's nothing to tell. Now let's get back to my reason for calling you."

"Alright, if you insist," Carl teased. "You should tell Lindsey tomorrow, since she knows your time travel story. Then start asking Aunt Sue questions about your Aunt Lucinda and see if she puts two and two together. Let her be the one to figure it out."

"Great idea," Katie hoped it would work. "Hey, I've got to go. I have another call. I'll let you know what happens."

Waiting for Dusk

"Take care. I really mean that in every sense of the word."

"Yes, I will. Thanks for everything." Katie hung up with Carl and answered her second call.

"Katie?" It was Tyson. Katie was silent. "Katie, are you there?"

"Yeah, I'm here."

"I'm calling to say I'm sorry…for everything." Ty sounded a little depressed.

"It's alright. I want to stay friends with you."

"You do? That's great! I made the basketball team." Katie guessed Ty didn't want to hang up and was thinking of things to say.

"Great, Ty! I'm so happy for you."

"Katie? Do you think you could ever love me?"

"I don't want to go there again. Please, let's end this conversation in a good way. If you can't just call to talk, then don't call me."

"Okay. Sorry, again. When are you coming home?"

"Monday. I've got to go. Someone is knocking on my door." Katie lied.

"I'll let you go, but promise me you'll come to my first game," It sounded like he was begging.

"I promise."

Katie couldn't hang up quick enough. She got ready for bed and set her phone alarm. She didn't want someone knocking on her door, telling her to get up. She wanted to be up and ready to go.

Katie was the first one downstairs in the morning. She smelled bacon cooking and coffee brewing, and it was a beautiful, sunny day. On the deck, she saw Anna sitting in a rocker. Katie went out to join her.

"Hello, Grandma J. Nice day, isn't it?" Katie wasn't sure if Anna remembered the conversation they had the night before.

"Oh, Kathryn, knock off the Grandma J crap and sit down here." Anna patted the chair next to her.

Katie laughed and said, "Where did you learn to talk like a trucker?"

"You don't live one hundred years and learn nothing. I have many grandchildren and great-grandchildren you know."

"Anna, don't you wonder why I look the same and you knew me many years ago?" Katie was thinking about that all night.

"Yes, I do, Kathryn, but decided not to question it. The Lord works in mysterious ways. I have you back and that's all I know."

"I'm glad to have you back too. I missed you so much. I was afraid it was all a dream. Can I ask you something?"

Anna nodded.

"Did you ever hear of or know a Jack Woods?" Katie wanted to get to the bottom of that and maybe Anna could help her.

"Why, yes, I have. He was a very famous writer and visited the canyon a lot in the twenties. I have some of his books. One is a journal he wrote of time spent at the canyon. Would you like to read them?"

"Oh, yes, please, Anna, I would. My dad's a writer, too. Not as famous as Jack Woods but he does pretty well. Have you heard of Jackson Roberts?"

"I have some of his books too. His writing is quite similar to Jack Woods. Your dad must be a fan or student of his."

"Actually he never mentioned him. Andrew…" Katie stopped short.

"Andrew wanted to take you to one of his lectures," Anna finished for her. "He was a big fan of Jack Woods. Jack became a mentor to Andrew. They were almost like brothers. You will be looking for Andrew today, won't you?" Anna placed her hand under Katie's chin. They looked at each other for a long moment, their eyes locked. Time had not come between them. "That's love, Kathryn, true love. To always look for the one you love."

Lindsey came out on the deck. She squinted in the bright morning sun. "Hi, Grandma J, you're always up bright and early." She walked over and kissed her on the cheek. "I'm so glad you like my best friend."

"She's delightful and the perfect best friend for you, Lindsey. Now you two go eat your breakfast and be on your way. Have a fun day. If you'd ask Grandpa Dan to come out and help me in, I'd appreciate it."

Katie leaned over and kissed Anna on the cheek. "You're also my best friend. See you later."

After breakfast, Katie went up to her room to finish getting ready. She sent text messages to everyone back home, including Ty, and one to Carl. She ran down the stairs and entered the large family room ready for the day. Sitting on the sofa with his back to her was a young man with dark hair that just covered the top of his shirt.

"Drew!"

Waiting for Dusk

Chapter Twenty-Eight

The young man stood up and turned to face Katie. "Sorry, my name is Charlie," he said with a cute little grin.

Charlie was definitely not Drew. He had dark hair but that was all they had in common. Charlie was shorter and thinner. He had the beard that all the guys wore—thin, from ear to ear traveling across the jaw line—and a faint mustache too. He wore a band t-shirt and jeans with a plaid hooded sweatshirt. She liked it. Nothing was designer but well thought out. Katie was surprised to see someone dressed that way out west. She expected cowboy boots and hats. She saw why Lindsey liked him. He had an easy way about him, and a killer smile.

Katie put out her hand. "Hi, I'm Katie."

Charlie shook her hand and said, "You ready for some hiking today? I got boots in the jeep."

Katie wasn't sure about hiking. She only went on a short one with Drew. The next one would have to be with him, too.

Lindsey walked in at that moment. "I think we'll be doing other things while you two macho men hike the canyon." She walked up to Charlie and hugged him.

"Good to see you, Lindsey. How's Ohio treating you?"

Katie saw Aunt Sue walk by and decided it was the perfect time to plant a seed. "Aunt Sue, do you have a minute?"

She stopped and put the laundry basket she was carrying on the stairs. "Sure, I do."

"Have you ever heard of Lucinda Hasting?"

"Yes, of course. She lives quite near here. Or I should say lived."

"Well, she's my great-great aunt and I was wondering if there would be time to drive me over to see where she lived?"

Aunt Sue looked a little shocked but seemed to be taking it all in.

At that moment, Brandon came racing down the stairs. "Come on, let's go!" he said, and then ran out the front door. The rest of them followed.

During the drive, Katie learned more about Brandon and Charlie. Both were seniors, planning on going to the University of Arizona. It was far enough away from home that they couldn't commute, so they planned on rooming together. They both played baseball and were avid hikers and climbers. Brandon was hoping for a baseball scholarship. Katie thought they were great guys. It seemed Charlie wanted Lindsey to attend UA too. He practically said so. He kept asking her about where she would go to college, mentioned how it be fun if they were all on campus together. He included Katie in that comment, probably just to be nice. Katie could tell Lindsey really liked Charlie, but she understood why she was holding back. Too many choices. The boys were going to college the next year, and Lindsey and Katie would be high school seniors.

Katie let out a big sigh. Everyone laughed.

"What's going on with you?" Brandon poked her playfully as he pulled into the parking area.

They all jumped out of the jeep and looked around. Brandon had parked in the familiar South Rim Village area. It was like being home to Katie. Charlie pointed out to Lindsey where he planned on hiking. She heard him asking her to come along. Lindsey declined, being true to her friend, insisting they would have time together later.

Finally Brandon and Charlie grabbed their gear and took off down the designated path. They all agreed to meet back in the parking lot in about three hours, then head for a restaurant.

"Hey, Brandon," Lindsey called after him. "Can I have the car keys?"

Brandon dug in his pocket and tossed the keys to her. The girls ran toward the jeep. Lindsey jumped in the driver's seat, looked at Katie and said, "Where to?"

Katie guided her to the boardinghouse. Her heart raced at the thought of seeing it. She knew the place had been sold but hoped for the best. As they grew nearer, they saw a sign for Erickson's Riding Stables.

"So it's just a place to go riding. Turn here. This is it."

Waiting for Dusk

They pulled onto a road that was y-shaped. The right road led to the stables and the other road had a sign that said Erickson's Bed and Breakfast. Choosing the road to the left, they drove past a modern one-story ranch house and continued on. Then right in front of her was the boardinghouse, her beloved boardinghouse. It had been turned into a bed and breakfast. What a great idea for the place. Katie loved that it looked so well taken care of. It still looked like the original building.

"Well? Do you want to go in?" Lindsey parked the jeep and looked at Katie.

"No, I don't think I can. It's just so wonderful to see it's still here." Katie couldn't help but stare at the place that held so many memories for her. Tears filled her eyes. She pictured the old Buick sitting in front of the house. She pictured Loretta and Lucinda chasing each other and dancing around in the yard. She heard Anna calling to her to get in the house before someone saw her with Drew. "Lindsay, why didn't you ever tell me your great-grandmother's name was Anna?"

"Like we ever talk about our great-grandmothers! Oh, let's compare grandmas. What's your grandma's name?"

"Okay, you're right about that. But don't think I'm strange or anything with what I am about to say, promise?"

"I promise. You know you can tell me anything."

"I know your great-grandmother."

"Of course you do. You spent a lot of time with her since we got here."

"No, not like that. I know her from my dreams. She's the Anna from my dream, which I'm pretty sure now are not dreams." Katie squeezed her eyes shut. She waited for Lindsey to tell her she was crazy.

"O…kay…"

"Lindsey, your grandmother knew me. She called me Kathryn and talked about Andrew. She was so happy to see me. We talked like we were old friends."

"Well, Grandma J likes to live in the past and we did say you looked like the Kathryn in that wedding picture. Maybe she's just confused. Old people are like that you know." Lindsey sighed. "Or maybe you're right. It could be more than a realistic dream."

"There's one more thing. We are cousins, long lost cousins." Katie put her hands over her ears waiting for Lindsey to yell or scream or something. There was nothing but silence. Katie looked over and saw her friend griping the steering wheel. She seemed deep in thought.

"Let's go over to the riding stable and rent some horses to ride. Then I'll fill you in on everything." Katie patted Lindsey's shoulder. "I know this is a lot to take in for one day. I've had more time to process all of this."

"Really? Just like that? I'm supposed to buy into this?" Lindsey slapped the wheel. "Wow, sorry about that. Give me a minute." She wiped her forehead, then started the jeep and headed down a back road to the stables. When she parked, she jumped out and walked around to face Katie.

"You're my cousin?" She hugged Katie as tightly as she could.

Katie was so happy by her final reaction. She understood.

On their hour-long ride, Katie did the best she could to fill Lindsey in on all the details. Katie told her that her grandma, Dan's wife Amy, was Lucinda's daughter and Katie's cousin. It took them awhile to piece everything together.

"How come our moms never figured this out?" Lindsey wondered.

"I asked myself the same thing." Katie was glad Lindsey took it well. That part was believable and could be proven. She didn't know how she could prove she knew Anna when she was young. For then, it was good enough. They returned the horses to the stable when the hour was up, jumped in the jeep and headed back to the canyon.

"Where next?" Lindsey asked.

"The Village, and then Yavapai Point."

They parked at a visitor center and walked to the spots that were so important to Katie. She wanted to show Lindsey all the places she had been with Drew. Katie stopped at Kolb Studio. She remembered how excited Drew was for her to meet Jack Woods. A cold shudder went through her. When she saw Jack, she knew it was her father and had to avoid him. Now all she had to do is prove that Jack is Jackson. For the time being, she would enjoy showing Lindsey all her favorite places.

The next stop was the piece of land that jutted out just a little further than the rest in front of El Tovar. It was where she and Drew had stood to first view the canyon and she knew the exact spot. She stood with Lindsey and retold the story of her first date with Drew. They turned around and headed back to El Tovar. Katie ran up the stairs and sat on the front porch. She remembered thinking she'd be in trouble for eating her lunch there with Drew. It seemed like such a distant memory.

Waiting for Dusk

Finally they headed down to Yavapai station. For some reason, they were the only ones there. A bus pulled away with a group of tourists.

Katie looked at Lindsey. "Don't think I'm crazy but there is something I just have to do." She walked up to the edge, took a deep breath and in her loudest voice yelled out, "Drew!" It felt really good so she did it again.

Then Lindsey joined in. Together they yelled his name out into that beautiful, magical canyon over and over again. They didn't notice another bus pulling up and people getting off. Katie looked at Lindsey and they burst out laughing. They ran all the way back to the village, and threw themselves down on the grass in front of El Tovar.

Lindsey took out her phone. "I just got a text from Brandon. They're on their way to the parking lot. Let's go meet them. I'm starving."

* * * *

The four teens found a great place to eat and then hung out for the rest of the day. It was getting close to dusk when Brandon suggested they head for home. They piled into the jeep and drove home in silence, a good silence. Katie made sure she sat in front with Brandon again so Charlie and Lindsey could be alone in the back. For some reason, Katie knew that Charlie was the one for Lindsey. She wondered if Lindsey knew it too. It was just like Anna and Daniel—meant to be.

When they got home, the front door flew open and Megan came running out. "Mommy says you're my cousin." She hugged Katie tightly.

"Really?"

"Come on. We have something to show you!" Megan pulled Katie into the house and everyone followed.

Aunt Sue sat at the kitchen table with Anna. They had a poster size paper mounted on the wall so everyone could see. At the top of the paper were Lucinda and Anna's names.

"Did you kids have fun?" Aunt Sue had a big smile on her face. "Sit down and I'll get you all something to drink. Megan, Grandma J and I have been at this for awhile. Katie, I can't believe we didn't figure this out sooner!"

She had her head in the refrigerator as she was talking and came back to the table with sodas and bottles of water.

"Mommy, can we start now?" Megan clapped her hands and her face was flush with excitement.

"Sure, you do our family." Aunt Sue gave her the go ahead.

"First, I want to say that Grandma J was a big help to us," Megan said. "Grandma J, also known as Anna, married Grandpa J or Daniel Jenkins. Then Anna and Daniel had Daniel Jr." She pointed to the family tree as she spoke.

"Grandpa Dan or Daniel Jr. married Amy Hasting. That's where you come in, Katie," She turned to Katie smiling, "Amy is your cousin." Megan then pointed back to the chart. "Dan and Amy had four kids, my mom Sue, Lindsey's mom Beth, and the twins Scott and Steve. So we're all related! That's the family history." Megan took a bow.

Lindsey and Katie clapped, looking at each other as only best friends with their own secrets can. Katie noticed Lindsey was holding Charlie's hand under the table. She gave her another knowing look.

Aunt Sue stepped in. "Today Katie asked me about Lucinda and their family ranch. I couldn't believe she knew Lucinda, my grandmother, let alone was related to her. It's such a small world. We had to put it all down on paper for it to make sense to us. Our heads are spinning! Grandma J was determined for us to get it right and insisted on making the two family trees. Luckily she was there for all of this. She lived it."

Sue touched Anna lovingly on the shoulder. Katie locked eyes with Anna, hoping she could read the love in them. She wanted to cry, sing, scream—she didn't know which one she was so excited. Katie didn't have that big of a family. Her dad had no living relatives. They did have her mom's side of the family back in Ohio and the Hastings but now they could add all of these people to Joanna's family tree.

Sue continued. "Lucinda married Henry Hasting and they had three daughters, Henrietta, Lucy and Amy. My Aunts Retta and Lucy still live at the ranch." She looked at Katie. "And by the way they can't believe you're here and are friends with Lindsey. They want us to come over for a quick visit tomorrow morning." She then pointed back to the family tree. "Now this is where the two families connect." There was a line drawn from Amy to Dan's name. "Katie, you finish the rest." Sue handed Katie a marker.

Katie stood up and went over to the poster board. They left room on Lucinda's tree so Katie could fill in the rest. She uncapped the marker and wrote in Loretta's name, connecting it to Lucinda since they were sisters. She continued on with the rest of her family, working from

Waiting for Dusk

Loretta's name until present day—Loretta's two children, Richard and Sandra, then Richard's son and Sandra's children, Will, Michael, and her mother. Finally she wrote her name under her mom's. Her name looked so lonely at the bottom of the tree. She wanted to write Drew's name in a new column and connect it to hers. "So as you can see, we are all cousins." Katie sat down.

Everyone talked at once, trying to figure out how they were connected. Katie took it all in. It felt so good to get some of the secrets out and share them with others. Only Anna knew all her secrets. Well, almost all of them. Katie didn't tell her she tried to stop Lucinda from marrying Henry. If she had succeeded, most of the people in this room would not exist. Tears filled her eyes as she gazed around at everyone. She hated herself for trying to play some type of god.

"Are you alright, Kathryn?" Anna stood over her now. "Would you like to come back to my sitting room and have some quiet time? I think I need a little rest."

"Yes, I would like that." Katie got up and walked with Anna down the hallway. Anna did pretty well for someone about to turn one hundred-years-old. She used a cane for support but was still able to keep up with Katie. They sat together on the loveseat.

Katie decided she had to tell Anna the truth. "I need to tell you something. You're going to hate me after I do. It's fine with me if you decide to never speak to me again. I deserve it."

"I doubt that, but go ahead, child." Anna took her hand.

"On the night of the wedding rehearsal, I was determined to stop Lucinda's wedding. I felt she didn't love Henry and would be in a loveless marriage. I wanted her to think about it before it was too late. And if I got through to her?" Katie covered her face with her hands and whispered, "There would be no Jenkins family tree." When she was done, she couldn't look at Anna. Katie realized they were still holding hands.

Anna brushed a piece of hair away from Katie's face. "Is that what's been bothering you? Kathryn, you were only thinking of your aunt and her happiness. You couldn't see into the future. What a loving and kind thing you tried to do. You cared so much about Lucinda that you wanted her to be happy, as happy as you and Drew are. There is nothing wrong with wishing someone happiness."

Katie looked at Anna. "How can you say that? How can you forgive me so easily?"

"There is nothing to forgive." Anna patted Katie's hand. "Now go and have fun with your young friends. Stop living in the past."

"There's a part of the past I never want to stop living."

"I know. I know, but you need to live your life in the here and…" Anna faded off to sleep, resting her head back on the loveseat. Katie sat with the sleeping woman for awhile. Sleeping Beauty, Katie thought. She's waiting for her Prince to come.

Anna did get her prince, Daniel. Her fairytale did come true, and so would Katie's. She was determined and felt better than she had all weekend. Katie was ready to join the family and see what could happen next in Arizona.

Waiting for Dusk

Chapter Twenty-Nine

It was a gorgeous Sunday morning. Aunt Sue drove Katie and Lindsey to the Hasting ranch. Katie looked up at the sky through the SUV's sunroof. The sun shone brightly and it was the kind of day Lucinda wanted for her wedding—bright blue skies and white puffy clouds. It was the perfect day to head for the ranch.

When they arrived, Katie noticed a circle with an 'H' in it. The 'H' almost looked like a Roman numeral. Lindsey's family ranch also had a circle with a 'J' inside. The font for the 'J' was a beautiful script. She wondered if there was some meaning behind the naming of the ranches.

The description of the house from Katie's dream was so exact that Lindsey gave Katie a 'how did you know' look when they arrived. Katie shrugged and jumped out of the car. There, on the 'be right down' balcony, were two older women, possibly in their late seventies. They were smiling and waving.

"Be right down," one of them said. Katie couldn't help but smile.

The door opened and Katie entered the familiar house. The Persian rugs were gone but in their place were beautiful rugs with modern designs, again matching perfectly with each of the rooms. As they entered the foyer there was a hallway to the right and one to the left of it which Katie knew connected to other living quarters. She wanted to run down the long center hallway and exit the backdoor to the garden, but knew better.

"Oh, Katie, we've only seen you in school pictures that your mom puts in the yearly Christmas card. It's so good to finally see you in person. You look so much like family, especially Aunt Rett." one of the women said as she hugged her. "I'm your cousin, Lucy, and this is

Henrietta or Retta." She pointed to the other woman standing next to her. Katie hugged her too.

After everyone said their hellos and were introduced, the two women escorted them to the back porch which now was partially enclosed and turned into a sunroom. There was a tea service on the table and some scones.

"Please sit and let's have some tea," Retta said kindly.

Katie's heart pounded as she walked through the back door. The garden was still there and so was the gazebo. To the right of the garden was a pathway to a large deck and in ground pool. That was definitely new. It was all still so beautiful, making it hard for Katie to stay in the here and now. She wanted to daydream about the wedding and the night Drew spent in her bedroom.

"So, Katie? What do you think?" Lucy poured her some tea.

"Beautiful, just beautiful. I can see why you never want to leave."

"We like to leave, trust me!" Lucy laughed. "That was my mother who didn't like to leave the ranch. It became part of her."

"Could you tell me about the circle with the H in it?" Katie thought she should be polite and ask some questions about the ranch.

"That stands for the Circle H ranch, just like the Circle J ranch." Retta told the story. Pointing to Sue she continued. "Our grandfathers, Noah Jenkins and Henry Hasting Sr., came out to Arizona together. Well, Sue, I guess they both were your great-grandfathers," Henrietta laughed. "It's hard to keep it all straight. Well, anyway, their dream was to buy land, build ranches and get rich. They did pretty well. They came up with the idea together how to name their ranches. They both chose circles with their initials in them, forever connecting them."

So the Hasting and Jenkins families always had a tie to each other. That made sense to Katie. "And," she pointed to the gazebo. "That's where your parents got married."

"How did you know that?" Retta seemed surprised. Lindsey shot Katie another look.

"I found a picture in our attic of your mother's wedding, and my mom told me all about it." Katie was quick with a white lie.

"Yes, she was right. Don't think it strange of us but we found our mother's wedding dress and decided to put it on display in their bedroom. We can't really bring ourselves to use their room. So I guess we turned it into some sort of museum, not a shrine as Kirsten calls it!"

Waiting for Dusk

"Kirsten?" Katie was thrown by a new name with so many to remember.

"She's our cousin. Our Uncle Clifford married a Swedish girl, Frieda, who used to work on this very ranch. She missed her homeland so much that they moved back there. They had a daughter, Kirsten, who lives in Sweden but comes to visit quite often. We love to go there, too."

"In the picture, there was another man that my mom said was Gilbert. What happened with him and Arlene?" Oops, I did it again. Katie would act like her mom told her about them if they questioned it.

"Uncle Gilbert and Arlene never had children. During the Depression a young boy, Trevor, of about nine or ten came looking for work here. Gil gave him a job but mostly let us all play together. One night, he found Trevor sleeping in the barn and questioned him about why he hadn't gone home. That's when we found out he didn't have a home. He was an orphan. So Gil and Arlene adopted him and he moved into the ranch. He learned all sides of the business and became our ranch manager.

Sadly Arlene passed away at a young age. Gil was devastated and never married again. We were so thankful he had Trevor. When Trevor married, my parents had him move into their old wing of the house because by then they were living in the main house. Trevor and Mary still live here. Their son is now the ranch manager and he lives in Gil's side of the house which he swears is haunted, in a good way, by Gil.

It has been great for Lucy and me. We could never run this ranch without them. My mom could have done it alone, but not us. We're grateful for the help."

So finally Katie knew what happened to all of her friends. Some good, some bad but in the end their lives went well. Katie learned that life continued on in a fluid motion that she never thought about before. There was always a new story to replace the old. The thing was to remember everything so that there would always be that flow of life. Katie stopped. She was getting a little too philosophical, even for herself. She still wanted to ask one more question.

"Is it alright if I see the dress? Your mother's wedding dress?" "You want to see the dress? Yes, of course. We would be thrilled for you to see it!" Lucy's eyes lit up. "We don't want to keep you too long because we know you have to get back for Anna's party. We'll be over soon, too." She stood up and took Katie's hand and studied her face. "You seem so familiar." Lucy touched Katie's cheek.

They followed Lucy into the house, heading for the curved staircase. Katie stopped on the step where Lucinda crumbled many years before. She remembered how she got up and brushed herself off, determined to become Mrs. Henry Hasting. That determination struck her the most from that day.

The master bedroom was at the end of the hall. They passed the guest room where Katie stayed, and she couldn't resist stopping to look at it. She couldn't help herself, she had to go in. It was all redone of course, but still decorated in beautiful shades of purple, lavender and pale green.

"This is a beautiful room!" Katie spun around as she spoke.

Again, Lindsey gave her a 'what are you doing' look.

"Glad you like it. It's a special guest room. We hope you'll stay there one day." Retta put her arm around Katie. "Now on to the shrine!"

A huge glass, display case rested against the farthest wall. It was centered in the middle with pictures on either side. Katie knew what the dress looked like before she even reached the case. She had the picture, and saw it in person. The two sisters had done a good job with the display. The dress was on a pink velvet headless mannequin. The veil hung from the top of the glass case and draped over the dress. There were lovely floral framed pictures of the wedding mounted on the backside of the case. A tiny white wrought iron table with a tea set and flowers was also in the case. A garland of white silk roses trailed across the top and down the front sides of the cabinet. It was quite beautiful.

"Lucy, Retta, you two did a wonderful job!"

The two women seemed pleased. Then Katie noticed they kept staring at her and then at the wedding photos.

"Katie, you look amazingly like my mother's friend, Kathryn. Here, look at the picture closely." Lucy pointed to the group wedding photo.

Katie didn't have to look because she remembered posing for the picture. She didn't understand exactly how it happened but she was in that wedding that took place in 1927 and came to accept it. In fact, she loved the idea.

"Everyone says that," Katie responded.

"Yes, I even said it," Lindsey piped in. "I first saw the picture at Katie's house. I couldn't believe it!"

Aunt Sue looked at her watch. "We really need to get back, girls.

Waiting for Dusk

Thanks for having us, my favorite aunts. We'll see you later."

She put her arms around Lindsey and Katie walking them to the bedroom door.

Katie wanted to look around more. Her cousins were certainly correct about the bedroom being a museum or shrine. She noticed they had mounted baby clothes in a frame and there were so many more pictures to see. She hoped to come back some day to spend more time with Lucy and Retta. And stay in her room…that wonderful room.

Back at Circle J, everyone got ready for the big 100th birthday party. Katie knew that it was just a weekend trip, but was sorry to see it end so soon. The next day she would be boarding a plane back to Ohio. Maybe she'd ask the cousins if she could live with them.

Who am I kidding? I need to get back to my life, somehow break into Maya's house and get a book before Thanksgiving. Whoa! That didn't sound good. Now she was resorting to breaking the law. She laughed at herself and hung up another balloon.

People started arriving mid-afternoon. It would be an early party for Anna because she rarely stayed up past nine. Katie was overwhelmed by all the people, but suddenly noticed someone in the crowd that looked vaguely familiar. Could it be? Another face from the past? She had to find out.

"Thomas? Thomas Cook?"

Chapter Thirty

Thomas looked at Katie with teasing eyes. "Yes, I'm Thomas. And you are?"

"I…I'm Katie, Kathryn., Do you know me?" she stuttered.

"No, but I do now! Nice to meet you, Katie, Kathryn," Thomas stuck out his hand.

Katie shook it, and kept staring at him. "You look so familiar…" She couldn't let go of his hand.

"Everyone says that about me. My father, grandfather and I all look very much alike." He kept shaking her hand with a slight smile.

"And your name is Thomas like your…?" Katie didn't finish.

"My grandfather and father, that's right. I'm Thomas the third but since they're both gone I guess I'm the only Thomas."

"Oh, I'm sorry to hear." Katie pictured her Thomas cooking and singing in the kitchen. He was one of Drew's best friends. Now he was gone.

"Please don't be. They had full and rich lives. Plus that is the circle of life."

"I'd love to hear more about your family later. If you'd excuse me I have to help with the party." Katie couldn't wait to hear what happened to Thomas Sr.

It was the typical birthday party. There was eating, opening presents and the cutting of the cake. Katie kept herself busy by serving the guests and helping Anna with her presents. She passed out the cake or wrapped it for people to take home. The day passed quickly and before she realized it, the party was ending. People began leaving in the early evening.

Waiting for Dusk

"Katie?" Anna called to her. "Would you mind helping me to my room?"

"Of course, Grandma J." Katie rushed over to help her.

Then Katie whispered to her, "I know, knock off the Grandma J crap."

"I saw you talking to Thomas Cook earlier. Quite eerie, isn't it?" Anna looked at Katie and saw she was puzzled. "The resemblance! He looks just like our Thomas! Thomas was a good man. Daniel wanted him to come and work here at the ranch full-time. We just couldn't steal him away from the Park system."

When they got to Anna's apartment, Katie discovered that the sitting room continued on into a bedroom and bathroom; it was like a little apartment. Anna picked up a Vera Bradley quilted-flowered bag and handed it to Katie. "Something for you from me," she said.

Katie looked in the bag and saw three books. "The bag is lovely. Are these your Jack Woods books?" Katie couldn't believe it. "I can't take them."

"I want you to have them. You will appreciate them, especially if you think Jack Woods could be related to you somehow." Anna sat down on her loveseat. "I think you know more about Jack Woods than you're letting on. "Do you have something to tell me?"

Katie sank down beside her. Anna didn't miss much. "I don't want to leave you. You know me so well! Too well."

"You always have Lindsey. Never forget that. You'll always have me, too, no matter where I am. I may not be long for this world, Kathryn, but I will be with you."

"Stop it; you're not…going anywhere. I need you. I plan on calling you all the time."

"Then you better give me your phone, and let me put my number in." Anna held out her hand.

Katie stared at her with her mouth open. "You are awesome!" She gave Anna her phone, and they sat quietly for a moment.

Anna handed the phone back to Katie. "Now, go ahead. You want to tell me something."

Katie couldn't believe how the words came rushing out. She told Anna everything—the dreams, the book, Carl telling her the dreams were real, seeing Jack Woods who looked like her father and that Maya lived next door to her in the 21st century.

"Mrs. Johansson lives next door to you? She is something. I always knew she was special," Anna slapped her leg. "So that's how you came to 1927. Well, I'm glad you did. I don't understand it all either, but it is fascinating. When are you planning on going back?"

"The Wednesday before Thanksgiving…if I can get my hands on a book."

"Lindsey will help you. You can trust in that." Anna sighed. "I'd love to hear more and talk all night but this old lady needs her sleep. Remember, those books belong to you now. My legacy to you." Anna lightly kissed Katie on the top of her head as she stood up to go into her bedroom. "Good night, my sweet Kathryn."

"Good night, my sweet Anna." Katie let out a laugh. "Will I see you before I leave tomorrow?"

"Of course. You know I'm an early riser."

Katie went back out into the main house. There were only a few guests left. She was glad to see that Thomas and his wife were among them. Thomas' wife was helping Aunt Sue while Thomas watched the boys play video games. Katie sat down next to him on the family room sofa.

"Good to see you again! I was just watching the boys play a little football. That's my son, Dante." Thomas smiled at Katie as he pointed to a boy playing the football video game with Brandon and Charlie.

"I wasn't going to let you leave without telling me some family history." Katie then realized that was a strange request so she quickly made something up. "I'm doing a history of our families and I was told your grandfather was friends with Daniel."

"Oh, yes. Yes, he was." Thomas seemed to be deep in thought. He shook his head and said, "Daniel, Andrew and Thomas…just like these three boys. Good friends."

He mentioned Andrew! Katie tried to get Thomas back on track. "Would you mind sharing a bit?"

"My grandfather always wanted to be a cowboy. Back east he knew he had no chance of becoming one. He came out here to see if he could get a job on a ranch. No one would hire him, so he got a job cooking at El Tovar. He was a skilled chef, actually, and got to know many of the ranchers that way. When one of the ranchers sent back their compliments for a good meal, Grandpa always made sure to go out and meet him. Grandpa Tom was very personable that way. Then Andrew Martin

Waiting for Dusk

showed up at the Grand Canyon and they became fast friends. Andrew got to know Daniel and the rest is history."

"History?" Katie wasn't quite sure what he meant by that.

"They became friends, great friends until the end." Thomas was quiet for a moment. "When the Great Depression came, the restaurant cut back hours on Grandpa Tom and the rest of the staff. Daniel offered him some part-time work here on the ranch. He jumped at the chance. He learned to rope and herd cattle. Grandpa already knew how to ride and had been helping out at the canyon stables when he could. He even helped out a Mr. Johansson at his stables back in the day. Daniel's father, Noah, offered my Grandfather a full-time job here. By then Grandpa had married my Grandmother Rachel and knew that wasn't the life he wanted for her. He didn't want to be gone on cattle drives. Plus when the restaurant heard he might leave, they offered him his job back with a chance for advancement.

After working at the National Parks for so long, Grandpa had another dream—to become a park ranger. So he decided to stay on at the restaurant and see what happened. He also served in World War II, can you believe that? He didn't have to. He was older, in his thirties, married and had three children. He felt it was his duty, so he enlisted. When he came home, everyone helped him fulfill his dream to become a ranger. My father, Thomas Jr., became one, too. I can proudly say I followed in their footsteps."

"Wow!" Katie thought that her Thomas had a great life. He did love the canyon and it sounded like his life turned out quite well. "Thomas was a great guy," she said without thinking.

"You sound as if you knew him," Thomas laughed.

"Anna has told me so much about everyone, I feel like I do! Now you mentioned an Andrew, one of Thomas' friends? What do you know about him?" Katie tried hard to not sound too curious.

"Andrew...he was a very good friend to grandfather. I think that Grandpa really tried to stop Andrew from—" Thomas was interrupted by Lindsey.

"Hi, I hate to break this up, but we are leaving early tomorrow. We need to pack and get to sleep." Lindsey grabbed Katie's hand.

"Thank you, Thomas. Thank you for sharing." Katie shook his hand.

"Very nice meeting and talking to you, young lady." Thomas smiled, then patted her hand.

Lindsey and Katie ran upstairs. Katie was a little upset that she didn't get to finish talking to Thomas. He was about to say something more about Andrew. She filled Lindsey in on all that had happened.

"I'm sorry, I didn't know." Lindsey gave her a pouty face.

"That's okay. We were almost done. I did add a few pieces to the puzzle tonight. Plus Anna gave me some old books to read written by Jack Woods." Katie remembered she left them in the downstairs kitchen. "Don't let me forget them!"

* * * *

The next morning came too quickly. Everyone ate a quick breakfast together and then Aunt Sue and her husband drove the girls to the airport. Katie hated saying good-bye to Anna. They hugged, cried and hugged some more.

Everyone piled into the cars for the ride to the airport. Katie liked that Megan insisted coming along and sitting in the backseat with her and Lindsey. There were more good-byes at the passenger drop-off point and finally they were on the plane, taking them back to Ohio and to her other life.

Waiting for Dusk

Chapter Thirty-One

Katie's and Lindsey's parents met them at the airport. The girls couldn't wait to tell them they were all related. They planned on Katie running and hugging Lindsey's parents and Lindsey running to Katie's. That should confuse them.

"What's going on here?" Katie's dad held out his arms. "I've got the wrong daughter!"

"Mom, Dad," Lindsey pointed at Joanna and Katie. "Meet our cousins."

"What?" Lindsey's mom covered her mouth. "I have no idea what you're talking about."

"Lucinda, Lucinda Hasting." Katie tried to read her mother's face as she said it.

"Lucinda is my great-aunt," her mother replied. "What does she have to do with this?"

"She's my grandmother!" Lindsey's mother grabbed her daughter. "When did this all happen?"

"At the ranch. Katie mentioned her aunt, I don't remember exactly how."

Katie's mother kept repeating over and over, "I don't believe it." Then she looked at Beth. "Why didn't we compare notes?"

"I have no idea but this trip was meant to be. I've always felt close to Katie and now I find out she's my cousin. You, too, Joanna!"

There was a group hug and everyone talked at once.

"Time out!" Katie's dad made the hand signal for it. "Let's go back to the house and discuss it there. I'm sure the girls would like to get home."

"What a surprise!" Her mom wrapped her arm around Katie's

shoulder as they headed for the car.

It turned out to be a great night. Although everyone had Thanksgiving plans, they decided to set aside a day during the Christmas holidays for their new family.

"It could be called the 'Long Lost Cousins Christmas'," her dad said.

Katie noticed how excited he was, like he finally had a connection to the past. He was animated, smiling and acting like his usual self, not the brooding and overprotective dad she got used to over the past few months. She was happy to have her old dad back.

Katie yawned. "Oh, sorry. I'm enjoying this but am very tired. Mom, is it alright if I stay home from school tomorrow?"

Katie's mom and Beth looked at each other. They knew both of the girls would have to do the same thing. "Sure," they both said at the same time.

Lindsey's mom stood up. "I think it's time to be going. This has been so overwhelming for all of us, but has opened a new chapter in our lives. Lindsey, you look tired, too." With that, she pulled Lindsey up from the chair. Everyone exchanged hugs and good-byes.

"I'll call you tomorrow," Lindsey whispered in Katie's ear.

After they left, Katie's dad put his arms around her and her mom. "It's been quite a day, girls. Let's all get some sleep." They headed up the stairs together.

Katie shut her door behind her, and flopped on her bed. She was tired but didn't think she could sleep. She looked at the clock. It was a little after ten. Since it was two hours earlier in Arizona, she knew she had time to call Anna. She should still be up and awake. Katie took her cell phone out of her pocket and went to her contact list. There was Anna's name, still hard to believe. She pressed 'send' and waited.

"Kathryn?" It was good to hear Anna's voice.

"Yes, it's me. I know it's close to your bedtime, but I wanted to let you know we arrived safely."

"I know I'm old but don't rub it in!" Anna laughed. "I'm so glad you're home safely. Now do well in school and call me when you can. I can't wait until Thanksgiving to hear what happens for you. Also, tell my young self that I say, 'Hi'."

"You are too funny. Could you see me doing that? She would freak out, plus I don't know if she would believe me. Speaking of that, do you

Waiting for Dusk

think I should tell Drew the truth? I really want to."

"It's up to you. Be careful how you explain it. I think Drew can handle it. This might be the best thing that could happen to him because..." Anna yawned. "I'm sorry, I'm getting tired."

"That's alright, Anna. Get some rest. I love you." Katie ended the call.

That was odd. It seemed like everyone wanted to tell her something important about Drew, and never finished. Or maybe she was reading too much into it.

She grabbed the quilted bag Anna gave her, took the three books out and laid them on her bed. She thought she might have a chance to read a Jack Woods book on the plane, but never had time. There were about six weeks until Thanksgiving so she could read the books to help pass the time until then.

One of the books had a cover that was very similar to the set that Maya had locked away in her house. All of a sudden, something dawned on Katie. She could switch the book with one of the books from the set and Maya would never know it was gone.

Opening to the first pages, the copyright was 1925. "Well, I guess this is the first book I read." Katie hugged the book to her chest. "I hate to give you away, but it seems like it was meant to be."

Katie's phone started to play the Carl music. She quickly answered. "Hey, Carl!"

"Good, you made it home. How was your flight? Tell me all about the trip. Did everything work out for you?"

Katie told Carl everything that happened. She told him that his idea of letting Aunt Sue figure everything out was genius. She told him Anna knew everything, too. Katie was still surprised Anna was so accepting of it all.

"The older you get, the more accepting you are," Carl said philosophically. "Katie, you aren't planning anything that I don't know about, are you?"

Katie decided to keep Carl in the dark. She knew he would feel obligated to tell his mother what she was up to. "No, Carl. You know I would tell you if I did. There's something I want to ask you. What's going to happen to the set of books, you know, when Maya..." Katie couldn't bring herself to finish. She never wanted to picture her life without Maya in it.

"...passes away?" Carl finished the sentence for her. "I thought long and hard about that. My mom said she plans to give the books to me. I will probably burn them."

"Burn them! You are kidding." Katie was shocked. Her plan to take one of the books was definitely on. She would keep that book and never give it back. Carl would never know it was missing.

"Yep, that's right. I will burn them. Let the past stay the past." Carl sighed. "I won't keep you any longer, kid sis. Take care and get some rest. Love you."

"Love you, too."

Katie put her phone on her nightstand. She had some thinking to do. She needed to make a plan without confiding in anyone. She was all alone in this. No one could stop her from seeing Drew. Then she heard Anna's words in her head telling her that Katie could trust Lindsey just as Kathryn trusts Anna. She would help, keep the secret, too. Katie would talk to her in the morning, and they would devise something together. That's what best friends, and cousins, do. She slipped into bed and fell asleep from exhaustion before she could think of anything else.

When she woke up the next morning, Katie was relieved she didn't have to go to school. She decided to stay in bed and pretend she was still asleep. She grabbed her phone, and got under the covers. The time on the phone was about eleven am and she hoped Lindsey was awake.

"I've been waiting for your call," Lindsey whispered. "What's up?"

Katie told Lindsey about her idea to steal a book from the set and replace it with one of the old books Anna gave her.

"That's a great idea! Only how are we getting into Mrs. Johnson's house?"

Lindsey said 'we'. She's in on the heist. "That part is easy. Our family has a key to her house. All you and I have to do is wait until Maya's out of the house. I will need a lookout."

"I can do that job."

"Do you mind helping me? If you think you might get in trouble, I understand."

"I'm totally in. You're not doing this without me!"

Katie and Lindsey explored a few ideas together. They knew they had time to put the plan in motion. Then they talked about getting their homework done, the people at school, the upcoming basketball game—all the things Katie now found boring.

Waiting for Dusk

"I guess I'm going to start the dreaded homework," Katie said. "My mom has a class at one, so I'm pretending to be asleep until then. I just want to be alone in the house. Talk to you later. Love you, cuz."

"Back at you. I have things to do, too. Maybe even text Charlie."

Katie looked around her room for her schoolbooks. She didn't see them. They must be downstairs so this would be a good time to start reading one of the Jack Woods' books.

She got out of bed, went over to get the bag and grabbed the one on top. It appeared to be nonfiction. The title said it all, The Nature of the Southwest. Not the greatest title, but she jumped back into bed, and began reading it.

Surprisingly, Katie found the book interesting. She thought it was a little different from the usual nature books. Of course, it talked about the types of plants, scenery and animals that one would see out west, but it went beyond that.

It categorized nature into different elements, like color, balance and texture. It described how to bring those things into your home wherever you lived. Katie was quite impressed. She thought she might buy a few small cacti and try one of the ideas.

Then she thought about her own backyard. Didn't it have some of these same ideas incorporated into it? The deck was surrounded by color. The back of the yard contained a rock garden with a variety of hostas and tall grasses interspersed, giving a feeling of texture. Even the small side garden where Ty and Katie had their first beer was in balance.

Yes, her dad and Jack Woods were quite alike. She continued looking through the book. There were a number of beautiful pictures. Too bad they were in black and white. Jack Woods put together a beautiful book. Katie closed it and hugged it to her chest. Dad, this was great.

Nancy Pennick

Chapter Thirty-Two

The weeks until Thanksgiving plodded slowly by. Katie thought the day would never come. She tried to keep occupied but it was hard. She hung out with her friends at school but then came directly home. She talked to Anna daily, calling it her 'Anna' fix, then did her homework to pass the time.

Every day she got out her stationery box and wrote Drew a letter. She put the month and day at the top of each letter, but was careful not to put the year. She told him about her day or something that happened to her. Sometimes she wrote about the weather, like the day the sun was shining on the autumn leaves, reminding her of the canyon. Katie also liked to remind him of days that were special to her when they were together, like the night of Lucinda's wedding. Whatever she wrote, she always ended each letter the same way, "I love you—across the miles, across time." She knew Drew would not know what 'across time' really meant. He'd probably think it had something to do with time zones.

When she was done with each letter, she put it back in the box. The letters were tied together with ribbon so she would always carefully untie and then retied the packet. Katie put the lid back on the box and ran her hand across the top. The box was beautiful. It was pale blue with an embossed butterfly in one corner. All the stationery matched the design on the box. She stared at the box for a long time. Finally she snapped herself back to reality, and decided it was time to do something else.

Katie thumbed through the second Jack Woods book. It was a travel book describing where to stay and what to do at the Grand Canyon. There were suggestions on camping and hiking. Again, the book was more interesting than she first thought it. Jack had researched the Indian

Waiting for Dusk

tribes of the area and there were stories about them.

Many pictures were included in the book, mostly of scenery. Whenever Jack was pictured, he always wore a hat of some type making it hard to see his face. It was almost like he made sure of it. There were other people in the pictures, too. Katie got a magnifying glass out to see if she recognized any of them. She swore Thomas was in one of them. She wished her father would tell her the truth. She'd love to know her parents' story. It was probably just as good as Maya's.

Katie had not seen much of Maya lately. She put the book down, and decided to pay her a visit before it got dark. Katie walked across the Katie Path and found Maya in her garden.

"Maya!" she called out to her.

Mrs. Johnson looked up with a smile. "So it's Maya now, is it? I guess you are old enough to call me that now."

"Oh sorry, MiMi. It just sounds so childish to call you that…you know, MiMi," She didn't feel like a little girl anymore either. She hoped Maya understood. "Is it alright if I call you Maya?"

"Of course it is. It always was. Your mother was the one who insisted on protocol. I have to admit I will miss being MiMi, though."

"I'm sorry I haven't seen you as much as I'd like. I've been busy."

"That's what happens once you start high school. You just do well and I'll be proud of you."

"I've been calling and texting Carl. He said you might come out there for Thanksgiving." Katie hoped it was true.

"I have decided to go and stay for about ten days. I leave Friday. I don't want to be part of the Thanksgiving crowds."

Friday? Katie couldn't believe her good fortune. This would make it much easier to get into Maya's house. "That sounds nice. Will you have Thanksgiving with Carl and then Carl Jr.?"

Maya nodded. "Now don't go passing that on to anyone."

"I won't."

Katie was glad Maya came to accept she knew the truth about the time travel. Maya didn't try covering anything up or made excuses. "I hope the weather stays mild like this. It's been a beautiful fall. I won't mind you leaving for California if it stays like this."

Katie waved to her, and ran back to her house. She flew in the backdoor, then up to her room. She looked around for her phone, finding it on the floor. Katie sat in her yellow chair, then pressed speed dial for

Lindsey.

"Katie, we just got home from school. Has something happened?" Lindsey sounded a little worried.

"No, but I have good news! Maya's leaving for California almost a week before Thanksgiving. So I thought on Saturday we could break in." She hated thinking about breaking into Maya's house and taking one of those books. Nothing was going to stop her though. She needed that book more than ever, especially since she learned Carl planned to burn them all.

"Sounds like a plan. Just promise me you'll keep me informed on what you're doing."

"Promise." Katie was ecstatic that the first part of her plan was in place.

She looked around her room. She didn't have any homework, had already read one of Jack Woods' books and really didn't feel like reading much more of the second one. That would be saved for when she was really needed a distraction.

There were four more days until Maya left so she still needed something to keep busy. One more book was left in the bag, so she decided to read it. The book was on the bottom of the pile. Katie hadn't really looked at the titles. She just grabbed the one on top and began reading. This last one was the journal Anna told her about. It was not surprising her dad kept a journal. Every Christmas since she started school, he gave her one. Her father encouraged her to do whatever she wished with them, draw or write, he just wanted her to be creative. She promised herself right then and there she would take up writing again.

Katie opened to the first page of Jack Wood's journal and started reading. It gave more of an insight to Jack, recounting his days at the canyon and the discoveries he had made. He wrote how the first thing people have to do is set aside their pride and respect nature. No one can control it. Humans can only be a part of it.

His goal had been to go white water rafting on the Colorado River, his biggest challenge. He had practiced by going on short trips with some of the men at a base camp that had been stationed at the bottom of the canyon right by the river. Jack had stayed there for days and had gone out with the men whenever he could. He wrote about how many times he had fallen in the river and had been pulled, exhausted, to the bank.

Jack had learned a lot about himself in those days at the canyon. He

Waiting for Dusk

had loved to go off by himself to a quiet spot and just listen to the silence. It had been a different kind of silence than sitting quietly in a house. He likened it to the dawn of time when there was no one on Earth, no animals, no people. He had spent hours by himself quietly walking, writing and taking pictures.

There had been something that had stopped Jack from totally giving himself to the canyon. Katie read that entry over and over to herself:

The canyon is part of my soul. I never seem to get enough of it. Yet, there is something holding me back from completely giving myself to this wondrous place. There is something that has a stronger pull on me, something that owns my heart and my soul. I always have to go back to her and leave you behind, my dear canyon. The love I have for my dearest Joanna exceeds whatever I feel for you. So I will always visit you, my friend, but I shall not stay forever. You see, it is love that has the stronger pull and will always win out. I would be nothing without her; I would not be the man I am today. I could not tackle your highest peaks or white foaming waters without her in my heart. She is my heart and I will always go back to her.

Katie wiped her eyes. That was her mother's name. It certainly made sense if Jack Woods was Jackson Roberts. It was a beautiful passage. Katie marked the page with her bookmark. It gave her insight to her father. Everything he did was out of love. He stayed in the present because he loved his wife and daughter. Nothing was more important than that. What didn't make sense was that her dad was so angry about her going to the canyon and back to 1927. If he loved it so much, he should be happy she was having the same great experiences. Katie decided the time had come to confront her father.

Just then her phone buzzed. It was a text message from Tyson.

Call me. That's all it said.

She hadn't heard from him in awhile. Tyson and Erin were the new 'it' couple at school. Girls were jealous of Erin and the gossip was she had everything a girl could want. She was the captain of the basketball cheerleaders and had the star of the team for a boyfriend. It was interesting that everyone called Tyson a star because the season hadn't started yet. There were rumors he was really great in practice and the team could make it all the way to the state finals.

Katie thought she better see what he wanted. "What's up, Ty?" Katie tried to sound light and cheerful.

"Just wanted to let you know the first game is Saturday. Wanted to make sure you'd be there."

Everyone knew that the first big game was always the Saturday before Thanksgiving. It was more like a preseason game. It didn't count, but it was a big event for the two small towns that played against each other. It was a tradition that started long ago, and something everyone looked forward to. After the game, there was a dance in the gym.

"Of course, I'll be there, wouldn't miss it." Katie wanted to see Tyson play. She knew he would be very good.

"I was just calling to remind you, that's all. Wish you were cheering on the sideline with the other girls."

Katie was glad she didn't have to cheer at the games. "You have Erin cheering for you. I'm sure she's your biggest fan."

"I hope you are, too."

"You know I am. I always want the best for you."

"Do you?"

"Of course, Lindsey and I will be in the stands to cheer you on."

"I haven't seen you in awhile so do you want to go to the dance with me?"

Katie couldn't believe what he just said. "Aren't you going with Erin?"

"I think she wants to go home. We don't have to go to the dance. I'll be hungry after the game. Promise me you meet me and go out for a quick bite."

"If you're sure Erin's going home."

"Positive. Are you going to leave me starving and lonely after the game? Some friend."

"Fine, I'll meet you by the locker room."

Waiting for Dusk

Chapter Thirty-Three

"Big day today for our little town!" Katie's dad was wearing a sweatshirt with her high school logo on it.

"I'll be glad when it's over." Katie was not as excited as her father was.

"Thought you were looking forward to the game. You couldn't get there fast enough last year."

She didn't want to give the real reason why she wanted it over. "That was last year." She rolled her eyes so he'd think she was having the typical teenage reaction to something that was so last year.

What she really cared about was that Lindsey was coming over in the afternoon. They would get the book, then have dinner with Katie's parents and head to the game.

She waited all morning for her parents to be distracted or go out. No such luck. They read the paper and drank coffee. Katie thought she would get them moving. "What are we having for dinner tonight?"

"I haven't thought about it yet," her mother said. "What do you want?"

Katie wished she looked in the freezer to see what was in there. She would have picked something that was not available. "Well, Lindsey does love salmon. She loves the way you cook it on the grill, Dad."

"I'll need to go get some fresh fish, then." Her father grinned. "Always appreciate it when someone enjoys my cooking. Joanna, let's get some breakfast going and then go to the market."

Homerun, Katie thought. She would be the sweet, helpful daughter until they left. They didn't seem to suspect a thing.

As soon as they left, Katie sent a text to Lindsey to come over. She ran to the key cupboard in the kitchen. Maya's key was on an apple keychain hanging in its designated spot. She sat at the kitchen table and waited.

Lindsey tapped on the back sliding glass door. She wore a black hoodie and sunglasses.

"Too funny." Katie wished she dressed in black, too. "I'll be right back."

She ran upstairs and grabbed the Jack Woods book to replace the one she'd be taking from the set. It was going to be hard to part with one of his books but it had to be done. She ran back down. "Let's go!"

The two girls ran across the path to Maya's house. Then Katie suddenly stopped. "We have a problem. This is the key to her front door." They looked at each other. That would make things a little harder. Tyson lived across the street plus there were joggers and people walking dogs all the time. And someone could drive by and notice.

"We can do this." Lindsey ran up the side of the house. "Come on!" As they approached the front, she said, "You go in and I'll stay out here and watch for anything suspicious."

Katie ran quickly to the front door, unlocked it and went inside.

"Hello?" she said meekly. She tiptoed to the family room. Although she felt extremely guilty she continued on. As Katie bent down to open the bookcase, she remembered it was locked and that Maya had the key on a chain around her neck.

Why didn't I think of that? Katie went into the kitchen and grabbed a butter knife. What else would work?

She felt like she had been in the house too long already. Nervously, she rummaged around for a few more things she thought would work—a letter opener, a paper clip. She took everything to the bookcase. The butter knife was too big. The paper clip was too small. The letter opener was just right. She felt like Goldilocks only she hoped the three bears would not return home and surprise her.

The books all looked alike. They were all a dull black color so the book she brought would blend in nicely. Katie made the exchange and locked the case. Returning to the kitchen, she made sure everything was back in order.

Then she ran to the front window and looked out. Across the street, she saw Lindsey playing basketball with Tyson.

Now she had to somehow get out of the house, without him seeing

Waiting for Dusk

her. Katie saw Lindsey flashing looks over at the house. Lindsey needed to know she was ready to leave. Katie left her phone at home. She decided to wait for the next time Lindsey looked over, and would quickly open and close the front door.

After a few more minutes, Lindsey stopped playing and rested her hands on her knees as if to get her breath. Katie opened the door and then shut it. She watched through the window again and saw Lindsey had Tyson by the shoulders and was talking to him. He faced his house, and she faced the street. Katie made a break for it. She locked the front door all the while looking over her shoulder. She ran over to the side of Maya's house and across the back yard. Then she entered her own house and rushed to the front door.

She called to Lindsey, "Sorry I didn't hear you!"

Lindsey waved to Tyson, then crossed the street. Tyson waved to Katie and went back in his house.

"That was a close one! He came out as soon as you went in the house!" Lindsey was out of breath. "I knew he saw my car in your driveway. I was afraid he might come over to your house. I ran around to the back of the houses and came out the side by your driveway. I went across the street and told him you must be doing something because you didn't hear me knocking. Ty suggested calling and I said I did that. So I just challenged him to a game while I kept an eye out for you. I swear he must keep tabs on you 24/7!"

"Thanks so much." Katie hugged her. "I got the book. It's mine forever! I need to find a good hiding place for it now."

They ran up to Katie's room. Lindsey looked around and then spotted the quilted book bag that her Grandma J gave Katie. "Why not hide it in plain sight?" She pointed to the bag.

"Good idea!" Katie placed the book underneath the other two.

By the time Katie's parents arrived home, it was dinnertime. Everyone enjoyed the meal and the talk was about the game. Katie was in a good mood, especially since she was in possession of the book. She forgot all about promising Ty to go out after the game.

Katie and Lindsey left before Katie's parents. They wanted to see Jordyn. It would be her first game, and she was a little nervous. When they got there, Jordyn was with Matt. "Do you mind if Matt sits with you guys?" she asked them.

"Of course not! We'll be your cheer section!"

Jordyn was called away for practice. Erin gave Katie an evil stare.

"What did I do now?" Katie asked Lindsey.

"I think she knows Ty asked you out."

"Ooo, forgot about that. I don't really want to go. Plus it's just going out and getting something to eat after the game. We're friends."

"Did you forget about the dance, too? I think Erin planned on going with Ty,"

"The liar told me she was going home. I'll handle it. I'll tell Ty to go to the dance."

Matt, Lindsey and Katie got a seat a few rows up behind the bench. The cheerleaders sat under the basket and would come out onto the floor during timeouts. The team was already practicing on the court. Brian and Ty were both in the starting line-up.

"Oh, Lindsey, there's Brian." Katie poked her playfully.

"We're just friends," Lindsey said sincerely. "And he knows it."

"Okay, I wished that worked for me," Katie put her head on Lindsey's shoulder.

The game was exciting. Lots of people were there. Jordyn was doing well as a new cheerleader. Her moms sat with Katie's and Lindsey's parents. Katie watched everything as if it were a movie. The basketball players jumped and drove to the basket in slow motion, the cheerleaders yelled out but she didn't hear the cheers. She found herself clapping with the rest of the crowd and not really knowing why. Katie wanted the night to be over. She wanted it to be the start of Thanksgiving vacation. She planned to go to the canyon on Tuesday night, knowing it would be Wednesday there. Then she'd return for Wednesday in the present, then go back for Thanksgiving. Feeling like a ping-pong ball, she wished she didn't have to go back and forth. She wanted to spend her vacation there, returning on Sunday. It just couldn't be done though. She had to live two lives during the break.

"Wow, if looks could kill…" Lindsey whispered in Katie's ear.

Katie was still daydreaming. "Huh? What?"

"Erin! She's been shooting you looks all night!" Lindsey pointed at her.

Katie grabbed her finger. "Don't point! That's all I need! What else could she do to me anyway?"

"Why? Has she done something to you already?"

Katie told Lindsey her thoughts on not making the cheer squad.

Waiting for Dusk

Lindsey nodded her head in agreement. "Oh, definitely, I think you are right."

The game was close to the end. Their team was winning. The gym was loud and rocking. Katie and Lindsey stood up for the end of the game yelling and screaming for their friends.

At the end of the game, Tyson looked up at Katie, nodded, then pointed to where they would meet. Lindsey waited with Katie since she promised Brian she would go to the dance with him. They watched all the people being ushered from the gym. It had to be cleared and quickly cleaned for the dance.

Brian came out first and he and Lindsey headed off together. Finally Tyson came out of the locker room.

"Hey, didn't know if you'd be here or not." Ty looked good. Katie hoped to get her old friend back.

"Why wouldn't I be? I always keep my promises."

"Let's go. Where do you want to eat?"

"Wait a minute, Ty. How about if you just drive me home then come back to go to the dance with Erin. I don't think she's too happy with me. I don't think she planned to go home."

"Everything's cool with Erin. She knows I just want to talk with you. And I do need to eat. I'll come back and hook up with her later."

Katie decided to go out for a short time with him. "If you're sure, I don't want to cause any problems."

They walked to Tyson's brand new SUV his parents bought him after he made the varsity team. Katie thought it was a little much but maybe they were hoping he would be good enough to get a college scholarship and it was incentive to keep playing.

When they got in the car, Tyson put his arm around Katie, pulled her toward him and kissed her. Katie couldn't believe it. "What are you doing?"

"Just one kiss? For winning the game?" Ty gave her puppy dog eyes.

Katie couldn't believe she did it, but she leaned in to give him a quick kiss on the cheek. Instead he turned and kissed her on the mouth.

Katie pushed away from him. "If you're going to keep doing this, take me home."

"Why? Because you have a boyfriend? I haven't seen you with anyone. Does he go to this school?" Tyson was getting worked up.

"No, he doesn't go to this school!" Katie had enough. She slammed the car door shut.

Tyson turned the key in the ignition. "So you do have a boyfriend? You're finally admitting it?"

Katie reached for her seat belt and then realized it was caught in the door. "Ty…"

"What, Katie, what? Are you going to tell me some more lies?" Tyson screamed as he put the car in reverse.

Just as he stepped on the gas, Katie opened the door to free her seat belt. The car flew backward. When Tyson saw the door open, he slammed on the brakes. Katie rolled out of the car and fell onto the parking lot pavement slamming the side of her head on the black asphalt.

Waiting for Dusk

Chapter Thirty-Four

When Katie woke up, her mother was sitting next to the bed. "Mom, what are you doing here?"

Her mom took her hand. "Hi, how are you?" She looked tired, like she hadn't slept all night.

"Mom..." Katie tried to sit up but her head pounded. She put her hand to her head. "My head really hurts."

"Don't try to sit up, Katie. Lie still."

She heard her father's voice and turned her head. He was sitting on the other side of the bed.

"What happened to me?" Katie asked, although it was coming back to her.

"You were in an accident. You hit your head on the pavement and now you're in the hospital. You have a concussion." Her dad looked worried.

"Oh, that's why my head hurts." Everything flashed before her—Tyson, the fight, the seatbelt. "What day is it?"

"It's Sunday, honey. You've been in and out of consciousness since last night. We have been here all night. So has Tyson. He was so worried about you and blamed himself for everything. He told us how your seatbelt was stuck in the door and you didn't tell him in time. Katie, why did you open that door without telling him?"

"Joanna, I thought we agreed not to talk about that. All we want is for Katie to get better." Katie's dad held her other hand.

Katie worried about getting back to the canyon. She didn't care if her head hurt or not. "When do I get to go home?"

189

"We'll talk about that later," her dad answered. "They want to keep you for observation. I said you could stay till Thanksgiving to make sure."

Katie was upset. "Oh, no. That's way too long. I'm not staying in the hospital until Thanksgiving."

"Now who is making Katie get worked up?" her mom eyed her father.

"You're right. No need to think about that. All we care about is you getting better and coming home whenever you can."

Just then, Tyson appeared in the doorway with a large bouquet of flowers in his hand. Katie moaned. She really didn't want to see him.

"Are you okay? Should I get a doctor?" Her mother frantically looked for the call button.

"No, I'm fine." Katie then realized her mom thought she was groaning in pain, not from seeing Tyson.

"Tyson, I can't believe you're back already! Did you get any sleep?" Her mother got up and took the flowers from him. "How sweet of you. Wasn't that thoughtful, Katie?"

"Uh-huh," was all Katie could get out of her mouth.

"Katie just woke up and I don't think she's in the mood for company," Jackson stood up and crossed his arms. "Let's give her some time to herself."

He got up, went over to the other side of the bed and ushered the other two out of the room.

Katie was glad to be alone. She couldn't think clearly and it hurt to move her head much. She wanted to talk to a doctor to see how long she'd have to be in the hospital and how long the concussion would last. This wasn't in the plans. If only it would all go away. Katie wished she never went with Tyson last night. She'd be at home in her own bed, not this hospital one.

Her parents returned and took turns sitting with her. Somehow her father managed to talk Tyson into going home. Katie was grateful for that.

Her mom decided to go home for awhile and Katie was alone with her dad. This was the perfect time to talk to him.

Her father was standing with his back to her, looking out the window. "Mr. Woods, Jack Woods?" Katie said softly. He spun around and looked at her.

Waiting for Dusk

"How do you know that name?"

"It's you, Dad, isn't it? You're Jack Woods."

"I knew of a Jack Woods, yes, of course. He was a famous 20th century writer. He…"

"Stop it. I know it's you. I saw you. And I have a feeling you saw me, too."

"Now is not the time to talk about this. We will talk, I promise. I just want you to get better."

"I'll drop it if you admit one thing, that you're Jack Woods." Katie was tired of waiting for answers. It took her so long to get to this point. She was determined to find out today.

"If it will stop you from talking and get you to rest, then, yes, I'm Jack Woods," her father walked over to her bed and sat down. He looked in her eyes. "You're in love, aren't you, Kate?"

Tears filled Katie's eyes. He said Kate. He knew. He knows.

He knew all along and was trying to stop it for some reason. She was determined to find out. For now, she could accept this. She needed to rest and needed to get better. "Thanks, Dad," she closed her eyes.

When Katie opened her eyes again, she saw Lindsey sitting in her room.

"I hope I didn't wake you! How are you? What happened? I should have never let you go with Tyson!"

"Calm down, this isn't your fault, it's mine. I should have known better." Katie looked at her friend with a very serious face and motioned her to come closer.

"Don't tell anyone what I'm about to tell you,"

"Sure, of course not."

"Ty and I had a big fight in the car. My seatbelt was stuck in the door. I tried to tell him but he kept yelling. He threw the car in reverse and raced back out of the parking spot. I think it was at the same moment I was opening the door. He saw the door open and that's when I felt the car jerk to a stop. That's all I remember."

"Oh, I'm going to…" Lindsey couldn't even finish. "That's not the story he told your parents. He is blaming you…in a nice way. He said you just opened the door without telling him. There was no talk of putting the pedal to the metal!"

"Well, in a way, he's right. I didn't tell him. I didn't get a chance to tell him," Katie could not believe how Tyson was manipulating her life.

"You've got to promise me one thing. You have to help get me out of this hospital the sooner, the better."

A doctor arrived at Katie's hospital room. He tapped on the open door. "May I come in?"

"Sure." Katie tried to nod but it made her a little dizzy and nauseated. She really wanted to talk to the doctor. Lindsey got up and went out into the hall.

"That was quite a fall you took, Katie," he said as he flashed a light into her eyes. "Anything you want to tell me?"

"No." Katie was hesitant. She probably could get Ty in trouble but what good would that do? She decided to stick to his story and there would be no problems. As it was everyone was being overprotective.

"Then let's talk about this concussion. What you have is called a mild concussion. It should disappear in seven to ten days."

"Seven days! I have to stay here all that time!" Katie was overwhelmed at the thought.

"No," the doctor laughed. "If everything looks good tomorrow, you can go home then. I gave your parents a list of things to watch out for. Are you having any symptoms? Lightheadedness, blurred vision, vomiting, difficulty concentrating? These are a few of the symptoms; there are more. You just need to get some rest and no physical activity for a few days. Do you think you can manage that?"

"Yes, I can do that, especially if I get to go home."

"What? You don't like the hospital food?" the doctor smiled at her.

"Actually I haven't had any yet. I don't have an appetite right now," Katie placed her hand on her stomach.

"Feeling a little nauseated? That's normal and should go away. We'll talk about your symptoms some more tomorrow. Keep track of them for me. If anything feels like it is getting worse, use that call button."

Katie tried to nod but it was too much. She just smiled at the doctor. Lindsey came back in the room after the doctor left. "I can go home tomorrow!" Katie smiled weakly.

Lindsey gave her a high-five in the air being careful not to really hit Katie's hand. "I better get going. I'll see you at your house after school. Lucky dog, you get to miss school!" She waved and disappeared out the door.

Katie talked her father into going home and getting some rest and a

Waiting for Dusk

change of clothes. She was glad to have the time to herself because she knew both her parents would be back soon.

After dinner, Joanna and Jackson returned. They saw Katie's tray with the untouched food. Her dad pulled a bag out of his jacket. "How about some of your favorite ice cream?"

"Chocolate chip cookie dough?" That sounded good to Katie. She enjoyed the rest of the evening with her parents. They fussed over her and fed her ice cream. Katie noticed that there was no Tyson and smiled appreciatively at her father. She knew he had something to do with it. When they finally left, Katie realized how much she loved them and how they were always there for her.

Although what she had to do next, she'd have to do alone. She turned on the TV, dozing as she watched.

Tyson came into the room. He sat quietly by Katie's bedside. He couldn't stop looking at her. He picked up the remote control and turned off the TV. He gently kissed Katie on the cheek. "Goodnight, my love," he whispered in her ear. "I love you."

"I love you, too," she whispered back in her sleep and then murmured, "…Drew."

"Well, I finally have a name. I'll show this Drew. I've known you longer. Where is he now? I'm here and he's not. I can watch over you day and night. I'm just right across the street, love. Drew might just be a phase but I'm the real thing."

Chapter Thirty-Five

When Katie woke up the next morning she felt a little better. She rubbed her forehead and tried to recall the strange dream she had last night. Tyson was talking to her and telling her all these creepy things. Good thing it was just a dream.

Her parents were already by her bedside, sitting quietly in the room. They both jumped up when they realized she was awake.

"I get to go home today," Katie smiled at both of them.

"If the doctor says so, honey," Her mother took her hand. "How are you feeling?"

"Better, the doctor said not to move around too much. I can do that at home, right?"

"Let's just wait and see."

That afternoon the doctor gave the all clear for Katie to go home. She was so excited she couldn't wait. Her mom brought fresh clothes for her to wear home and helped Katie get dressed.

"Slow down, Katie! We're just going home, not to the Royal Ball or anything like that."

If only you knew, Katie slipped her top over her head.

Her dad pulled the car up to the front of the hospital while a nurse pushed Katie in a wheelchair to the front door. Joanna helped Katie into the front seat and jumped in the back and Jackson headed for home. School buses were on the road so that must mean school would be out soon. Katie needed to talk to Lindsey about her plan. She hoped Lindsey would come over right after school.

Jackson helped Katie up the stairs and Joanna was already in the bedroom making things ready. After Katie was in her bed, she said to

Waiting for Dusk

them, "Your work here is done. Fine job!" She really wanted them not to hover and they respected her wishes.

After awhile there was a knock on the door. Lindsey slowly opened it. "Hey, how's the princess?"

"Get in here! How was school? Did Tyson go today? Was Erin mad?"

"First things first, you didn't tell me how you are." Lindsey sat down on the end of the bed.

"I'm feeling much better, now go ahead."

"Tyson did come to school today. He was acting like he was the hero who saved your life. All he did was call 9-1-1. Erin was upset at first but is putting on a good show now. She's standing by her man and all that."

Typical high school. Kate was glad she wasn't there to see it. "Wow, I should have guessed. Now, I need your help. When I go to see Drew I won't be here. Since I was just in an accident my parents are going to keep checking in on me. I need someone to sleep in my bed."

"And you want me to do that. I'll have to tell my mom I'm sleeping over here and hope she doesn't tell yours. We'll have to make up something so she won't tell. You were just in an accident so she'd probably say yes. This could work."

"My parents have to think you're going home on Tuesday night. Then we'll sneak you back in," Katie had planned most of this through while she was still in the hospital.

"I'll see you tomorrow then, after school. I hope you're doing the right thing. After all, you just had a concussion. What if something happens back in good ol' 1927 and you don't make it back?"

"Don't worry, I'll be fine."

"You know I believe all this stuff. You're really going to the Grand Canyon and I won't be able to help you. Grandma J is also your friend and she'd never forgive me if I didn't lecture you."

"I told you I'll be fine but thanks for worrying."

"I'll let you rest. See you tomorrow. And don't do anything stupid until I get back." Lindsey closed the door as she left the room.

It was almost dinnertime and Katie wanted to go downstairs to join her parents. She needed to practice moving around. She picked up the baby monitor which she couldn't believe her mother still had—you never know when you might need it she had said--and called to them. "Mom,

Dad, you there?"

Before she could even finish her request, her father was at her door.

"I'd like to come downstairs. I'm bored up here and need to move around." Katie looked at him with her pouting face that always worked.

"There you go again with your famous boredom speech," her father put out his hands. "I'll help you up."

Jackson carefully guided Katie down the stairs and put her on the family room sofa. She was happy to be sitting up in a regular seat. It felt pretty good. Katie still had one whole day to get better before she left.

Her mother was in the kitchen making dinner and soon they were sitting at the table eating and talking. Katie planned on being extra good and was on her best behavior. She didn't want her parents to suspect a thing.

"You guys don't have to check on me every five minutes now when I go to bed," Katie teased. "I'm getting much better, really."

"Then we will check every ten minutes," her father teased back.

They watched TV together and then her mother helped Katie back upstairs. She gave Katie her phone and the remote control. "No laptop today, it may make you dizzy. No reading for awhile."

"Okay, Mom, goodnight, or should I say see you in ten minutes?" Katie was feeling a little tired. She planned on sleeping and nothing else.

* * * *

Immediately turning on the TV the next morning, Katie wanted to be distracted until Lindsey came over. She mindlessly flipped channels. She was awake pretty early and most of the channels had news and morning shows. Katie decided to watch the weather channel for awhile because she needed to know what the weather was like in Arizona for some reason. After hearing about the mild November that Ohio was having no snow, not much rain, and temperatures in the high fifties they finally got to the national map. Flagstaff, Arizona was also having high fifties and sunshine. That was the only difference, gray here, sunny there. That's one thing Katie missed the most, the sunshine and the blue skies. She was starting to sound like her Aunt Lucinda. Ohio didn't have many sunny days in the fall and winter. Well, she would be there soon enough.

Katie's phone rang, playing the Anna music. She excitedly picked it up because she would have someone to talk to about her plans.

"Kathryn! Are you alright? Lindsey called me last night and I just about fell off my chair when she told me what happened to you. Here I

Waiting for Dusk

thought you were busy with school and that's why I haven't heard from you. I don't think I like this Tyson fellow very much. He's bad news."

"Anna, take a breath and let me talk! I'm much better today. Tyson's not a bad guy, just a teenager like the rest of us. Don't be too hard on him. I really want to discuss my plan with you because I need your help."

Anna and Katie talked the morning away. Katie filled her in on everything but was surprised by what Anna said as they ended their conversation.

"Maybe this should be the last time you do your time traveling. Enjoy the here and now. Tell Drew you will always love him and explain you live in the 21st century. I'm sure he will understand."

Katie could not believe what she was hearing. Anna was a romantic who believed in love. Now she's telling Katie to just live in the present. She thought Anna understood she couldn't do that.

"You think I should tell him I live in the future? Won't he think I'm a little crazy?"

"Maybe not, you need to give him more credit. How is the Jack Wood's book reading coming along?" Anna completely changed the subject.

"Fine, two down, one to go," Katie didn't have the heart to tell Anna she used one of the books as a decoy at Maya's house.

"Which one is left?"

"The journal, but I have started it." Just then Katie heard her mother coming up the stairs. She was probably bringing lunch. "It was so nice of you to call, Grandma J, and check up on me. I'm doing fine, really."

Katie's mom entered the room and said, "Tell Anna I said hi."

"Mom says hi," Katie could just picture Anna's face after she called her Grandma J.

"Okay, kid, I get your mom is there now. I'll let the Grandma J go this one time." Anna was too funny. Then she said, "I will be praying for you. Have a safe journey. Also, Happy Thanksgiving."

"Happy Thanksgiving to you, too, and tell everyone there we send our love," Katie hung up her phone. 'Thanks for lunch. I think I'm going to rest again after eating.'

Katie planned on conserving all her strength and quickly dozed off after lunch.

* * * *

"What are you doing in here?" the sound of Lindsey's voice woke Katie up. She opened her eyes and saw Tyson and Lindsey in her room.

"Katie and I are working on a science report for class. It's done and on a flash drive. I was just looking for it here on her desk. Her mom said it was okay if I came up. It's due next Monday. Gosh, Lindsey, you don't have to be such a brat."

"When it comes to Katie, I can be more than a brat! You're not one of my favorite people right now, Ty."

"Sorrr – ry! Geesh! I'm only trying to do her a favor."

"It's okay. Ty and I are working on a paper together," Katie chimed in. She remembered signing up for a certain topic and Ty made sure he did, too. They were assigned to write the paper together by the teacher. Katie made sure they met at school or at the library to work on it. She forgot it was due Monday.

"Thanks, Ty. I think we just need to proofread and print."

"You're not supposed to be reading so I thought I'd take it home and do it. Take care and have a good Thanksgiving," Ty came over and took Katie's hand. He kissed it lightly and left.

"You're too nice to him!" Lindsey clenched her jaw. "You need to be a little meaner, cousin."

She walked over to Katie's bed. "My mom thinks I'm sleeping over at Jordyn's. I didn't want her calling here at all. Jordyn knows I'm doing you a favor and will cover if she has to. I'll drive over there and she'll bring me here. Then in the morning she'll come back to get me. She was great, didn't ask any questions. Maybe we need to bring her in on all of this."

"Not yet," Katie wasn't up to trying to explain anything to anyone. "Make sure you say good-bye to my parents and they see you leaving. Call me when you are on you're way back tonight."

Katie lay back on her pillows. There were butterflies in her stomach and she knew they weren't all from the concussion. It seemed like hours before she heard from Lindsey. "Finally! I thought you'd never call!"

"It's only nine o'clock! Are you planning on going to sleep already?"

"Yes, I am! Dusk was over three hours ago. I could've been gone already!"

"Well, you better say goodnight to your parents. They're guarding the nest you know! Almost there, Jordyn's dropping me off about three

Waiting for Dusk

houses away."

"Tell her thanks and I love her! See ya in a minute!" Katie hung up and went downstairs. "Mom, Dad? I'm going to sleep now. I want to get rested up for Thanksgiving."

"We can come up, honey, and watch TV in our room so if you need us we'll be close by," her mom got up. "Come on, Jackson. Let's go."

"I'll be there in just a minute. I want to get a soda," Katie hoped that would work and they'd go without her.

Her dad walked through the kitchen and said, "See you upstairs."

Katie tiptoed to the front door. She opened it quietly. Lindsey was already standing there, again wearing her black hoodie. It was hard not to laugh at the sight of her. She slipped in and the two went up the stairs trying not to make a sound.

Katie hid Lindsey in her bathroom. She handed her the soda and closed the door, then put on pajamas and walked to her parents' bedroom. She climbed in bed with them and hugged and kissed them goodnight hoping it would be enough.

"I'll be fine tonight, don't worry about me," she hugged them one more time and headed back to her room. Lindsey was in her bed when she got back.

"You have to stay in the bathroom until I'm gone. What if you end up going with me?"

"I hadn't thought of that. This is kind of scary!" Lindsey shivered.

"You don't have to do this, I'll understand," Katie rubbed Lindsey's shivering arms.

"No, let's do it. I'll be fine," Lindsey walked back to the bathroom and closed the door.

Katie went to the bag and got out her book. Then she walked over to her desk, found all the letters she wrote Drew and tucked them in the book. Climbing into bed, she opened the book to start reading. After a few minutes, Katie felt tired and a little dizzy so she put the book down to rest for a minute.

Chapter Thirty-Six

Katie looked around at the familiar surroundings. It was so good to be back. She quickly searched around in the bed for the book, sighing with relief when she found it. The letters were inside. They made the trip with her. Katie slipped out of bed and into the hallway searching through the little closet that contained her clothes. The smell of Swedish coffee filled the air. Mr. Johansson must be in the kitchen. Katie grabbed an outfit and ran back to her room. After she was ready she entered the kitchen.

"God morgon, Mr. Johansson," Katie remembered to use the Swedish he taught her.

"Flicka! I did not expect to see you already," Mr. Johansson came over and gave her a big hug.

"Could I ask a favor?" Katie's heart was pounding. She just wanted to get to the canyon.

"Of course you can! Anything for my wife's favorite girl," Carl smiled like a proud papa.

Favorite girl? Maya must have talked to Carl about me. Katie liked that. "Would you be able to drive me over to El Tovar?"

"Let me have my coffee and we will head over," Carl headed over to the stove. "Ruthie and Molly have to work today but not until the dinner shift. They're sleeping late."

"What about Anna?" Katie was unsure if she wanted to see her or not.

"She's not working today. I believe she's going riding with Daniel later," Carl sipped his coffee.

Anna was probably sleeping, too. That was a good thing. Katie needed to stay focused. She sat at the table with Mr. Johansson while he

Waiting for Dusk

had his coffee with a cinnamon roll. It looked good but Katie's stomach was not in the mood for eating. She just made small talk and hoped he would hurry and finish.

Finally Carl stood up and said," I'll find my hat and we'll get going."

Katie ran outside, and jumped in the Buick. It was a beautiful day. The sun was shining and the air was cool. She hoped Drew was already here, and they could enjoy this day together.

Mr. Johansson dropped Katie off at the back of the building as usual. She waved good- bye, and told him not to worry about her. Katie didn't know if she should go inside or not. She would love to see all her friends, but seeing Drew was more important. Just then, Thomas came out the backdoor.

"Well, if it isn't Miss Kate," Thomas said with one of his wonderful grins.

"Thomas, I'm so glad to see you. Do you know if Andrew is here yet?"

"Yes, he is. I guess you want to know where he is." Thomas teased. "I believe he's over at the Studio. He's helping out there today, preparing for the big lecture."

"Thanks so much, you are the best." Katie started running.

"Come back and I'll have lunch ready for the two of you." He called after her.

Katie couldn't run fast enough. She waited too long for this moment. The Studio came into view. She hoped Drew was there. Katie didn't take time to look around or gaze into the canyon. Her mind was focused on only one thing. Drew. As she got closer, she saw a familiar figure. The dark hair caught her attention first. Then those eyes met hers. Katie continued to run, feeling like she was in a movie. Her feet just kept moving as if someone else was controlling them. The young man began to run, too, and she heard her name being called out.

The next thing Katie knew, she was in Drew's arms again, and he was swinging her around in the air.

"Drew, Drew, put me down." She was a little light-headed and did not want to discuss the concussion with him.

"I didn't think I'd see you until later."

They sat down right where they were to catch their breath. Their eyes locked, soaking in the essence of each other. For Katie, all was right with the world for now. She reached out her hand and placed it on Drew's cheek.

"It is so good to see you," she leaned forward and kissed him.

Drew stood up and pulled Katie to her feet. "Let me go tell them that I'm taking a long break and I'll be back."

Katie decided to walk back to El Tovar knowing Drew would catch up with her. Before long, they were both sitting on the porch of the hotel, talking about their time apart.

Drew told her about his studies and playing sports. He was the football team's quarterback last year but gave that up after planning on being at the canyon for a longer time this year. "I couldn't let my teammates down so I stepped aside. They asked me to still be on the team and play when I could, not as quarterback though. Since I missed summer practice and some games I thought it wasn't fair but they insisted. It kept me busy so I wasn't always thinking of you.

Also I'm planning a trip down the Colorado soon. I've been practicing this summer with the men at base camp. Thomas and I may go off on Friday for one more short practice run. Now, what about you? What did you do that you were too busy to write?"

"Drew, stop teasing. I did write to you, almost every day. I brought all the letters with me."

Drew looked lovingly at her, "I can't wait to read them."

"I pretty much did the same as you. I went to school and did my homework."

"That can't be all, come on, I want to hear more."

Katie told him about trying out for the cheerleading squad and how she thought Erin didn't want her on the team. She told him all about Jordyn and Lindsey, her best friends. She explained how she grew up with Tyson and how he was now the star of the basketball team. "Ty asked me to Homecoming…"

"Homecoming?" Drew said it as if he didn't quite understand.

"Yes, it's a weekend when alumni come back for a football game and …"

"I know what Homecoming is. I'm just surprised you could go out with another man."

"He's not a m-man," Katie stuttered. "He's a teenage boy and a friend."

"He must like you if he asked you to Homecoming," Drew seemed agitated.

"But I don't like him; I only care about him as a friend. He got a little carried away. He thinks he's in love with me. Tyson is immature and very emotional; he will get over it."

"Did he try to kiss you?" Andrew took a deep breath.

"Yes, he did, he did kiss me," Katie knew that sounded bad.

Andrew put his head in his hands. "I thought you loved me, Kate. I thought we had something special."

"I do…we do," Katie pulled at his hands. "Look at me. I'm here. I came all this way for you. I don't care about Ty. I thought it was just a casual date to the dance. Please believe me!"

Drew took Katie into his arms. "I don't want to be jealous or have a jealous relationship. I want us to be a couple forever."

Katie wanted that too. She was so choked up she couldn't answer him. She only could hold on tightly.

"Come on," Drew took her by the hand and they went around to the back of the hotel to the kitchen door. "I'm starving and I'm sure my good friend has lunch ready."

Thomas came to the door and handed Drew a pail with a cloth napkin over it. "Enjoy, you two."

They strolled for awhile talking about nothing important. Relieved to have her Andrew back, Katie hoped he understood. She didn't explain things very well and would like to start over from the beginning but there wasn't time. Instead, Katie told Drew about visiting the ranch in October with her friend, Lindsey. She wanted to tell him about Anna but didn't think he would believe her.

"What if I told you I was from the future?" Katie baited him.

"I would think you are half crazy but the other half was quite beautiful."

"No, really, would you believe me?"

"Yes, I would believe you. Didn't Jules Verne write Journey to the Center of the Earth and H.G. Wells, The Time Machine? Those books are thought provoking."

"Then you are a student of science fiction?" Katie hoped that would help him understand.

"Is that what you call it? Well, yes, I am. Who knows what can happen in life?" Drew sat down on a grassy spot in the sun. "Are you ready to eat lunch?"

It was a perfect day for Katie. She could not have imagined it any better. She was so happy to see Drew and so in love. Schoolgirl crushes came and went and this was not one of those.

When they were done, the couple walked back to the barn where Drew kept his horse. The sun was lower in the sky and he wanted to get Katie back to the boardinghouse.

The ride was wonderful. Katie's arms were around Drew's waist, and she rested her head on his back. The word perfect kept popping into her head.

They arrived too soon; the ride went so quickly. Drew jumped off his horse, and Katie slid into his arms. They kissed for a long time, and Katie did not want him to stop.

"I have something for you," Drew went to his saddle bag and pulled out a long, blue velvet box.

"Here, put these in your bag." Katie pulled her letters out from her jacket pocket.

Drew put the letters in the bag, and turned to Katie. "Since you said you never would take the necklace off, I got you something different."

Katie slowly opened the box and inside was a charm bracelet. Two charms were on it, a crescent shaped moon and a star. "Oh, Drew, it's beautiful," Katie loved the charms he had chosen.

"The moon is to remind you I'm always here for you. I added the star because you are my shining star. I would give you the moon and the stars, if I could. I hope to add more charms in the future. This is just the beginning," he kissed her softly.

"Would you put it on for me?" Katie couldn't wait to wear the bracelet. She held out her left arm. Drew clipped it on, and slid his hand into hers. "What's this?"

She felt him tap something on her ring finger. She looked down at her hand and gasped. There on her left ring finger was the tiny diamond promise ring that Tyson gave her the night of Homecoming. "I don't know what that is. I don't know how it got there! Drew, you have to believe me!" Tears began to fill her eyes.

"Believe you? I don't know what to believe! You don't know how that got there? Did that Tyson fellow buy this for you?"

"Yes, yes, he did."

"So if he bought you a ring like this and you're wearing it on your left hand, it must be pretty serious," Andrew yelled.

Waiting for Dusk

"No, it's not like that at all," Katie was panicking. She felt like Drew was not listening to her.

"All this time I loved you and you were playing me for a fool. Was I just a summer fling?" Drew had tears in his eyes.

"No! I did not play you for a fool. It's hard to explain," Katie stumbled over her words.

"It's not that hard to explain. You have a boyfriend back home and one here. Well, this one is leaving. Good-bye, Kate." Drew started walking away from her and then turned back. "I'm setting you free. Do what you need to do. Maybe if I let you go now, maybe someday…someday you will come back to me." He got on his horse and rode away.

"Drew, wait a minute, don't go!" Katie sobbed. She fell to the ground wailing.

It was all so confusing, and then she remembered Tyson was in her room on Tuesday afternoon when she woke up and was standing by her desk. She had put the ring box in the top drawer of the desk when he wouldn't take it back after Homecoming. He must have found it, and slipped the ring on her finger when she was asleep.

Finally Katie sat up. She ran to the barn and saddled up Flicka. She would find Drew and explain. She could fix this.

Katie stopped at El Tovar, and Thomas said he hadn't seen Drew although she knew he had. He was just being a good friend. She went to all the spots Drew loved and couldn't find him anywhere.

As she rode around looking for him, Katie began to feel a little angry. Drew hadn't let her explain or finish what she was saying. Why were men like that? She would let him cool off for a day or two and then come looking for him again.

She decided to stay home and not come back for Thanksgiving although she'd love to share it with Molly, Ruthie, Anna and Mr. and Mrs. Johansson. It was probably better this way; she'd just want to find Drew the whole time she was here. It was better to stay away.

The sun started to set and Katie knew she needed to get back to the boardinghouse but first there was something important she had to do. She slid off Flicka, tied her up and ran to the canyon's rim. She took the ring off her finger, and threw it as hard as she could into the air. Good-bye, Tyson, good-bye for good.

Chapter Thirty-Seven

Katie woke up with a start. She flung the blankets back and jumped out of bed. She looked over at the bed and saw a large lump. Lindsey! Oh my gosh, I completely forgot about her!

She knew she had to wake her up and get her out of her bedroom. "Linds, Lindsey, wake up!" Katie shook her.

"Katie, you're back. Oh, what a night! You really leave you know. That was weird. I'm still trying to process it all. Your parents are still on patrol, too. I had to sleep the whole night under the blankets with my head covered."

"I'll make this up to you, I will. You're the best friend anyone could have," Katie sat back down on the bed. "Now you have to get out."

Seeing the humor in that statement after all she went through, Katie picked up her pillow and lightly hit Lindsey with it. They both started laughing. Lindsey put a call into Jordyn and made arrangements to be picked up. While Lindsey got ready, Katie filled her in on what happened.

"So Drew is mad at you. You can take care of it when you go back," Lindsey was supportive. "I think giving him a few days to cool off is a good idea. And what's up with Tyson? I knew something was going on when I found him in your room while you were sleeping. He's turning into an obsessed stalker!"

Katie may have agreed with her before the time travel, but didn't now. She just felt sorry for him. She remembered how Lucinda felt about Daniel, and this helped her understand his situation.

Katie slowly opened her door and looked around. "I think my parents are gone. That's strange."

Waiting for Dusk

Lindsey threw on her black hood, ran down the stairs and out the door. Katie saw a note on the kitchen counter. It said they were out Thanksgiving shopping and would be back in an hour.

Katie planned to sleep the day away. She wasn't in the mood for small talk with her parents. They would let her sleep because of the accident. She would come down for dinner, then back to bed. Somehow she would get through the next day with the family, too. Katie intended on leaving Thanksgiving night and wasn't going to try to cover it up. Lindsey did not need to sleep in her bed again. Her plan was to talk to her father on Thursday night to finish the conversation they started in the hospital, then leave for the canyon.

* * * *

Katie got through Wednesday with no problem as planned. Her parents reacted exactly as she thought they would and left her alone.

Now Thanksgiving was here and became another task for her to complete before dusk. She heard voices downstairs that sounded like Grandma Sandra and Grandpa Mitch. They always came over early to help with the dinner. Her uncles and families were coming this year and the house would be filled with people. That might be a good distraction.

Katie got ready and went downstairs. "Hi, Grandma, Grandpa."

"How's our little angel?" Grandpa Mitch sounded a little worried.

"I'm fine, Grandpa, really." Katie liked his big bear hugs, feeling safe and loved.

The doorbell rang and Katie walked to the door and opened it. It was Tyson.

"Hi, you got a minute?"

Katie stepped out on the front porch. "I don't know if I do. That was pretty sneaky slipping that ring on my finger."

"So did it work?"

"Work? You mean have Drew see it and get angry? Yes, it worked."

"Good, then he's out of our lives."

"No, he isn't, I'm going to fix this. This doesn't change anything."

"Katie, I love you!" Ty didn't seem to be hearing her.

"I know you do and I understand that. You have to realize I just don't love you that way. I hope one day we can be friends again."

"I hope we can, too," Tyson rubbed her arms. "You're cold. You better get inside. Thanks for putting up with me."

Katie went back in the house. Everyone looked at her, but Katie didn't say a word. Grandma Sandra walked over and guided her to the sofa. "You just rest on the couch and we'll do all the work this year. Can I get you anything?"

"No, I'm fine."

That's how the rest of day went. People fussed over Katie and kept asking how she felt. She played with her little cousins and hung out with the older ones. They all ate too much turkey and hardly had room for dessert. Katie noticed the sun had set although she knew it was still early. The sun set by five in late November. She just had to be patient. The apple and pumpkin pies were set out for anyone who wanted dessert. Katie hoped people would then want to be headed home.

Another hour passed before the aunts and uncles began to leave. Kids were getting cranky, some adults had to work the next day and others had another Thanksgiving to attend. It was all very typical of a holiday.

Katie felt like she just went through the motions during the day. She was so glad to see everyone leave. Her mother got a call from Beth and went to the bedroom to talk.

Katie decided to take advantage of the opportunity to talk to her dad. "Well, we have time to continue our discussion. In the hospital you told me you were Jack Woods and said we would talk later."

"I never said I was Jack Woods, honey, I said I heard of him. A lot of people know who he is."

This was not how the conversation was supposed to go. Her father was not being truthful with her again.

"Dad, you said we would talk. You know Andrew and you are Jack Woods!"

"Think of what you are saying. That just isn't possible."

The calmer he seemed, the more furious Katie got. She wanted to do something to make him as mad as she was. She stormed into the kitchen and opened the key cupboard. There, dangling on its special keychain; was the key to the Mustang. Katie grabbed it and her coat and was out the door in a flash. She couldn't believe she was doing this. She could hear her father's voice in the distance.

Katie entered the code to the garage and ran and jumped in the car. It started quickly, and because it was always backed into the garage, she could pull right out. She flew passed her father as he approached the car.

She had no idea where she was going. She only had her temporary

Waiting for Dusk

license but didn't care. She was just so mad she needed to get out of the house. What better way to get to her father, than to take his car?

Pushing harder on the gas pedal, Katie felt the car gliding down the road. It felt good to be going this fast. Let's see how fast this car can go!

Everything was whirling past her in a blur but not because of the speed; her eyes were filled with tears.

Katie thought she saw headlights in her rear view mirror. It could be her dad. She wasn't sure. She decided to pull into the park with the walking trail. It was a good place to calm down and think.

The car behind her pulled in, too. Jackson jumped out of the car and into the passenger side of the Mustang. "What were you thinking? You could have been hurt! You don't even have your license!"

"You only care about your precious mustang, Dad," Katie stared straight ahead wiping away a tear that rolled down her cheek.

"No, you don't understand. I care about you. I care about you more than you know. I love you with all my heart and soul. That's why I stay here."

"Then you admit you're Jack Woods from 1927."

"Yes, yes, alright, I'm Jack Woods. Now I am Jackson Roberts who lives and works in the 21st century. I have the most amazing wife and daughter that keep me grounded. I have to be here; I have to live here…because I love you and your mother. Love is what keeps you grounded, Katie."

"Then you should understand why I want to go back. I love Andrew."

"We need you here more. We don't completely understand the power of these books. We only know the book always takes us back to 1927 but we end up back here in the present time. No one has stayed passed December 31st because we're afraid we may not be able to come back. We might have to live our lives out from there."

"Would that be so bad?" Katie was thinking that going back in time to 1927 over and over again was like that movie where the person had to live the same day over and over again until he got it right. It might be nice to continue on into the next year.

"For some of us, no," Her father was now very serious. "But for some others, it would be. So, Katie, please, don't go back again. End it now. This is the perfect time. You have great memories, don't you?"

"Yes, I do. Can we talk some more tomorrow? I'm getting tired."

Katie was getting good at lying. "I want to hear your story--yours and Mom's."

"Okay, it's a deal. But I drive the Mustang home," Her dad handed over the keys to the other car.

When Katie got home, her mother was pacing back and forth in the family room. "Oh my gosh, what happened?"

Jackson signaled to her that everything was okay. Katie kissed her mom and went upstairs. She dug around her bag for the Jack Woods journal and the other book. She got ready for bed but was not really tired and decided to finish the journal. When she came to the last chapter, it was just called, Andrew. Katie couldn't wait to get started reading.

Andrew Martin was a young man who came to the Grand Canyon with his family at the age of fourteen. If he had his way, he never would have left.

Andrew was part of the Martino family from Italy. Many of his family members were famous seamstresses and tailors in Italy. They started their own design house in Milan. The House of Martino is a well-known fashion industry there.

Andrew's grandfather decided to come to the U.S. and expand the line. He started a small clothing store in New York City and it has grown into the popular chain of Martin's Menswear. He runs it along with Andrew's father, Nicolas. Andrew was supposed to follow in the family footsteps of design and tailoring. He was being groomed to run the family business and attended a private boy's prep school on the East Coast.

Once Andrew saw the canyon and all the nature surrounding it, his destiny was sealed. He chose to use his creative talents, which indeed he had, on photography instead of design. He could not get enough of the canyon and begged his parents to stay longer. His family could not deny the devotion he had to it. That is when his father set up an endowment for the park. It also enabled Andrew to come and go at will. His grandfather built him a cabin on the park grounds for his use only. I believe they did all of this to appease Andrew, hoping he'd come to his senses one day. They wanted him to stay in New York with the family and enjoy visits to the canyon; only they did not realize this was not just a piece of Andrew, it was his whole life.

Each summer Andrew would return by himself for longer and longer periods of time. I would take him with me and help him take

Waiting for Dusk

photographs with his state of the art 35mm camera. Each year he brought a newer, better one with him. I am ashamed to say I was jealous of his ability to purchase the newest and latest models of cameras, but Andrew's likeability and unpretentiousness always won me over. He never asked for favors or expected anyone to do things for him.

Eventually I felt like I had gone from mentor to friend. He was almost like a younger brother to me.

Andrew had another good friend at the canyon, Thomas Cook. Thomas was very interested in learning everything about the canyon that he could. I believe he had aspirations to become a ranger. We had a good laugh about that since Thomas would first have to learn to get over his fear of heights. The two boys would accompany me on many adventures trying to learn everything they could about the park.

The summer of 1927 I decided I needed to tackle one last challenge. I wanted to go down the Colorado River and experience the river and its rapids. I knew this was something that would not be easy. You had to respect the river and learn how to live with it, not fight against it. My young friend, Andrew, wanted to join me in this latest endeavor. I was not too keen on the idea but could not dissuade him. We did many practice runs that summer. There were camps set up along the way for us to stop and stay overnight. My ultimate dream was to photograph and write about my adventure.

Little did I know that my dear friend, Andrew, was planning a trip down the river with his friend Thomas all on his own. It was scheduled for the Friday after Thanksgiving during Andrew's extended holiday. I was a newlywed and would be with my beloved wife and had scheduled my return for the weekend after the holiday. When I arrived on Saturday, I heard of Andrew's departure. I was surprised he did not confide in me but I also knew he was a proud young man and wanted to accomplish something on his own. The only trouble I had with this trip was that his friend, Thomas, was unable to go at the last minute. Still I had faith in Andrew and knew he would be careful and use all safety precautions. He was only to be gone overnight and return the next day.

Sunday was a long day for me. I stayed at the bottom of the canyon, watching for Andrew's return. Dusk was setting in and no sign of him. I was hoping he was at one of the camps and not able to return because of the shorter daylight hours. Monday turned into Tuesday and finally almost a week had gone by. There was no Andrew. I decided I would go looking for him. There were many volunteers so I had much help. Poor Thomas blamed himself for not going along and was beside himself with grief. We all knew the outcome of this trip was not good.

We never found him…my friend, my brother. I will never forgive myself for not being able to find him. He sleeps now in his beloved canyon. He is a part of it now, part of the nature of the canyon. Sleep well, my friend, God speed.

Katie was shocked. She couldn't breathe or think straight. Was this why her father didn't want her going back to the canyon? Drew is going to die? She decided she didn't have time to cry or panic; she had to stop him. From all the information in the book, it sounded like she had time. He left on Friday and she intended on being there.

Waiting for Dusk

Chapter Thirty-Eight

Katie woke up as dawn was breaking. There was not a minute to waste. She jumped up and ran down the hallway.

Anna's door flew open. "There you are! We wondered what happened to you. You missed Thanksgiving. I said you were probably celebrating with Andrew. Were you, Kathryn?"

"Anna, I don't have time to talk. I had a fight with Andrew and I have to go find him. Please help me."

"Say no more. I will go saddle up Flicka and you get dressed. I'll meet you in the barn," Anna went back in her room and grabbed her coat.

Katie was ready so quickly Anna barely had time to saddle on the horse.

"Anna, thank you. I'll explain everything later when I call you."

"Call me? I'm right here. You just need to come to my room."

Katie nodded her head as if to agree and wished she could explain what she really meant. She wanted to talk to the older Anna, the one who knew everything. Before she mounted the horse, Katie ran over and hugged Anna. "Thank you, again. I love you so much. I hope you know that. I want to tell you something that I don't want you to ever tell anyone else. Don't even tell me until I ask."

Anna nodded and Katie whispered something into her ear, then jumped on Flicka and headed for the canyon. There was no time to waste. She would stop Drew and tell him everything. She was going to let him make the decision for them. Should she stay or should he come with her? There was so much to decide. They were young and had their whole lives ahead of them. She was not going to let him die.

The first place she stopped was El Tovar. She hoped Thomas was there for the breakfast shift. She tied up Flicka in the barn and ran to the kitchen door.

"Thomas! Thomas? Are you in here?" Katie yelled and cried all at the same time. It was still very early and not too many people were there.

Miss Betsy came in from the dining room. "Why, Miss Kathryn, are you doing all this yelling?" She did look sympathetic as she said it.

"I'm looking for Thomas, Miss Betsy, is he here yet?" Katie tried to calm down.

"He should be here shortly."

Before Miss Betsy could even finish talking, Katie was outside scouring the landscape for signs of Thomas. She thought she saw him walking off in the distance and started running toward him.

"Thomas!" Katie waved her arms frantically.

Thomas ran toward her. "Kate, what is the matter?"

"I have to find Andrew. Please help me," Katie was out of breath.

Thomas stopped and looked at her carefully. "I don't think that is a good idea."

Katie decided she had to tell him something that would make him help her. "His life could be in danger."

"Follow me." He turned around from the direction he had been walking. This time he ran. Katie tried hard to keep up with him.

All of a sudden, they were standing in front of a wonderful looking cabin. "Is this where Andrew lives?" Katie put her hands on the walls of the cabin.

"Yes." Thomas felt around the top of the door.

"How are we going to get in?" Katie pounded on the door.

"I live here, too," Thomas produced a key in his hand.

The cabin was silent. It was just one level with a large living space. There was a fireplace in the living area and the kitchen and dining room were off to one side. There was a small hallway that led to two bedrooms. Thomas came out from the back rooms and shook his head.

"He's already left. He's probably halfway down the trail by now."

"Weren't you supposed to go with him?"

"Yes, but they needed me at work. I will take any extra shift I can. I'm saving up for a ring for Rachel."

Rachel. Thomas III told Katie the story of his grandfather marrying someone named Rachel. She couldn't blame Thomas for wanting to do something out of love.

Waiting for Dusk

"Why did he still go?" Katie was beside herself.

"I asked him to postpone. I really did. I wanted to go with him." Thomas sat down on one of the chairs.

Katie melted into another one and began to cry.

"He'll be alright, trust me."

"No, no he won't." Katie tried to figure out what to do next. She never walked the entire path to the bottom of the canyon. If she did, would she even make it in time? There were no phones at base camp or any way of contacting Drew. She had to give up.

Thomas and Katie slowly walked back to El Tovar in silence. When they got there, Thomas told her he would let Drew know she was there and wanted to see him. Thomas expected Andrew back on Sunday or Monday at the latest. Katie thanked him. She knew there was nothing else he could do.

She walked to the barn and got on Flicka and rode to the edge of the canyon. She sat on the horse and called out into the open canyon, "Drew, come back to me!"

Tears slowly rolled down her face. Feeling defeated, Katie turned the horse toward the boardinghouse and slowly trotted back.

She slid off Flicka and into the hay next to the stall and wept. She never cried like this in her life. She couldn't stop. She decided to stay there until all the tears were gone. Her father, and now come to think of it, even Anna tried to stop her from this hurt. Perhaps it was meant to be. Katie got up from the hay and brushed herself off. She could never come back here. It was too painful. Everything reminded her of Drew. She would go back to the boardinghouse, sit in her room until dusk and go back home.

Chapter Thirty-Nine

Katie woke up sobbing. She just couldn't stop. She wished this really was a dream because it has turned into a nightmare.

How did this happen? Why didn't someone stop Andrew from going down the river by himself? She already knew the answer. No one stops Andrew. He is strong and determined. She wished she had a picture of him right now. He never had his camera with him when they were together. If she had known he was a photographer she would have had him take pictures of them--too late now for that, too late for anything. Katie buried her head in her pillow and began crying again.

There was a knock at her door. It slowly opened and her father popped his head through the opening. "Are you alright? I thought I heard you crying."

She didn't answer.

"Katie? Your mom is going over to the college to do some work at her office. We thought that would be a good idea so you and I can have some time together."

"Why didn't you stop him?"

"Stop who, pumpkin?"

"Andrew, Dad, Andrew!" Katie could barely get it out of her mouth.

"Stop him from doing what? Who is this Andrew?"

"Come on! You know what I'm talking about! Andrew died! You could've stopped him! You could have saved him! Why did you wait so long to go looking for him?" Katie burst out crying again.

Her father walked over to her bed and sat down. "How did you know? How did you find out?"

Katie pulled the journal out from under the blankets. She waved the

Waiting for Dusk

book in front of him. "From this," she pushed the book in his face.

"How…what…" He stumbled over his words.

"Anna gave me her books written by Jack Woods. She thought I might like reading them," Katie sniffled.

"So that's how you know," Her father had tears in his eyes. "I loved him, too, you know. He was like a brother to me."

"Obviously you didn't love him enough! You let him die!" Katie was angry now. She knew she shouldn't blame her dad but he was there and Andrew wasn't.

"I've blamed myself for his death since it happened. You will never know how much." He got up and walked over to her window. "You know how every year I'm gone on the Friday after Thanksgiving?"

"Mom always says you're on a book tour or giving a speech or something like that," Katie was now surprised he was still here.

"That's not what I'm doing. Every year I go back and try to stop him. I try to save him year after year. It's torture for me. And, yes, I try to talk him out of it before that day but it never seems to work. I just hope to catch up to him on that Friday to stop him," Her father put his head in his hands. "One year I could see him on the trail in front of me. I called his name over and over. That was a very bad year for me."

Katie got out of bed and walked over to her father. Her heart was breaking, not only for Andrew but for her father. "I never knew," She said softly, feeling terrible for accusing him.

"That's why I was trying to stop you from going back. I didn't want you to feel like I do. I didn't want you to feel guilty about anything. I had mixed feelings about you meeting Andrew. He was a great guy; I would be proud to have him as your boyfriend. I knew how it was going to end; and I wanted to spare you all of this. Please forgive me."

Katie looked at her father. There was so much pain in his eyes. She made this all about her, not thinking of his feelings at all. "Dad, there's nothing to forgive. I love you. I can't believe that every year you go back to look for him… I went, too."

His eyes flashed with a look of hope.

"No, no luck."

They both sat down on the bed and didn't say a word. Then Katie jumped up. "Dad, we are not giving up. If anyone can find him or stop him, it's you. You're going back there to try again."

"It's too late, honey. Andrew has a day's jump on me. I always went back on Friday. I stayed here to talk to you instead."

"Don't say it's too late. You're going to do this. I have faith in you. Go find your book and we'll make all the arrangements. Dusk comes early in November." Katie ran into her bathroom to get ready for the day.

Joanna came home and was filled in on their plan. "Jackson, you better get over to Maya's, if you know what I mean."

"Mom, there are no more secrets. I know that Maya has a set of books." Katie was starting to feel better about all of this.

Jackson went to the key cupboard and grabbed the keychain with the apple on it. "I'll be right back."

"The cabinet is locked!" Katie called after him.

"Don't worry, I got it," Jackson called back as he went out the door.

Dusk could not come soon enough. Katie paced back and forth in the kitchen. She kept looking at the clock, willing it to move. Her father explained he could be gone for days and she was not to worry. She had to promise she would go on with life and attend school as if everything was normal. It was hard but Katie promised.

Joanna told her that they would talk and she would fill in all the blanks for her and finally answer any questions Katie had.

As the sun started to set, Katie went out on the deck. She saw the moon faintly in the sky. *Andrew, if you can hear me, we are coming for you. I know that you are looking down on me now.*

As she watched the moon grow brighter in the sky, the first star appeared. "I will give you the moon and the stars", that's what he had said to her.

Katie clutched her bracelet tightly. *If only wishes came true,* she thought.

Again, one of those fairytales popped into Katie's head. You can wish upon a star and your dreams come true. That was now a childhood fantasy. Things don't always work out and you can't depend on a star to solve your problems. Katie knew who she could depend on, her father. She was putting all her hopes and dreams on him. Maybe that wasn't fair, but that was all she had left.

Her mom came out onto the deck. She put her arms around her daughter and whispered in her ear, "He's gone."

Waiting for Dusk

Chapter Forty

Joanna told Katie that she would be sleeping in Katie's room or that Katie could sleep in hers, it was Katie's choice. Joanna said she didn't want her to be alone at a time like this but Katie knew the real reason; Joanna wanted to make sure she didn't use her book and join her father.

They made plans to stay up late and talk. They got drinks and snacks and took them up to Katie's bedroom pretending everything was normal.

"Start from the beginning. How did you meet Dad? Are you from the past?" After Katie said that she realized it didn't make sense. Her mom had parents and brothers here in the present.

"No, I'm not from the past. I'm right where I'm supposed to be. Maybe that's why you fit so easily into both worlds. You have one parent from the past and one from the present. We can't figure it out-- how you seem to have a life in 1927 and one here. You are in that wedding picture; I know that's you, but how? I guess we will never know or understand it all."

"So you really think it's me? I guess I do, too. Anna recognized me when Lindsey and I went to the ranch," Katie decided to tell all, too.

"Really? That's unbelievable. But we're getting off track, if you want to hear my story."

Yes, please go ahead," Katie wanted to hear this story more than any other one.

"Your father met Carl in the winter of 1927. Well, it was one of many winters for Carl as you know. Carl was married to Maya and Carl Jr. was a young boy by then. Maya stayed in the present all the years Carl was growing up and Mr. Johnson would travel back and forth because he needed to be in both worlds. Maya always understood that.

Nancy Pennick

I met Maya in the library when I was a freshman at the college. She was always helpful, took me under her wing and we became friends. I got a part-time job at the library because, as we know, all college students need cash. One day, Carl showed up at the library with a young man. He was extremely handsome and very curious about everything. He spent hours looking at the books and walking around the library and campus. We met briefly but Maya seemed intent on keeping us apart. That made me all the more interested.

I was heading down the library stairs at the end of my shift when I ran into Jackson. We chatted and then he offered to escort, yes, he used the word escort, me home. Wow, handsome and a gentleman, I thought. We ended up making tea and talking for a few hours but when the sun began to set, he got nervous and said he had to be going. I asked if I'd see him again and he was very vague. I liked him and I hate to admit falling in love with him already.

The more I asked Maya about him, the more agitated she got. I dropped it and just hoped I'd see him again." Her mom sighed and got a far away look in her eyes. Katie patted her mom's arm to say she understood.

"At the canyon, Jackson was staying at the boardinghouse for free room and board. Carl finally decided he needed help around the boardinghouse to get it up and running and had placed an ad in the local paper. It took him many winters of 1927 to figure that out!" Joanna laughed and then continued. "Your father answered the ad. Anyway, one night your father found Carl reading the book and being an author himself asked a few questions about it. Carl said it was an old book he discovered in the house which made your dad all the more curious. Carl hoped Jackson would leave well enough alone but your father was an avid reader, too, and said he'd love to read it when Carl was done. Carl promised him that he could have the book when he was finished with it."

Katie giggled. "Dad didn't give up, I take it."

"No, he didn't. Of course, we know that Carl was just trying to appease Dad and would never give him the book to read. After that, they said goodnight. Your dad then remembered one more thing he wanted to discuss, returned to Carl's room and discovered he was gone. Your father is a smart man. He stayed in that room until Carl returned the next morning. That's when he got Carl to explain everything and made him promise to take him to the future. Carl agreed to do it just once. He

Waiting for Dusk

didn't know your father would meet me.

So that's the story, boy from the past meets girl from the present, they marry and live happily ever after!"

"Mom, there's more to it than that." Katie knew there was always more to the fairytale now.

"Of course, there is. Jackson and I got married after I graduated from college. It was a September wedding. He stayed here with me in the present, going back to the canyon for a day or two here and there. After Thanksgiving he wanted to stay longer and asked my permission and I gave it willingly. I didn't want him to be homesick. When he got back from that trip, it took a long time for him to recover from the tragedy of Andrew's death. That's when I agreed to go back with him and have him show me his world. We told the family we would be traveling because of Jackson's job and would visit as often as we could. We spent a lot of time together in his past.

He took me to New York to meet his family. His father's name was Robert. That's how we came up with his new last name--Jackson Roberts. Mainly, we would stay at the canyon because that's where your father liked to do most of his writing. It was an interesting time, almost dream-like."

"Wow, you've been there. Don't you love it?"

"Not really, I haven't been back since you were born. That's why your father always says I don't take it seriously. He thought I saw it as an extended vacation that I'm done with now. It's not really true. I just like living in the present and being with my family, it's my preference. Your father is free to come and go as he chooses; I don't stop him.

This summer he wanted to start a new book and planned on being gone for awhile. That's how he saw you, Katie—you and Andrew at the canyon. He knew it was going to end tragically and tried everything to keep you apart but you already know that."

Katie was happy to have the final piece to her puzzle. Her father did see her at the canyon. For awhile, this story kept her mind off Drew and what was happening right now. "Mom, do you think Dad will find him?"

"If anyone can, it will be your father. Now let's turn off the lights and call it a night."

Chapter Forty-One

Katie was flying down the rapids being tossed around like a rag doll in the boat. She hung on for dear life. Only one thing was important to her, finding Drew. She kept calling out his name as she clung to the boat. Then the boat flipped over and she struggled to hang on to the side of the boat. She felt herself going under but was able to scream for Drew one last time.

"Katie, wake up! Are you alright?" Her mother shook her. "Katie, please, you must be having a terrible nightmare!"

"Drew!" Katie sat up in her bed and looked right through her mother.

"No, honey, you're here with me at home. I'm sorry to say, you have to get ready for school."

Katie sunk back in her pillows. The dream was so real. She felt like she was going to drown and never see Drew again. In a way, she was glad she was at home.

Katie couldn't believe it was Friday already. Her father had been gone a week. She tried to focus on school but it was hard. Lindsey was trying to help her through the best she could, even using a little humor. "Earth to zombie," was now one of her favorite sayings.

Katie spoke to Anna every day after school. Last night Katie decided to finally ask her about their last conversation at the boardinghouse.

In a way, Katie still needed validation that this was all true. If the Anna from the past told Katie in the present what the secret was, she'd know for sure this is all one hundred percent real.

"Anna, do remember our talk in the barn? The one when you

Waiting for Dusk

saddled the horse so I could find Andrew?"

"Yes, you said that Jack Woods was your father which didn't make sense at all. Now it does. You said not to tell anyone, not even you, until you asked. That's why I bought those books and took an interest in him. I was thrilled to be able to pass those books along to you. I was conflicted because I knew you'd read the journal and find out about Andrew. Then I decided if anyone could stop him, it would be you."

Katie thought about that phone call over and over now as she got ready for school. Anna thought she would have the powers to stop Andrew. Well, obviously not. Plus Anna didn't know Katie would have a huge fight with Andrew, and he would feel he had to let her go to find herself.

Find myself! I didn't find myself until I met you! If only she could tell him.

Katie went begrudgingly off to school. At least it was Friday. As she entered her first class, American History, she saw Mr. Dallas getting a DVD ready in the player. Good old Coach Dallas was reliable. Every Friday the class watched a DVD or a television show. She knew he was getting ready for the Friday night football game instead of being interested in teaching the class. She appreciated the truthfulness of it.

Everyone loved having Coach Dallas for a teacher. He didn't care where they sat in class and they were free to have juice or a breakfast bar. Katie headed for the last seat in the middle row. It had become her new favorite spot. The teacher couldn't really see her and everyone else seemed to know to leave her alone. She put her head down on her books until class started.

"Class, we're getting a new student today. He should be here shortly," Mr. Dallas announced. "Looks like he might be a good quarterback for me next year."

The class laughed. They knew that coach loved football. His team was in the playoffs, and he was preoccupied with that.

Great, Katie thought, another jock. He can be friends with Tyson.

There was a quiet tap on the door. That got Katie's attention, and she sat up. The school secretary and a tall young man entered the class. He was wearing a sweatshirt with the hood up over his head and jeans.

Typical. That hoodie is either designer or has his old high school's name on it.

The secretary introduced him to Coach Dallas and the class. "This is

Andrew Kelly, everyone."

Andrew? Why did his name have to be Andrew? Katie moaned a little too loud.

Mr. Dallas looked around. "Miss Roberts? Is that seat open on your left?"

"Yes," she answered and put her head back down on her books.

Mr. Dallas gave a short speech about how he liked to follow up his lesson from the week with the DVD he was about to show—the same speech he gave every Friday. As he went to turn out the lights, he turned back and said, "Mr. Kelly, we don't wear hoods in my class. Please be so kind as to remove it from your head." The lights went out and the show began.

Katie couldn't help herself. She just had to look at the newest jock. His dark hair peeked out from until the hood. He raised his hand to his head and pulled back the hood. He looked at Katie and smiled.

She gasped. It couldn't be true. He looked just like Drew. She just kept staring as tears filled her eyes. It was Drew. Her father rescued him and brought him here. She just couldn't believe it.

"How?" she started to say.

"It was because of you, Kate," Drew whispered. He scooted his desk a little closer to hers. "I started to read your letters when I got to the bottom of the canyon. I couldn't stop, and the time got away from me. I had to wait until the next day to leave. When I got in the boat, I had such a peaceful trip—being one with nature—but my mind just kept going back to the letters. I couldn't stop thinking about them. I wanted to finish reading so when I got to the first camp I went ashore. I unloaded everything and tied up the boat or so I thought I did. While I was reading your letters, the boat drifted away and I was stranded. I knew that the men would come looking for me, especially Jack. Jack's great, but I suppose you already know that."

Tears welled up in Katie's eyes as she nodded. Her wonderful father always had her back; he never let her down.

"I spent my time reading your letters over and over. That's when you came back to me."

"I never left," Katie put out her hand.

"The moon and the stars..." Drew looked down at her bracelet.

"You already gave them to me," she smiled.

Andrew took Katie's hand. "I love you—across the miles, across time. Those words brought me home."

The End

Nancy Pennick

About the Author
Nancy Pennick

After a great career in teaching, Nancy found a second calling as a writer. Her debut novel, Waiting for Dusk, was a surprise to her as much as it was to her family. Watching a PBS series on National Parks, her mind wandered to another place and that is where the characters of Katie and Andrew were born.

Nancy's called Ohio her home for all her life but loves to travel the U.S. She enjoys reading and writing young adult novels with a good cup of tea nearby.

www.facebook.com/nancy.pennick

Waiting for Dusk